A FOREIGN COUNTRY

Francine Stock studied languages at Jesus College, Oxford. She is a radio and TV journalist who was a reporter and presenter on BBC2's 'Newsnight' and 'The Antiques Show'. She now presents Radio 4's nightly arts programme 'Front Row'. She is married, with two children, and lives in London and Hay-on-Wye.

FOR ROBERT

Francine Stock

A FOREIGN COUNTRY

VINTAGE

Published by Vintage 2000

2 4 6 8 10 9 7 5 3 1

Copyright © Francine Stock 1999

The right of Francine Stock to be identified as the author of this
work has been asserted by her in accordance with the Copyright,
Designs and Patents Act, 1988

First published in Great Britain in 1999
by Chatto & Windus

Vintage
Random House, 20 Vauxhall Bridge Road,
London SW1V 2SA

Random House Australia (Pty) Limited
20 Alfred Street, Milsons Point, Sydney
New South Wales 2061, Australia

Random House New Zealand Limited
18 Poland Road, Glenfield, Auckland 10, New Zealand

Random House (Pty) Limited
Endulini, 5A Jubilee Road, Parktown 2193, South Africa

The Random House Group Limited Reg. No. 954009
www.randomhouse.co.uk

A CIP catalogue record for this book
is available from the British Library

ISBN 0 09 927350 0

Papers used by Random House are natural, recyclable
products made from wood grown in sustainable forests.
The manufacturing processes conform to the environ-
mental regulations of the country of origin

Printed and bound in Great Britain by
Cox & Wyman Limited, Reading, Berkshire

1

THE AFTERNOON had not been without its trials. In the greengrocer's, the recycled carrier bag finally expired. Brussels sprouts bounced at wild angles across the black and red tiles. Then, as she made her way home, the back tyre developed the sinister drag of a slow puncture. Day by day she felt the card index of her life, the register of interests, tenderness and fears, slipping out of order.

But for now she must address herself to the struggle ahead. Every day the same – these last painful revolutions of the pedals, the jolt of downwards, the lurch of upwards, along the lumpy tarmac. Feet, in thick socks and tennis shoes, click and whirr, their joints a counterpoint to the arthritic old bicycle. The portly Jack Russell canters alongside, swerving towards the wheels. Damn dog. One, two, three – another burst of laboured breaths until the track swings left, away from the double file of brick bungalows and runs along the sea-wall. Every day that turn brings the breath back; it shakes off the seaside and delivers the sea.

Safe now to lift the eyes. Impossible, until then, not to be preoccupied with the earth-bound – plaster griffins on pilasters guarding the Vauxhall or Nissan, leaded lights under pale green tiles, borders and hanging baskets studded with the acid pinks and yellows of petunias and marigolds. Impossible not to recite the names burnt into slices of varnished wood – The Willows, Simla, the ever-optimistic Sea-View, ludicrous Loch Fyne – until tarmac gives way to unmade gravel and sand.

At the turn, the corset of south-coast retirement is cast off. The road becomes track, private access to a series of Edwardian railway carriages that lie in a disjointed line like a toy snake. Each was decades ago refurbished or disembowelled. Some boast gardens, some simply sit on the shingle that runs into farmland. Some are modernised (in a Fifties, Sixties, Seventies way); others strive for period credibility. All have an uninterrupted pioneer's view of sea and sky. From each veranda or window the view wraps itself round for 180 degrees and more.

The panorama today is the colour of polished pewter, darker at the shoreline lightening to ivory overhead, just a faint horizon. Some fifty yards from home now, time to prepare to halt. Don't remember when these messages first started so far in advance, like Christmas. First ease off the pedals and let the ache creep along the thighs. Squeeze the brakes and send pain shooting up the forearms. Now the co-ordinates come faster – feet bounce along the ground, head down, torso braced for the impact. With luck, the bicycle slews to a halt.

Bugger it. Seventy-four, bugger it. Too old for a bicycle, she thought. But too old to change.

The landing was bumpy; her feet shuffled clumsily to gain balance. The dog wheeled around, barking. Damn him for announcing the fiasco. She negotiated the bicycle through the wicket fence and fumbled in the pocket of her faded trousers. The key stuck in the front door, as usual. On the veranda, as she struggled, she could hear the phone ringing in the kitchen. The door finally yielded with a blast of a familiar yet unwelcome smell – food, gas, maybe a touch of drains. Each time she returned the house delivered the same brief armpit shock.

The phone had stopped, of course, just an echo reverberated on the linoleum. The dog skidded on leaflets from the pizza shop. No second post, thank God. The main rooms, fashioned from the original railway carriage, were hot and stuffy. An afternoon of May sunshine had picked out the dust on the windows and stirred up the odours of upholstery and carpet. The place looked tatty.

Once it had seemed splendid, a beach house fit for the general who had built it. Now, two generations later, worn away by summer after summer of sandy feet, shell collections dumped in armchairs and wet clothes hanging in the bathroom, it needed an overhaul. It needed paint for protection against sea and wind. Most of all, it needed a new champion.

She had always been the champion of the Hut, as the children called it. Weekends and school holidays she had packed them into the old Rover and headed south. Later they came to despise the surroundings, if not the house or the view. Now they came again, affecting irony and enthusiasm in equal measures – her elder son Richard with his own children; her younger boy, Oliver, often in a state of exhaustion that returned him close to infancy. Only she remained here, suspended between land and sea, between then and now.

The light was fading; it was well past seven. As she sat with a Scotch on the veranda scrutinising the inner tube, a tortoise plodded into her peripheral vision. Her next-door neighbour made steady progress towards his second swim of the day. He was over ninety, with scrawny neck protruding from his towelling robe; a towel with violent magenta and grey swirls was draped over one arm. In rubber shoes, he picked his way over the shingle.

Since his retirement, thirty years ago, he had kept to this routine, through the seasons, his wife's death, the weather's excesses. Each morning she saw him as she walked the dog. Sometimes he hailed her as he emerged from the waves, underpants waterlogged, pink-grey penis just peeping through the Y-front. Sometimes he kept aloof, spitting contemptuously into the foam.

The young couple who'd taken over No. 6 had marvelled at his health and vigour. One Christmas they'd invited him to venture from his terracotta-painted bungalow with the sinister garden into their home for some cheer. Seated at their Ikea table, he vomited a torrent of racial hatred, nothing personal of course. It was rather strong for their taste, they'd confided to her, their icon of old age tarnished. Between neighbours, they called him Oswald.

No warmth left in the day now. Oswald was returning in the gloaming to his overgrown lair. She went inside to the kitchen and switched on the strip light. The balance between inside and out was suddenly reversed. During the day, the vast sweep of sea and sky dominated the interior. Now, the darkening sea was passive, lapping at a deferential distance from the glow-worms of the houses, as the occupants watched their evening rituals reflected in the windows.

The phone rang. She broke off from chopping onions and potato.

'Hello.'

There was a wheezy pause before Kenneth spoke.

'And how are you?' The emphasis, as ever, on the 'you'.

'Not so bad,' her voice assumed the guarded sing-song of the long-time spouse. 'Yourself?'

'Oliver phoned here. Couldn't get an answer from you. Is it tonight his . . . thing is on?'

'I was at the shops. Half-past nine, I suppose. Is he all right?'

Gradually, in overlapping phrases, vital information was extracted. Son still in the Soviet Union, snippets about friends and acquaintances, small outrages of etiquette at the doctor's surgery, questions repeated and unanswered – a gavotte of restrained concern and affection. Since his stroke, Kenneth made great efforts to communicate, as if the struggle to speak had made conversation more worth while. These days they shared the same roof for no more than a few months a year. The spells together, seasonal and family festivals, were diluted by visits from friends and grandchildren. It was a very British separation.

She lived alone because she could no longer bear conversations. With Kenneth, it was too painful, too great a reminder of what they had both lost. With strangers, she despised chatter. The most engrossing discussions were the ones she had with herself and there was no shortage of those.

How lucky she was, she thought as she ate, to still enjoy real food while her peers sucked on predigested pap from glossy supermarkets. On the radio a concert crackled; she watched the black water some hundred yards away. Now and again, a figure would amble through her gaze along the little road directly beneath the veranda. The usual mix – tanned taxi-drivers walked dogs; kids in anoraks, cigarette ends glowing, sauntered towards No. 19 at the end of the path for an evening of chemical escape; occasionally an elderly couple from the retirement estates would defy crime statistics and television reconstructions and venture a late stroll just to see what happened down this funny little road. The local policeman in his panda car crawled past and executed a practised three-point turn at the end. As he drove back, he waved to her.

How lucky. To have health, sanity and family at seventy-four could well be the definition of fulfilment. Or a great deal to lose.

Because it was late, she would watch Oliver's programme in bed. In readiness, she washed up and locked the doors. As a token security device, the dog was settled in its basket. The Hut had always felt safe, although only the most languid burglar could fail to breach its defences. These days, after some half-century of reflection, she did not so much fear the manner of her death. The fears came in different clothes now.

The bathroom tiles around the mirror were cracked here and there, but still white. The light was unforgiving – but what was to forgive? She was old. She fancied the reflection suggested vigour: eyes still grey, if faded and hidden beneath drooping lids; hair pulled back into a passable bun, passable from the front anyway; own teeth; dark eyebrows. Over the years the wide forehead and prominent jaw had become more pronounced; the nose was undeniably beaky. Strong face, people said, good bones.

She was in bed in time for the News, relayed on a small portable television – a present one Christmas from her younger son. She was a listening-post, a sounding-board for information – the newspaper, the radio, the television, the telephone calls, the letters. Wearily she turned it all over, passing it through the filter of her experience. Presiding over an ice-blue waste of studio, the newsreader intoned the day's events. For half an hour, the world was filed into pockets of significance and sensation, an arbitrary order for the evening. Occasionally, the divisions would strike her as so bizarre she would exclaim at the set. First came another threat of defeat for the government over Europe. The usual protagonists were paraded, depressingly familiar, their arguments reduced to lumps of gristle. Loss of sovereignty, boats missed, blame shifted – the argument bounced dutifully to and fro. She found herself glowering at the screen.

The horrors of war on the difficult fringes of Europe followed. The newsreader invoked maps like a magician's doves. In a gilded hotel, statesmen looked tanned and troubled. Finally, a report depicted the plight of villagers in one of the areas under negotiation. With a slight shock she realised that this must be material collected by Oliver and his team. He would have walked down that street. She searched for a clue, some slight reassurance.

On went the litany. In the box behind the newsreader's shoulders appeared the face of an old man with the graphic legend 'War Crimes' superimposed. A Pole living in the Home Counties had been arrested, together with some Lithuanians. It was expected that they would be variously charged with aiding the occupying Nazis fifty years ago. The old man was described as a brutal camp official. He had fine cheekbones. A young reporter explained wide-eyed to camera the magnitude of his guilt. The phrase 'Archangel of Terror' occurred, awkwardly, twice, like an attraction in some grisly theme park.

The phone rang. Richard, multi-media executive and assiduous elder son, was a busy man. There was time for telephone calls for pleasure or family duty only late in the evening. As ever, he reminded his mother of this. As ever, she listened to him as to a visitor from another planet. Richard spread the gospel of the dissemination of information. From the stream of facts on offer now, she picked out that he was just back from Tokyo and in the midst of negotiations. They were already five months into 1990; he wanted a deal by the end of the year. His speech was fast, almost jocular. At intervals he laughed as a social encouragement quite independent from any sense his words might have. Richard and his wife Joanna lived in south-west London, though Richard's dominion spanned the globe via satellite and cable. It was a network of networks, the key to the present and the gateway to the future. It did not, however, solve for them the problem of finding suitable schools for their children – boisterous Arabel and querulous Sam. Joanna had surrendered her job at the PR company to dedicate herself to their care.

Daphne stared intently at the screen. Her wristwatch lay on the bedside table. She squinted at it. Twenty-five past nine. She cleared her throat to halt the stream of domestic details. It was useless. With a mounting sense of panic and irritation, she broke in.

'Richard.'

'What?'

'You must stop. Oliver's programme is about to start.'

He paused, taking the blow on the nose.

'What programme? I thought you might want to hear about the children. They're looking forward to coming down, you know. Well, we all are, of course.'

'Yes, yes,' she passed a weary hand over her forehead. 'Let's talk about it at the weekend.'

'Well, I won't be here, but you could talk to Jo, I suppose.' His role as the pivot in this machine of family arrangements was suddenly redundant. 'They need me in Montana for a story-lining convention. Then I'm back via New York.'

'I have the impression that your work is all about speed – instant this, instant that. But most of your time seems to be spent throwing yourself in and out of planes. Hanging around airports. And why all this talking, talking, talking? Seems very outmoded. Don't tell me, I'll speak to Joanna.'

She replaced the receiver, leaving them both bemused and annoyed. For a clever man, he was remarkably obtuse. The programme had started.

It struck her that there were conventions in documentary making. Oliver subscribed to the theory that you needed one good witness – preferably English-speaking – to tell the story of conflict. This witness was a schoolteacher, aged around thirty, with a small daughter. Her husband was away fighting the Serbs. Her doctorate in English philology did not keep the power going in their flat, or draw water from the stand-pipe or deflect the sniper's bullet. Oliver's film was a study of education and liberal values powerless in the face of old hatreds. It was a film he often made in war-zones. It was beautifully made – elegiac, yet stopping a frame short of sentimentality.

Throughout the long passages of interview in the teacher's room Daphne strained to catch the occasional sound of Oliver's voice as he prompted her off-microphone. He sounded concerned and weary. His was a portrait of an elegant, reluctant victim. Just once did he touch the spring that revealed an adamantine heart of loathing for the enemy. Many people who had once been her neighbours had always, it now seemed, carried an invisible placard around their necks. They could be kind or generous or simply placid; they might even, by marriage, be relatives, but they were, for all that, a different tribe. It was a line Oliver chose not to pursue.

The programme built image upon image of domestic life destroyed. It lingered in the makeshift classroom where the little girl struggled with maths amidst other panda-eyed children. It followed her and her mother home across the potholes, past the bookshop that her grandfather used to run. It was there when news came of Muslim successes or Serb advances. Inevitably (and from the beginning this was as inevitable as Greek tragedy) it was there when the father's death was announced by the local postman.

As she watched, the cardigan did little to reinforce her nightdress, and her shoulders grew cold; a certain discomfort was the great companion of old age. Along with a recurring sense of guilt and loss; of things done and things not done.

All in all she disliked the television technique of pinning out people's lives on a dissecting table to provide fodder for dinner-party conversations. She couldn't be critical of the programme; with Oliver's work criticism was not an option. Her own capacity for criticism grew daily as targets presented themselves, with this one exception. Her younger son was protected by her passion. She'd been over forty when he was born. In those days that was an adventure in itself. Richard was already away at school and she had considered a return to work. The baby had pushed her back into the home and – against her will – seduced her utterly. He was tiny and golden and tender, very different from his sturdy brother, who strode through infancy accomplishing all targets at least two months ahead of time. Oliver was erratic and puzzling and as he grew from tanned boy to pale adolescent, she felt at once a mesmerising mix of distance and intimacy. Richard was clever, but Oliver beguiled.

The credits slid upwards. Oliver's name came last, just ahead of the television company. However many times she saw it, the form of those letters on the screen or in the newspaper brought a lurch of pride. Now it was safely over, she could relax, stop frowning and unclench her fists.

She approved of Oliver's confidence to order events together like that, to frame the world, although she often considered his conclusions wrong. She knew he would dismiss her argument with a grimace. He would disparage his own powers and claim to be no more than the messenger. But the messenger's skill was to gauge the spirit of the age.

It was shaping up to be another sleepless night. At two-thirty, she got up to ease the stiffness in her back and hips. She walked through the unlit corridor (sheer folly with brittle bones) past the dog, which raised a sleepy head and sank back. As a child, she'd wondered if death was like walking down a corridor in the dark. She made a cup of tea and sat in the front room, wrapped in her dressing gown, feet pushed deep into slippers. The blinds were open far enough for her to watch the shore while keeping herself hidden. The moon shone down on the pebbles, bleaching the yellow poppies that poked up here and there. The tide was high again now. It would have receded by the time the world woke. This was its secret visit.

A group of youngsters wandered back along the path, silhouetted against the bright moonlit pebbles. Girls and boys alike wore a uniform of black jeans, black silky bomber-jackets tied round the waist, white shirts flapping below. Hair was worn long, straggly and tied back. One or two wore crochet caps on the back of the head. A pair of girls walked arm in arm, their pale faces morose. They travelled so quietly that it seemed a soundtrack of waves had been laid over silent film.

A little behind the main group, two figures lolloped along.

One of them was large and ungainly. Daphne had not seen Jad since the previous summer when he had taken to helping her with rough work in the garden. At first he had not been a great talker, which suited her fine, but in time he developed a barrage of questions which she found at first annoying, then quaint. Richard had been horrified to find the marijuana plants in the shed, but she only guffawed, judging it a confidence more than an outrage. She had more tolerance, suggested Richard, for a gormless stranger than for her own family. That did make her laugh.

The group moved past, splitting and re-forming, relaxed and silent.

Unobserved, Daphne stood in the window. She gazed at the sea and shivered.

2

OLIVER SAT in a bath of golden light. The table was tucked around the corner from the main concourse of the restaurant. Wedged between plate glass and a pillar, threatened by a potted palm, he closed his eyes. He had to snatch a few minutes of warmth and drowsiness to himself; the rest of the day was assigned to the fixer and the phone and dreadful coffee and endless cigarettes. This was the day to chart the territory. First, there would be the courtship of the fixer, the local researcher hired to work on this next project – enquiries as to family, previous work, the current political situation. If all else failed, there were always anecdotes about the American networks to trigger despairing laughter and instant bonding.

In the meantime, he could gaze at the four-day-old copy of the *Financial Times* that had mysteriously found its way to the hotel reception this morning. He could admire the efforts at landscaping that three men and a bright yellow excavator were executing just yards from his table. This was the first joint-venture European hotel in this southern Soviet republic, the brainchild of an Austrian entrepreneur, and it threatened to have surroundings to rival Versailles. He imagined the architect's impression in the developer's office in Vienna. He looked at the three men; the excavator had been resting for some time at an alarming tilt. They were leaning on spades, smoking and chewing. Their dark, lined faces were humorous, their collarless shirts and baggy trousers barely soiled. It was ten o'clock; they must have been at work for at least three hours. Their impact on the bank of scrubby earth was imperceptible. A pile of saplings lay wilting in the sun.

towards the gorge. The
with the occasional dome
ow-piece buildings of the
monumental palaces to
ie cream-coloured apart-
erials, scarred with graffiti
of grass. Opposite, on the
oligatory television tower,
rusted.

sense of anticlimax that
charm or its architecture.
e sense of separation. The
he south-facing slope over-
to bring Austrian efficiency
to this most romantic and reluctant outpost of the Soviet
empire. It had been open only a few weeks; the staff were still
rehearsing for an inspection from their Viennese boss any day
now. The hotel's boast was that it had modern communi-
cations and food flown in from Western Europe. The fact was
that a veil of local muddle had already fallen. Cable TV in the
room perhaps, but sometimes no electricity. Marble in the
bathroom, but cockroaches in the basin.

He cursed himself for being booked in here. The hotel had
the luxuries of spoken English and a halfway decent message
service, but it had no sense of location. The smell of warm
newspaper rose from the table. He could feel his eyelids
closing when he saw reflected in the window the assistant
manager bearing down on him. The man was snaking
between the tables parallel with the ambitious breakfast
buffet, past the castle of bread rolls erected by an eager
waiter. In his hand was a telephone.

'A call on the satellite phone for you, sir.' He came to a halt
with a flourish and laid the phone like a game bird in front of
Oliver. 'A lady. From London.'

Oliver took the phone. It sizzled with static. Rachel's voice
came and went, making dialogue impossible. He gathered that
The Times and the *Guardian* had been warm, if brief, in their
reviews, the *Independent* less so. She was thrilled, apparently.
She wanted him home. He, naturally, wanted to be home, and

so on. The assistant manager smiled, his head on one side. There were days and days of this ahead. Oliver felt depressed.

Niki Gabounia was waiting for him in the atrium, wearing a dark navy suit. She might have been in uniform. The vast fig trees of the indoor jungle dwarfed her. Her shirt cuffs were too long, as was her fringe, which threatened her eyebrows. The rest of her hair was pulled back like a schoolgirl's. She carried a brown plastic briefcase. She shook his hand in an attempt at a businesslike manner. He ordered coffee for the room and they began the slow progress up in the glass lift.

Was she familiar with the new hotel? She shrugged, with a deprecating smile. It was a folly, of course, but Westerners would be glad of its comforts and its ability to insulate them from her country. She reached into the briefcase for a packet of American cigarettes. Oliver found his lighter and noticed the tremble in her fingers.

Niki Gabounia tended towards the Type B researcher. Type A was male or female, but young, pushy, garrulous and familiar. Type A was on the make, keen to form their own production company, and wore jeans, Italian shoes and plenty of hair, usually falling over one eye. Type A told you what you wanted to hear and, if they failed to deliver, apologised extravagantly and with great charm and minimal sincerity – or cried. Type B was an older woman, maybe no older than thirty, with a child or two to support. Anxiety underlined every Type B action, long lists were made, punctuated with sighs. Type B recognised the vanity and vacuity of television, but was through circumstances enslaved to it. She always knew best, but was reluctant to share the knowledge. The cameraman generally thought she'd be better for a good shag.

For six weeks Oliver would be locked into a contract of dependence with this woman. At first, in a bravura display, he would outline to her his (and by implication the programme's) view of her country. She would bite her lip and nod, perhaps making some token protest of hidden complexities. Gradually, in the long round of telephone calls and meetings, they would gain some common experience. They would develop nicknames for particular characters in their play, little jokes perhaps, the odd kindness. By the end of filming, there would be relief and professed affection. At the airport, there would be an embrace, a little stilted after the wrangle over fees (paid in dollars, cash). By Heathrow, she would be no more than a number in his book, which he would bequeath to television teams who followed later.

Oliver unlocked the door to his room, with its startling livery of peacock blue. They took up their places; he sat at the circular white table, while she perched on the bed near the telephone. He began his speech, distilled from the notes his London assistant had made. She listened, eyes down, extracting a notebook from the briefcase. When he had finished, she responded with a staccato list of desired interviewees. Oliver rapidly scanned his notes for familiar names.

'And of course, the President,' he added, almost sure his name had not come up already. 'How is the bid progressing?'

She grimaced. 'He'll do it. I'm sure he will. But you and I must meet with his adviser, Mekhusla; he's also minister for interior affairs. As soon as possible. Perhaps this afternoon?'

He heard himself launch into excuses. Just arrived, barely up to speed – he checked himself. 'That's fine. Just as soon as you like.'

The language was a problem. As he heard her make her first call, he was lost. A little knowledge of Russian would be no help here. Through the window, the sky was deep blue. He could make out the course of the river behind the houses. Everything through the window was washed with romanticism. It looked like no other republic he had ever visited in the Soviet Union; from here it resembled a painted backdrop of a town in Greece or Turkey – little more than a few hundred miles distant. He looked at the diagram in front of him. This was the way it was all going to look in a few weeks' time, thirty-nine minutes and fifteen seconds, including titles. That would make it real.

The taxi that took them to the Parliament building seemed to be travelling at full throttle. Almost before they had pulled the tinny doors shut and settled themselves on the back seat, it shot away from the hotel drive and hurtled down the cobbled hill towards town. Oliver watched the streets roll past, out of reach. Niki talked non-stop to the driver in a fierce tone, quite altered from the resentful diffidence she had adopted with him. The taxi bumped across potholes, vied with painted trucks and performed a slalom around the security barrier to deposit them in an impressive courtyard.

Niki led the way. Her walk was exaggerated by her shoes, which had heavy heels and were half a size too large. She strode into the entrance hall. Oliver, at least a head taller, followed. Inside, the carpet was red but balding and the lighting so dim that figures came almost face to face before they could recognise one another.

Accompanied by a heavily armed soldier they climbed the massive stone staircase. The corridor ran round three sides of the courtyard before it ended in a light wood-panelled room presided over by a queenly blonde. She sat behind a vast electric typewriter with a bank of ancient cream and green phones. Against the walls sat petitioners – an old man, a woman in black with two young men, and three grey-haired business types.

Niki made her case to the woman, who glanced at Oliver. Her eyes, magnified behind winged glasses, were lined in bright blue. A plump hand with crimson nails reached for one of the phones. She gestured to an empty chair. Oliver sat down while Niki stood by the desk chewing the side of her thumb.

Along the row of chairs he could hear the woman in black quietly moaning. Her head was covered with a printed scarf and her hands wrestled together in her lap. One of her sons rested his hand on her shoulder. The other sat straight, gazing at the carpet. Suddenly, the panelled wall beside the secretary began to rattle. Oliver noticed a door handle in it turn. The old woman broke free of her son's caress and rushed to the door, where a burly figure emerged.

She had been subdued, but now the woman chattered and howled hysterically. A young aide tried to push her away but the burly man restrained him. He put his large arms around her and muffled her sobs with his embrace. Over her shoulder he spoke to the sons, who stood awkwardly. His questions seemed quiet, casual even, against the intensity of her grief. Niki moved closer to Oliver.

'Her youngest son has been killed in the fighting. The family are trying to get the body back for the funeral, but the rebels won't let anyone from the family into the village.'

The aide was taking details from one of the sons. The burly man was cradling the woman's face in his big tanned hands and talking softly to her. She closed her eyes and turned her tearful face to kiss his palm. The tears glistened in the creases of her eyes. The other son gently disengaged his mother's grasp from the politician's jacket and led her out into the corridor, where her agonised breathing echoed against the marble. The minister smoothed down his coat and, after a brief word to his side-kick, approached Oliver.

'Please.' One confident hand to the upper arm and a firm handshake. 'Come into my office.' The minister rocked back on his heels, sweeping an untidy lock of black hair out of his eyes.

The office of 'Rambo' Mekhusla conformed to a pattern Oliver had seen a hundred times. Above the desk, a nationalistic portrait; in front of it, at right angles, a long veneer table flanked by uncomfortable chairs. They sat down. The minister, behind the desk, swivelled gently on his leather throne. He sat at an angle, one broad arm across the back of the chair. He was lazily handsome, just going to fat.

First of all, said Rambo, he must apologise for his English, learnt in his former career as a sportsman – an international judo champion. Some career progression: from black-belt to spin-doctor, remarked Oliver. Mekhusla smiled and proffered a dish of boiled sweets that lay in the centre of the table. He hoped he might be of assistance.

Oliver reinforced the message of his letter to the President. He sought permission to film in the disputed semi-autonomous region. For the purposes of the film, he would need to interview both government forces and rebels. The interview with the President would feature largely in the programme. Was it possible to set a date?

Without doubt, in due time, but the President's plans changed daily. The course of the war was unpredictable, the situation delicate. Oliver had perhaps noted the desperation of the woman outside. The rebels were capable of great barbarity; it was necessary occasionally for the President to travel close to the war-zone to reassure those most afflicted by the fighting. Perhaps, and here he glanced at his aide, Oliver might be able to accompany the President in the next day or so to see how the land lay. The aide got up and left the room.

Mekhusla expanded on his theme. Support for the rebels from Moscow was becoming more obvious. Russian troops had gathered on the northern border of the region where the fighting was. There had been threats to close the airport, or cut the supply of aviation fuel. He leant back in his chair, straining his shirt across his chest, and ran his hand again across his hair. The government was mindful of Moscow's power, but utterly determined to protect its people in the villages from this Communist-inspired insurrection. Oliver asked with some scepticism if the rebels were Communists. Mekhusla levelled heavy-lidded brown eyes at him. Little creases of concern appeared at the corners.

'Too stupid. You should understand, these are very . . .' an exasperated pause, 'simple people. Not sophisticated, barely political. They are being used.' He glanced at the clock. 'I am very sorry, but I have to leave now. We have a battalion of troops returning this afternoon.' He stood up, stretching his arms above his head. The short train of thought had slipped away. Oliver sought to regain the initiative by remarking on the collection of photographs that covered one wall – Mekhusla in competition, triumphant, receiving medals, meeting film stars – but the bonhomie was wearing thin. The adviser was already kissing Niki's hand in a show of gallantry that overwhelmed her thin frame.

On the return journey to the hotel, Oliver quizzed Niki, who had become mildly skittish from so much attention. Mekhusla was no more than forty. He had been, without doubt, a national hero for his sporting exploits, but he was no fool either. If he took to you, there would be no problems with the President. What problem, asked Oliver, I thought the President was a racing certainty. Sure, sure, she said, lighting another cigarette.

At reception, Niki called home while Oliver checked for

messages. He heard her interrogate someone and then lapse into a defeated, complaining tone. Sighing, she put the phone down.

'Who was that?' he asked.

'My lover,' she replied. 'My little boy,' she added hastily, wincing at her own joke. 'He's ten.'

'Then you'd better get home to him.' Perhaps a benign approach was best at this stage. He could be tough another day. 'We'll meet at eight tomorrow. No other calls I can make tonight?'

She shook her head, gathered her things together and walked in her heavy shoes from the sparkling foyer.

The vast peacock-blue tapestry in the atrium was reproduced in each room as a wall-hanging. It was no better in miniature, when the tree and strange beast shrank from bizarre to comical. Oliver took a beer from the mini-bar and opened some stale cheese biscuits. It was difficult at this stage to keep hold of the strands. Maintaining coherence in the face of local difficulties was the great challenge; with it came a numbing sense of not quite knowing where the party was, of being the professional outsider.

He turned over the pages of his notes and rang the retired editor of what had been described as one of the city's more reflective newspapers. The man's English had been acquired some decades ago in Tunbridge Wells; it was untouched by the American phrasing that was obligatory in anyone under forty. He had a grand manner, tossing out references to Conrad or Keats, not entirely without purpose. Oliver wanted to talk about the President; he had obviously hit on a distinguished supporter. The President came from a respected family of intellectuals. His father was a novelist and essayist; the son, a poet, had been imprisoned by the Communists. He was struggling to bring democracy to a country where notions of justice and decency had long atrophied. It was not easy. He needed to be strong: perhaps he should be stronger still. This war was a deadly trap. Moscow could crush them in an instant. The editor had seen the speed with which the tanks could arrive. He knew the tourniquet that could be applied to vital supplies. Your hotel, he told Oliver, would be no better than the most impoverished hovel in the mountains without power. When Oliver steered him back to the subject of the President, the editor was fulsome about the father but offered little that put features on the outline of the son. Oliver sensed a certain disappointment.

The telephone call had taken over forty minutes. Oliver took his hot ear and his hollow stomach down to dinner. He had been hoping the new contact might proffer some instant hospitality, and a glimpse behind closed curtains, but had known within seconds this was not the man. He would rather sit beneath the glass and steel chandelier in the deserted restaurant and read up on the formation of the nation in the fifth century than discuss back-numbers of the *TLS* with an Anglophile old queen. Rachel would smirk to see him at one of only five occupied tables as the staff practised an elaborate dining etiquette. Or perhaps she wouldn't. He was amused by absurdities; she was irritated. Three mouthfuls into the schnitzel (flown in the day before and as tasteless as an airline meal) came a worried girl from reception with news of another call from England. Oliver laid down his knife and fork, but took his book.

The indoor garden in the atrium was lit at night with green spotlights. As yet, only one or two were broken. From the phone came his mother's voice. She sounded as if she were a yard from the phone. He was suddenly anxious for his father.

'Is everything all right?'

'Fine. Yes. I saw your programme last night – rather relentless, but I suppose that was what you intended.'

'It's a rather relentless sort of place,' he said, predictably. 'Are you sure everything is all right?'

She sighed with exasperation. 'Yes. How are you getting on?'

'God knows. It's too early to tell. I've just got these few days of setting up, but I'll be back at the weekend.'

'Of course. Will you bring Rachel down to the Hut? She'd have to take pot luck with Arabel and Sam. Is she up to it?'

'I expect so. She's good at dealing with unpredictable situations without blinking. Did she give you the number?'

'No, I got it from the office. See you Saturday, then. Take care of yourself.'

This last phrase faded into a mutter, or perhaps he hadn't heard it at all.

As he returned to the congealed veal, he wondered what the sub-text of the call was. Beyond concern for his welfare and the bank holiday arrangements, there was something she wanted him to do. She never rang him when he was working. She was cheerfully scornful of his work, but then she was scornful of most things. What the hell was it? She couldn't possibly be lonely. Bored, perhaps, but she was so tough, it was almost impossible to tell, just as he found it near impossible to offer affection. It simply bounced off the surface and landed at your feet in an embarrassing mess. His father spoke occasionally of her sensitivity, though not, of course, in those terms. Oliver knew it existed, but most of the time he was damned if he was going to risk the fire to find it.

The call must be a whim. It sprang from an over-active mind rattling about in the body of a grandmother.

3

SHE WAS either too hot or too cold. Life's thermostat had gone haywire. The evenings were uncomfortably chilly, but by eleven in the morning the sun was too fierce for gardening. It was a curfew of sorts. Daphne paced slowly through the rooms. There was plenty to be done, always plenty to be done, but she dawdled in a hinterland of contemplation.

The heat amplified the musty smell. In the corner of the sun room lay some boxes, old stuff, stuff she hadn't looked at in years. This year – soon – she would really get round to it.

What did you do with all this stuff anyway? Memories and details that were clear in her head lay muddled in dusty scraps of paper in files and folders. She hardly liked to start.

It wasn't as if she'd forgotten. She had the kind of brain that constantly ran through, sorted and selected. But the selection didn't always make sense, and sometimes she couldn't sleep.

She didn't have to lift the spine of the old ledger, with its dog-eared corners and slivers of old gum, to remember that it was a diary of sorts, the confidante of those days.

Five decades ago – or five years, or five months, sometimes it seemed the same. Before then, everything made sense; afterwards, it was perfectly logical, she'd made sure of it. But for a few weeks, nothing was in its place.

She knew, without looking, what the first page said. In memory she could repossess her first official desk, the thick grain of the oak, split here and there, with rough fibres of wood pushing through the wax.

The first thing she wrote that spring, as Hitler drew and

quartered Norway and Denmark, was of the joys of filing. It gave her such satisfaction to despatch a pile of folders to their vellum cradles. Each was an achievement, but the real goal was to polish off all they could throw at her. She could prove she was sharper than the rest. And she had proved it.

That spring she had emerged from South London, swinging off the bus, blinking in the sunlight as she looked up at the stone bulk of the War Office. She was in the grip of a fierce excitement, like a desire to bite, that battled with total fear. I was unstoppable, she'd told the children. I marched in there and I showed them. As fast as they could put the work on my desk, I cleared it. That's the way to make your mark.

You had to remind them. Sometimes, they seemed so bland, so untouched. She had come from a tiny house – neat and clean, mind you – into this great edifice. What a journey. I wore my best, naturally, wool twist with a faint stripe and always a crisp white blouse and polished shoes.

That girl was magnificent, and terrified. She could see her poised on the steps, could feel the rush of details in the diary. She stared at books and files in the box. Could it have been that, even then in those first few weeks, those pages harboured a germ of disappointment?

Crashing into her thoughts came a clumsy knock at the door. The present clamped around the unfolding past.

'This one's a brute,' said the postman, breathing heavily. 'Crumpled too – the stamps are all over the shop, looks like a child's been at it. It's not, strictly speaking, properly addressed. There's no postcode and the surname is wrong. But the postmark's clear – Melbourne, Australia.'

His opinion was delivered ahead of the parcel, which he held firmly, just out of her reach.

'There's no writing,' he went on, 'just one of those adhesive labels. The coming of the computer has made life easier, no doubt about it, fewer indecipherables these days. The new scanners can even read handwriting, it's true, can take italic or Gothic or plain old scrawl and suck out the postcode. Amazing, you wouldn't believe it. But that isn't the problem here, of course. The problem here is that there is no postcode.

'And the real problem, if you take my meaning, is that this parcel is so big. It was a fine judgement as to putting it in the sack at all. Of the two hundred-odd days out of each year when I go down there, I reckon I see you at the far end of the beach for a good, what, hundred and sixty. Your dog-walking you could set your watch by. If it was up to me I'd leave it on the veranda, wouldn't come to any harm, but that's not the way these days. It's tick the little box, put the time, take it back to the Main.

'I missed you yesterday and on my way back, there you were, head down like the Wicked Witch of the West, or was it East, never could work that out, kamikaze mutt in tow, cycling all the way into town and then back again. Hope it was worth it.'

'Thank you,' said Daphne. 'Shall I take that from you?'

4

AT THE sluggish ends of the day, Oliver felt vulnerable. In the morning and evening, the very moments when he sought a little Buddhist distance, Rachel and his mother would try to drag him into engagement.

From different angles, their thoughts bounced down the corridors of cable towards him. Sometimes an observation or enquiry hit home, but more often he felt the heat as it shot past his ear, ricocheting off the walls – wasted. With his mother, he could understand a little more. She lived alone, she was questioning and restless. She was bored. But Rachel, with all the challenge of work around her, was a puzzle. Her response to him was increasingly a trajectory of disturbance and aggravation. He was, all in all, the most empathetic of men, and yet he would put the phone down and wonder – what did she want to do that for?

Rachel was calling him from the office. Minutes before she went on air she could do that, switch from preparation to last-minute diversion, as an escape. He could just hear in the background voices that came at her across the desolate landscape of the newsroom, skirting computer terminals and empty desks. Harassed editors, watching the engine of their creation running unaccountably towards the deadline, issued final, futile instructions before she went down to the studio, but she couldn't hear. Her anxieties were channelled down the telephone line to Oliver, 3,000 miles and three hours ahead. He knew he could only disappoint.

He knew that in a few minutes she would be twisting her ear-piece in place, pulling the wire down the back inside her jacket. He almost could hear her droning a few tuneless bars under her breath as she suffered the final ministrations of the make-up woman. He saw her fiddling with the keyboard on the computer that lay on the plasterboard table in front of her. Fretting, fretting – with no outlet for her anxieties and no target that he could discern.

What patently mattered most at this very minute was that she should be in the studio, on time, reading in a measured reassuring way, guiding the viewer from one headland of significance to the next. She did it well; some used superlatives about her performance. Newsagents, in particular, seemed appreciative. Cinema ushers sometimes recognised her. Her postbag reinforced this random sampling. So many letters began 'I have never written before . . .' that it almost seemed, against reason, that she must have touched some spot in the national psyche. Oliver appreciated that what mattered most at this moment was that she should look groomed (symmetry and convention being the touchstones of her trade) and speak clearly. She should be alluring, but not dirty, a goddess of a chaste hearth.

And she was. Morning after morning she chanted autocue to a grateful nation, as if the words sprang fresh from her own brain. Morning after morning, she'd once told him, she made lists in her head of things to do – meetings, lunches, dry-cleaning – while she recited death and deficits and record rainfall. Unlike some, who illustrated their readings with exaggerated mimes of concern or jollity, she had but the one expression. And it worked.

The hunger for young women to act as priestesses to the nation was never satisfied. Under thirty, the skin looked good. Over thirty, the audience listened to what they said. Rachel, as she often remarked, was twenty-nine.

Oliver was sceptical about all this populist, showbiz stuff, naturally. Not my thing, he would say, retreating behind the *New York Review of Books* or *Granta*. I deal only in minorities. But he recognised the power of the medium. He laughed at her appearance when she emerged from a television studio with grotesque make-up – the head of a pantomime dame on discreetly padded shoulders. He teased her for the turbo-charged air-hostess outfits she wore on-screen, but found them erotic when she came home.

Rachel's problem was not lack of success. She was blooming early and prolifically. Rachel's problem was that she had an inkling of her limitations. That gave her voice its nasal edge. When men gathered they said of her that her hair and her eyes had taken her to on-screen prominence. She had to silence them.

Oliver heard no murmurs. To him Rachel was articulate and capable; she was easily as good as most people around her. One day, given the right circumstances – and how much of this came down to luck – she would be excellent. All she had to do, as he had done, was to keep plugging away at the good stories, the right stories. What he found increasingly enervating was her anxiety about the tests that lay ahead. Was she making the right decision? What did he think she should do about this or that? If God opened a window, Rachel inevitably saw a hundred-foot drop. If Oliver tendered advice, it was pushed away, sometimes aggressively. It was easy enough for him to talk.

What was bringing the scowl into her voice this morning was an opening of sorts. Not quite God, but the head of department had offered her a couple of forty-minute slots – publishing space, he called it – within a strand of contemporary history programmes. What did Oliver think? Great, he thought, great; he was really pleased for her. Had she thought of what she might do?

There was tension, even hatred, in her silence.

For a few months now Oliver and Rachel had shared Rachel's flat, in an informal way. It had been a good buy, he'd encouraged her. Her parents weren't so sure; he'd watched how subdued they seemed on the day she showed it to them. Her mother's breathing had seemed a little constrained, as if the air might be tainted with some ancient plague. Her father had repeated 'Oh yes, oh yes' with an air of nervous cheerfulness as she opened doors and explained features. Oliver had noted the slow way they had entered the hall downstairs, stepping carefully on the brown nylon carpet, swivelling their heads like lizards to take in the doors of the other flats – each of which held unknown threats.

Oliver had helped her choose. Thanks to him, she knew

that this far north of Notting Hill was a good place to be, a street of tall, white stuccoed houses like ocean liners in dock. The view was fine even if the stairs were daunting. Oliver scorned the terraces of Clapham and Fulham, the domesticity of Chiswick, the political rectitude of Islington. Why, he wondered, shoehorn yourself into middle-age ahead of time? Why serve an unnecessary apprenticeship in streets clogged with child-commuting Volvos?

She'd responded with typical acidity. It was clearly better to fight for parking space not with family estates but with clapped-out old motorbikes and drug-dealers' Porsches, preferable to know that the needles discarded in the front garden might have belonged to a performance artist or conceptual architect. But once inside, up the sixty-seven stairs, Oliver saw that Rachel soon colonised the flat. The sweep of hardwood and steel that was the kitchen, the halogen lighting, the aqua of glass shelves – all her installations conformed to modern order and safety. Her parents approved of the place now. Very swish, said her father.

Oliver thought it touching that their approval mattered so much to Rachel, but it made Rachel angry. They had channelled so much energy and love into her that she somehow hoped the sheer force of it might propel her up beyond this need to please. By now she should be above their middle-England, middle-management aspirations. For their only child, they had made sacrifices for a more than decent education. Evangelists for the power of learning, they collected libraries by instalments. Her father was phenomenally well read, with the zeal of an autodidact.

Her university place was a cause for family celebration, but as she progressed into television, her parents' pride was clearly dampened by a certain caution. She had done well, of course, but somehow they had not anticipated anything so ostentatious. They had perhaps imagined a partnership in a law firm or something in the Foreign Office. What they got was a glamorous and clever daughter displayed for every cheap compliment and jibe that the world could throw at her. Rachel's parents knew that true reward came only from hard work. Television, for all its long hours, did not seem hard.

Sooner or later, her bluff would be called.

And that, Oliver guessed, was what Rachel feared. She suspected she was somehow inauthentic. The work ethic was as ingrained as the marbling in the bathroom, but in her present job she simply could not fathom how work could get results. The knack of journalism, yanking at the hangnail of what the public wanted to know, did not come easily. Others chased after causes and individuals, fired by a sudden certainty that *they were on the right track*. For her, she occasionally grumbled, most tracks ran parallel. He felt she was making an unnecessary fuss.

Once she had confided in him – or was it an accusation? – that she couldn't see the difference between a good story and a fashionable one. Oliver's sympathy was running out.

'Of course I've thought,' she was still talking, as the burble in the room behind her resolved into a few strangulated voices. 'I was up until midnight thinking it through. It's just so difficult to find a new angle. You know what these things are like. The researcher's been turning up some anniversary stuff about Italians in Britain in the war.'

'You mean POWs?'

'No, no, no,' she was impatient, 'internees. Civilians. There's not much, a few cuttings about the former detention camps, wartime memoirs by an intelligence officer, something just out of the Public Records Office. I don't know. Does anybody care?'

Oliver had just caught sight of his watch. Ten to. 'Shouldn't you be in the studio?'

'I'm going. Now. What do you *think*?'

'Well, it's very difficult. I don't know anything about it. What's the issue?'

'That British intelligence fucked up, that all sorts of people were interned who shouldn't have been, that Nazis, Communists, Fascists, anti-Fascists, they were all lumped together. That there were mistakes. We're trying to track down survivors.'

'Well, I can't say. It sounds like there might be something. Get that researcher to dig a bit more.'

She was edgy and querulous again. Why did she make life

so complicated? Why did she see every opportunity as a snare?

She had accused him of complacency because he enjoyed the ease of the insider. Oliver was hardly an insider. His own father had gone into business after generations of lawyers and doctors and military men. His mother's background was pretty humble. His family was neither brilliant nor particularly high-achieving. It was paranoid to suggest they were intimidating.

To his relief, she at last put the phone down. He was jumpy for her deadline.

How could she possibly think life was simple for him? He understood the pressure of expectations. The periodic phone calls at the tail-end of the day reminded him that nothing was ever good enough for his mother. Even excellence was greeted with the immediate enquiry, 'Can you keep that up, then?' The gongs he'd won over the years were gently derided. Now she asked him about the younger people coming up behind. She'd call it keeping him on his mettle; he called it exhausting.

All his life she'd stressed the importance of clear thinking. Don't be muddle-headed like the rest. Find the logic. Think it through. Then, when he did, she criticised his conclusions. She was so tiring.

He expected to be finished here by Saturday. He was travelling tomorrow to the war-zone. The date to meet the President had at last been fixed. And the weekend? Rachel would collect him from the airport and they could go on to his mother's the next day. No respite.

He had no evidence but he suspected there *was* something in the handful of newspaper cuttings that Rachel's researcher had turned up, a low fog-warning that might make a story. How many people knew about these detentions, the arbitrary line between those who were 'safe' and the undesirables who might not put the interests of Britain first? Who made these decisions? There must have been mistakes. It was a question of cutting a reasoned line through.

You should ask my mother, he had said to her; she might remember all that, she spent some time in the War Office.

5

THAT POSTMAN is a fat-head. He's one of those hale-fellow hearties with hamburger for brains. Cheerful enough, I suppose it goes with the job, but that relentless whistling, that optimistic beard, jovial raised eyebrows. I wasn't going to go any faster, you fool; damned shingle doesn't get any easier. I'll get there when I get there.

In his hands another package. Slight question in his voice – two in a week, yes, it's remarkable really. No, not a birthday, nothing like that. Thank you, thank you, good day.

Watch him go further down the road, winding between the puddles, sea to the right, houses to the left. This one is very bright, banana yellow, one of those ready-made package bags. Same postmark. Damn. Heart bouncing out of the chest like this. Sit down and have a cup of tea.

Daphne sat at the little table in the kitchen with her hands clasped together. In front of her lay the package. After a few moments she unfolded her hands and smoothed over the surface, framing the label bearing her address. She'd had little occasion to use her maiden name in over forty years. She took a mouthful of tea and turned the package over. These things were remarkably well designed. Unlike a milk carton or the plastic clip on a packet of bread, both enemies of stiff joints, this was child's play. And at the same time not easy at all.

There was a strip of paper printed with an arrow. Slowly she pulled it down and tipped the package. The contents remained snug inside. She reached in but her hands slipped on shiny paper. She lifted it and shook. A sudden cascade of white shot out, gliding off the waxed tablecloth to land in a fan shape around the legs of her chair. Whatever it was had landed with the important side down. Shaking slightly, she leant over to pick up the papers.

There were two items – a little pamphlet on cream paper and a single white sheet, with something, a picture of some kind, reproduced in the centre. She turned the pamphlet over. It was an anniversary, half a century. The publishers were a private association – San Michele and San Giovanni – in Melbourne. The single sheet carried an impression of an old photograph. The snapshot had been taken in strong sunlight; its contrast was deepened by the photocopy. A group sat ten or so together, in two rows like a sporting team. All elbows and crossed ankles. Their faces were little more than brows and dark sockets. Without warning, they would have meant nothing.

She looked again at the pamphlet. A memoir of Italians interned in Britain. This was not without warning. In the drawer of the card-table was another sheet of white paper. Sitting askew in the middle was another fuzzy photograph, a newspaper story this time, a column four or so inches long. A dismal little headline – Hundreds Presumed Lost. Things done and things not done.

She had been sitting for ten minutes or so, grey eyes fixed on the grey sea. She reached across the table for the old packet of Camels. Emergency rations.

6

OLIVER HAD been waiting for ten minutes when the military policeman swept up to collect him from the front of the hotel. The weather was keeping glorious vigil. Each day was warmer than the last and flourished skies blue enough to make the eyes water. By the time he returned with a cameraman it would surely be raining.

The little car was sprayed cream and pale blue, with no great finesse. On its roof was painted a large red number. From the driver's door emerged a small pigeon-chested man in a slate-grey uniform. He strode around the front of his vehicle, approached Oliver and saluted. Oliver took his hands out of his pockets and made some token gesture of greeting. The policeman nodded curtly and indicated the rear door of the car.

To Oliver's relief, Niki was tucked into the back seat. He had little enough idea of where they were going and the driver spoke no English. Within minutes they were on the main road that ran along the gorge and out of town. The driver was constantly busy with some activity unconnected with driving. Every couple of minutes, he spoke into a radio-handset, one of two on the dashboard. In between, he looked down at the tray between the two front seats and fiddled with the holster of his gun, which lay there by the handbrake. From time to time he reached inside the breast-pocket of his jacket to find a packet of cigarettes. The lighter was inevitably in the glove compartment, or in the shelf of the passenger door. Occasionally, his head would dip below the dashboard completely, leaving one stubby hand on the top of the steering wheel, while he searched for something under his seat.

Niki seemed unperturbed. She had spoken to Rambo's assistant this morning and they were to meet the President around midday. He was visiting a town on the edges of the disputed region. Before these troubles, the town had been quite prosperous, drawing on good farming land, but the news from Moscow was menacing; there was talk of closing the airport. Oliver felt momentary alarm but reassured himself. There was always such talk – southern republics thrived on the depiction of the bear from Moscow clawing at their borders. It sculpted their sense of national identity.

The road stretched out. The mountains edged back, allowing room for gentle plains. Along the road were trees already heavy with pink blossom. The sun broke through briefly in between, racing the car along the road. Magpies rose in twos and threes ahead of them.

In all likelihood it was beautiful, but Oliver was distracted. The policeman, given the run of the open road, drove like a maniac. When there was no traffic coming the other way, he pulled into the left-hand lane and overtook in bulk. Faced with opposition – large trucks, farm carts, overloaded Ladas – he seized the second handset in front of him. This was connected by a flex to a loud hailer on the roof. Into this he barked a series of commands, unintelligible even before the distortion of the sound system. What emerged from the roof was a cacophony which, to judge from the faces of the oncoming drivers, engendered only confusion and panic. Far from pulling over, the vehicles drifted towards the centre of the road, looking for the source of the row.

Trapped in the back, Oliver was on his third cigarette. He flicked the ash out of the inch of open window. Niki, by contrast, was drawing serenity from his discomfort. In the past few days, she had conducted a non-stop tour of the capital's political life, all the while appearing strained and exhausted. He was sure he could detect her cringing as she introduced the idea of each meeting to him, flinching once more as she made the introductions at the meeting itself. Yet they had talked to every colour in the rainbow coalition that was the post-Communist government and had even ventured into the shadows at its edges. She was nothing if not thorough. She had no energy to speak of and yet she was relentless.

And what was emerging? He was running out of time to soak up the information that these research meetings yielded. Tomorrow he would return to London; next week he must plan the filming schedule and in a fortnight return with the crew. But what did he know? He knew that the President and his entourage had a certain glamour – or at least had done when they came to power in the first, limited exercise in democracy. He knew that Moscow could still influence through its control of vital supplies. He knew that the war in the enclave was backed and armed by Moscow, that it had rumbled on for some years and was now approaching some kind of crisis. He also knew that the so-called rebels were the descendants of an ethnic group settled there by Stalin. They had nowhere else to call a homeland. They spoke Russian. They were despised and without supporters, except for their Russian army protectors.

The great disadvantage of the coalition government, from a documentary maker's point of view, was that it had no opposition. Gradually, however, fragments of criticism were drifting up. The President was autocratic and increasingly removed from the people who had brought him to power, the same people whose plight he had so emotively depicted in his poem cycle 'Lost Kingdoms'. This great work, Oliver found, as with many translations, read like early Leonard Cohen; he abandoned it after two pages. The President's appeal to liberal sympathies went back to his association in the Seventies with Western groups concerned with freedom of speech, but a new generation of political activists saw him in a different light entirely. What Oliver was finding increasingly difficult was that no two critics coincided in their criticism. The fat boy in the leather jacket who ran the university's political science department felt the President lacked courage to confront Moscow, but a young playwright couple claimed he was a Fascist and had driven their work underground. They growled something about the death of a colleague in detention but were evasive on details. Conspiracy theorists, fantasists, piqued former lovers, loquacious political analysts and taciturn former colleagues – each scraped a little from the enamel of the President's image, but the substance beneath was equally opaque.

But Oliver did not at this stage wish to make a film about the President, he wished to make a film about the war. He wanted to fix the President at least in some bracket politically, even if his personality was so fluid that he could simultaneously be ranked a weakling and a tyrant. Within a few hours, he hoped that his own assessment would nail the beast down.

The car swung down the right hand of a fork in the road. Hard to believe the fighting was only three kilometres away. The little town was set out in a neat grid; they passed by an ugly industrial plant, possibly a distillery or flour mill, to schools and blocks of town houses and came at last into a rectangular square. The plinth for Lenin's statue still stood at its centre. On one side of the square was an ornate three-storey building. From the first-floor window hung a limp national flag. On the pavement below stood perhaps forty or fifty people, all men, wearing old coats or belted leather jackets over baggy blue trousers. Some wore embroidered caps with flaps that pulled down over their ears. All were waiting. At the approach of their car, many looked up from their conversations. The buzz of talk faltered as Niki and Oliver got out, but resumed as they walked into the building.

In a first-floor room, an aide motioned them to chairs. Oliver could see the flagpole from the window. The room had high ceilings; it was painted a light but curiously bright shade of green, something he hadn't seen since childhood crayons. From the rosiness of the spring outside, he felt plunged into artificiality. On the other side of the room, behind a trestle table, he saw the President.

The first impression was slightly comical. The man was sitting with his elbows on the table. His chin rested on his hands. He was flanked by two women with browned faces and rough black clothes. The eyes that had stared out from a score of newspaper cuttings – large, bloodshot, baggy eyes – stared now at Oliver from under dark brows. The expression was both miserable and wary. There was too much of the man, his limbs seemed folded and refolded. Seated, he looked about seven foot tall. His hair was thick, its black compromised by grey. With a drooping moustache, neat beard and those huge sad eyes, the President made an unhappy photofit of Zapata and Chekhov.

As the women talked, the President's glance flickered to Oliver and Niki. Was this interest or distaste? He avoided a direct glance.

After a few minutes, the aide returned to the room and approached the table. The President grunted and stood up. As he came around the table, Oliver saw that he was indeed well over six foot. The suit was fashionable, with a slight sheen, incongruous in the dusty room. There was no smile, just a grudging nod. Oliver went to shake hands but saw that the President's remained firmly in his pockets, like a truculent adolescent.

'This is a difficult time,' the voice was tired.

'I appreciate that,' said Oliver, 'and we're very grateful for your time.' The President shrugged. 'I very much hope that over the next few weeks you'll allow the camera to be with you from time to time?'

Another shrug, but this time with an ironic smile. Encouraging.

'Are you going into the war-zone today?'

'No. I have come to listen to the people. This woman,' the President gestured behind him, 'we have returned her son's body to her.'

Oliver looked across. It was indeed the same woman. He glanced at Niki. 'Yes, we saw her the other day . . .' he began.

'It's a terrible, terrible situation,' the President cut across him. 'Terrible.' His voice tailed off. Oliver drew breath to speak. 'But we are determined.' This was almost a shout, with the eyes wide.

The aide appeared at the President's elbow, whispering urgently. The President turned and strode across to a phone on the table. He barked into it. Niki caught hold of Oliver's arm, 'It's Moscow, the Defence Ministry.'

Oliver had little need of an interpreter. After a short period of grim-faced listening, the President erupted into histrionics. He paced up and down on the short tether of the telephone, his eyes on the window. No, Oliver guessed, no, never, not a millimetre, by the blood of my forefathers, no. It was impressive; the two old women rocked gently to and fro. The call ended with a sustained burst of defiance from the President and a melodramatic slam of the plastic receiver. The President sniffed fiercely and went over to the window.

'The aviation fuel, they're going to cut supplies,' whispered Niki. 'They want him to withdraw his forces from the semi-autonomous region. He has to protect his people – it's our land by rights, anyway.'

'Can't he get fuel from someone else?'

'Sure, but he's got little enough to exchange for it. Some wine, a few films, a great literature – what do you think?' She inhaled heavily on her cigarette.

Oliver looked sideways at her. He wasn't altogether sure. More immediately, he trusted there would be enough fuel for his flight out tomorrow. Christ, what about getting back in? There was always a way.

A small group of men now filled the doorway. One of them shouted across the room and the women started towards them. The President turned away from the window.

'Come with me,' he declaimed to the room, although few but Oliver and Niki could follow his English. 'Let me show you what this war is doing.'

Obediently the group clattered down the wooden staircase at the back of the building. At its foot was a rectangular yard, depository for old crates and pieces of scrap iron. A chicken scratched at the sparse grass. Backed up to the staircase was a van with its rear doors open. Inside was a pile of crumpled blankets. It took Oliver several seconds to realise that the blankets were thrown around a naked body. He felt himself start and knew from Niki's stillness that she had seen it too.

He was a young man, perhaps no more than twenty. He lay awkwardly and at his temple was a dark wound. His cheek-bones and nose stood out in the pinched relief of death. One of the women was massaging his ivory foot and wailing. The men stood in an informal circle, their faces creased with emotion. Slowly, the mother pulled back the blanket. Niki looked away. The woman began to scream and Oliver saw the lacerations around his ribcage and the magenta burns at his groin.

'This is what they have done,' the President's voice was close to Oliver's ear. 'Do you understand?' The woman had now yanked aside the blanket completely and was gesturing desperately at Oliver to look more closely. He shook his head, whether from deference or disgust he couldn't be sure. 'She wants you to understand. You are the way for the world to know.'

Oliver nodded. The President's red-rimmed eyes were shining with tears.

At the front of the building, they were joined by Rambo Mekhusla for the journey to the edge of the war-zone. As they came out, he was talking to the throng of waiting men, serious but familiar, smoking. He broke away and ushered them to a large black car with tail-fins. The three of them sat in the cavernous back. The car swung through the streets and out to the north of the town.

'You speak with the President?' Mekhusla put his shoulder against the window and turned towards them.

Niki launched into a description of the telephone call from Moscow. When she was excited, Oliver was realising, her English improved. Mekhusla listened, clicking the joints in his knuckles. Oliver wondered if it was a breach of government etiquette to transmit news vital to the health of the state in this casual, gossipy way. The minister didn't seem bothered. Oliver asked if there were contingency plans in the event of a fuel blockade.

'There are always plans,' replied Mekhusla, the slow playboy smile unfolding. 'We have a little put by, a little here and some there. But the plans don't always work.'

'Aren't you concerned?'

'From the day I become minister, from before even, I live always with this worry. After some time, these things are no longer worries, they are simply the rules. You have to live this way. This is now the game. They will squeeze us and we will find ways to fight them – and in time, they go away, perhaps, because they have other worries, other people to fight, somewhere else. But that does not change the fact that at any moment they could crush us. The international community, you and the Americans and all our friends, would protest, but,' he paused for a morose smile, 'it would be done already.' He spread his hands on his massive knees.

The child and the warrior took turns in this man, Oliver thought. There must be times when the minister sat down and discussed strategy, yet he seemed so easily bored. Who was the guiding force behind the war, then, was it Rambo or the melancholy poet? He looked for evidence of their much-vaunted idealism.

They arrived at the border post. Around a dozen soldiers stood around with the ear-flaps down on their hats and chapped red hands resting on machine guns. The sergeant stepped forward to salute Mekhusla. He had a cough that shook the shoulders of his greatcoat. Mekhusla produced cigarettes and the two men lit up. This, explained the Interior Minister, was the southern entrance to the semi-autonomous region. Beyond this point, they had lost all jurisdiction. Villagers loyal to the government had been turned out of their homes just a few hundred metres from this spot. His troops went on patrols – as far as was possible – in armoured cars. From time to time there were skirmishes along the edge. The weapons recovered from the rebels were invariably of Soviet origin – he could show them when they got back. It was a fine haul.

Beyond the soldiers stretched a muddy road leading down a slight incline. The road bent around out of sight. Towards them trudged a couple of forlorn figures lugging bundles, their clothes spattered with mud. The fine weather seemed to have stopped just short of the border.

Oliver asked how dangerous it would be to go in independently without an armed government escort. Mekhusla put his large head on one side. 'It depends. Maybe you'll have no problem. But I can't say for sure.' He took a deep breath and turned to face Oliver straight on. 'This is not a rational situation. There is no Geneva Convention, no protocol. These people want the land and they know they have the . . . the . . .' he appealed to Niki for translation, 'the muscle of Moscow behind them. It makes them difficult to predict. But then again, you have the camera.' He put his hands together in a gesture of mock obeisance. 'Do you want to go in now?'

Yes, said Oliver and wondered why. It was no more than a public-relations exercise. There would be nothing to see.

The road was heavy-going, even for the tracks of the armoured vehicle. After a kilometre of countryside they came to a small village. Many of the houses were empty; the windows of some were blackened from fire. Stray dogs gathered at corners. Two boys of perhaps eight or nine watched them pass from behind a tree. Oliver saw a woman's face at an upstairs window. The sergeant kept in constant radio contact with the border post but there was nothing to report, only the grey mud spinning around the wheels, spreading like batter in their wake. The very absence of activity made Oliver nervous.

Back inside the smoky limousine Oliver's fears settled. Nameless dread was not easy to depict on-screen. He hoped the hostilities would in time show themselves in a more dynamic way, although he had little doubt that they would. He felt suddenly very tired and slightly sick.

Niki and Mekhusla were talking. The minister broke off to shout instructions to the driver. Food was needed, drink also, he suggested to Oliver, who made to protest that there was work still to be done; he was on the morning plane out; he and Niki had to sort out their schedule for filming. Just a short stop – you'll work better; there was no arguing with Rambo.

It was already dark when the car swung off the same straight road that led back to the capital. It followed a dusty track overhung with bushes for a few hundred metres and pulled up in front of a low pebble-dash building with a lean-to extension. Oliver followed Niki out of the car. She appeared to bounce into the building; he took longer, hit by the evening chill and his cramped joints. The interior of the building was brick, washed with dark brown paint; it smelt damp. There was one long table lit by candles in tin holders with a plastic tablecloth and bentwood chairs. From the direction of the lean-to, a man came towards them, brushing aside the beaded curtain. Within seconds, wine and tumblers were produced. Mekhusla sat on one side of the table, his guests on the other. They drank, toasting future co-operation.

The proprietor brought salads and steaks of river-fish, which swam now in oil and garlic. Oliver ventured some questions on the political situation. The minister, if he had ever been on duty, was most firmly not so now. Oliver's enquiries were returned unopened. He tried to get some leverage by engaging Niki in the discussion, asking her opinion on matters – the funding of the government's forces or the engine of the nationalist movement – on which Mekhusla must be the superior authority. His reward was negligible: nothing except an indulgent smile or a brief joke.

When they had finished eating, their host produced a bottle of brandy and he and the minister moved over to a side table. Oliver resigned himself to running through with Niki the preliminary schedule while the two men talked and drank. The matrix of staple interviews – the professors, editors, politicians, the dissidents and detractors, the zealots – must be laid over the vast uncertainty of the war and now, it seemed, of the President himself. As they juggled days and times, availability of interviewees and meal-breaks for the crew, Oliver wondered with a recurring sense of gloom whether it would all hang together.

Since they were shut out from the minister's conversation, he confided this to Niki. Her mouse's nose tilted up sharply, as if sniffing danger. That, he saw, was not a problem she wished to share. He poured himself another drink, grumbling.

Oliver began to despair of regaining his peacock-blue bed in the glass-and-steel ziggurat. It seemed impossible that in twenty-four hours he'd be in the Home Counties. At last, well after midnight, the minister knocked back the contents of his glass and stretched. The driver rose from his seat in the gloom and they went out to the car. Niki and Oliver sat in the back as before, but the minister installed himself up front alongside the driver.

The driver was better than the policeman of the morning, but the drive itself wore hard on Oliver's nerves. It was obviously the custom to drive after dark on side-lights only, and traffic in both directions used the line in the centre of the road as a guide-track. There were few vehicles travelling at that time of night, but to Oliver's alarm each took on a nightmare quality as it loomed ahead. After a kilometre or two, the minister began humming and fiddling with the radio. He growled at the results of his tuning and the bursts of static. Oliver and Niki sat quietly, like children, in the back.

The driver handed Mekhusla a cassette. He pushed it into the machine and sat back. The chipmunk call of Russian pop music rattled around the car. Niki's shoulders began to twitch to the frantic beat. Oliver stared at the fields rushing past to avoid the frightening spectacle ahead through the windscreen. In the darkness he didn't notice the minister take something from his jacket pocket and lean on the open passenger window. So he was doubly startled as the gun blasted nonchalantly into the night sky, a fanfare for their journey.

7

DAPHNE COULD imagine it.

Arabel felt sick. Arabel had been feeling sick for some miles now. At intervals, Arabel sang of her sickness in low moans and wails, complaining of the hurt in her tummy, of Daddy's driving, of Sam's stupidity and the need to stop, now.

Arabel, said her mother, Joanna. You are not going to be sick. Just be quiet. We're nearly there, and we can all get out and get some fresh air when we get to Grandpa's house. That's enough.

Joanna was probably feeling a bit queasy herself. Richard handled the four-wheel drive, 24-valve vehicle with panache. They were late, naturally. The journey from London to the Surrey hills was not long, but regularly became a race against the digital clock.

Kenneth, Joanna's father-in-law, Daphne's long-distance spouse, would spend the twenty-minute delay in the dark wood hall, gazing from time to time for the first sign of the car through the rhododendrons in the drive. He would sit on the hall chair, feigning absorption in the *Telegraph* crossword. Every few minutes he would get up, shaking his stiff leg. He would check the bolts on all the doors and windows, the note for the cleaning lady, the timed feeder for the cat. By the phone, in his crabbed hand, would be a list of numbers, with theirs at the top. Just before they arrived, he would try that number.

Richard brought the car to a halt with a turn on the gravel. Arabel was whimpering, aggressively. Joanna jumped down and opened her door, then went round to the other side of the car to let Sam out. As she opened the door, he threw up – a

43

piebald projectile down the metallic paint.

'Sam, for God's sake,' exclaimed his father.

The house had been built between the wars, a mock-Tudor construction with weathered exposed beams and sandy pebble-dash. The wisteria was just showing luminous clutches of young leaves. It was a house that in direct sunlight looked mellow and welcoming. It stood in direct sunlight perhaps only a dozen times a year. For the rest, it was sallow and sad, overhung by elm and larch.

Sam's grandfather was busily sympathetic. Come on in, old man. Let's get you a drink, he said as he shuffled around with concern. Arabel nosed about the kitchen, turning over the note for the cleaning lady, poking into the larder and pulling out a chair from the table on to which she clambered and swung her legs expectantly. The mustiness of the house was disturbed.

Within a few minutes the group had rearranged itself in the car. Richard helped his father up into the passenger seat, where he sat, huddled in his sheepskin coat. Joanna rode between the children in the back, sunk in a fuggy indifference.

In his conversations with his father, Richard had developed a kind of restrained, distracted tone, as if carrying out another task simultaneously. Face to face, they spoke as if on the phone. They ran through the approved list of topics – relatives, the garden, Richard's work – at a steady pace, punctuating them with comments about the car's perfor- mance or other drivers' inadequacies. Bloody fool, repeated Kenneth obligingly, looking down on the offenders from his elevated carriage. Bloody fool.

Richard was worried about Daphne. The cares of the family wrapped themselves around him. He had to contend with a mother who had taken herself off to a glorified beach hut in Sussex, abandoning his frail father. Then there was a brother who was never in the country, who had one broken marriage and a disregard for his own safety. Then there were his children, whose needs were, he supposed, special. His work made myriad demands; he was a partner in a multi- media company that would soon go public. Richard subli- mated his concerns to the strictly practical, since no one else in the family did. He kicked tyres to check their pressure, put an ear to central-heating boilers and opined on interest rates. Richard was everyone's executor.

He shifted the over-powered engine into fifth gear for at least a hundred yards.

At Heathrow, the arrivals gate in Terminal 3 was stale with expectation. For passengers, it was the end of a journey; for those meeting them, the beginning of an adventure or longed-for interlude. Sometimes it was even the other way round, but the perfect coincidence of lovers' embrace or grandparents' hug was rare.

Oliver was pleased to see her. Really, he repeated, stroking her red-gold hair, noting the occasional frown of recognition in passers-by.

On the motorway, he yawned and rummaged in the glove compartment of Rachel's car for a tape. He slipped Lou Reed into the player. The metallic refrain clutched at him, a bolt of nostalgic adrenaline. The nostalgia passed Rachel by; he saw a little muscle in her cheek contract as the chords ground out. Different songs but the same chord sequences; it took him back to sweaty rugby socks and a study painted a decadent dark brown. Some rebellion. He yawned again, liverishly. Rachel was humming to herself, her fingers drumming a different beat on the steering wheel.

It was strange to be home, at once exhausted and excited, but with little to share. His message service hinted at the hang-over from his last programme – congratulations mostly, but a gritty handful of complaints too. Various lobby groups accused him of bias. He would have to attend to them before they turned nasty. On Monday, anyway.

Before then he'd be facing the jury of his family. Professional plaudits were one thing – they came flavoured with office politics – but the careless opinion of relatives was truly Russian roulette.

Oliver noticed another flicker of recognition on the face of the hotel manager when Rachel checked them in. It was a mock-Elizabethan folly. She really was cashing in on her new celebrity. The four-poster, bottle of champagne – hospitable clichés piled up like guest soaps in little baskets. In the public areas waiters and chambermaids swam before him. No leaded window was left unswagged. When he came out of the shower, she was lying diagonally across the bed in an ivory slip reading *Vanity Fair*. Even in that undeniably attractive moment, Oliver had the uneasy sensation of having been choreographed. The sex was fine, yet as he lay, resting his head on her white thigh, he felt a sudden yearning for dark and tenderness and singularity – nothing on the menu here.

As they dressed, the phone rang. From Australia, reversed charge, came a contact unearthed by the researcher. Oliver could hear the woman's voice, slow and deep with the curve of its accent. He caught too the long pauses as she considered Rachel's enquiries and the caution with which she responded. Rachel lay back amongst the pillows with the telephone cradled on her shoulder. She wrote notes in a large book.

She replaced the receiver and took a long swig of champagne. 'Shit.'

'What is it?'

'She doesn't want to talk.' She sighed and read irritably from her notes. 'The Italian émigré community in Australia is doing fine, thank you. It was all such a long time ago. There's sorrow about the loss of life and the treatment at the hands of the British government, but it's private regret, not for public consumption. There would be little served, etc., etc. Bugger off, in fact.'

'You can't blame her.'

'I don't, Oliver, I really don't. We'll just have to try harder.'

'Maybe,' he ventured slowly, 'this is not so much an issue for them as it is for you.'

She looked at him doubtfully.

'I mean,' he added, smiling at her scowl, 'it's possible.'

'Bollocks,' her face was pinched, peeved. 'They don't want to rock the boat. But it happened; they can't deny that. That's all I'm trying to get them to say.' There was a touch of sulkiness now, another layer in a room already heavy with sweat and perfume and champagne. He thought of the President and the purity of his grievance.

'Come on,' he said, 'let's eat while we may, for tomorrow

we face my mother's cooking.'

Eight for lunch no longer holds any terrors, thought Daphne, except possibly for the guests. I see no point, at this stage, in departing from the trusted repertoire. Roast chicken or lamb, vegetables – string bean and carrots, roast potatoes of course – and an apple pie. Nothing that can't be got out of season, out of the freezer. Never been much of a cook, but with two boys there was never much point. They wanted quantity and convention – with gravy.

Amazing still how much six adults and a brace of children can eat in a weekend. Forced to take the car out yesterday to load up all those plastic bags stretched perilously thin with provisions to accommodate the children's fads and fashions, and Richard's ulcer. Joanna's the most sensible of that little tribe. Joanna's sense would drive most men berserk, but for Richard it's absolutely essential. She's a curiously solid creature. On her, somehow, leather trousers lose the lure of eroticism. On her, they look like cow's skin.

And the other one. What will she eat? Whatever Oliver does, I expect, and Oliver will eat in a kind of nostalgic haze, professing his devotion to my gravy or – less plausibly – my pastry. Then before cheese, he'll start to get restless. He'll begin to pay Kenneth elaborate attention, saying they must have a chat over coffee. But before coffee he'll be out walking – away from us all, her included.

She tries very hard; I've seen her doing her stuff on the box. On-screen she's a perfect ice-maiden, but face to face, irritating as hell. Every word becomes a chance to prove how good her education was. Sooner rather than later he'll get bored. Surely.

Celia was different. I did like Celia, but I can see that she and Oliver might feel bound to go their separate ways. Celia ploughs her own furrow. She's an odd fish, really, but I think she suited him. I think that now, anyway. He still sees her sometimes, he says, for a chat. I can't imagine what a chat would be like with Rachel, but I suspect chatting isn't high on the list of activities here. No, Oliver is enjoying a little reflected fame. He hates the idea of fame, naturally, but if it is forced upon him, he might as well bask in it. Oliver is not above a little hypocrisy.

Beds made up, vegetables in water, fish fingers laid out for the children. Time for a drink. There's something at the back of my throat I cannot shift.

And as I walk through the sun room towards the kitchen there is always a pain, a tension in my left side. As I walk back it transfers to my right. I cannot ignore it; it's to do with those damned things in the card-table drawer.

No one will arrive for another hour at least – and if they did, it takes only a second to sweep it all back. All what? A few sheets of paper – no message, no explanation, no accusation. Bloody nonsense.

I didn't need reminding. It's not by chance that I live by the sea. It calms, it rouses, it fascinates and intimidates as it might for anyone. But for me, it brings also the constant pounding of the cost of duty. I have been dutiful in my time – less so of late, it's true, but there are relatively few demands. For decades I applied myself sedulously to the discharge of my duties. Don't imagine that I was unquestioning. My questions were as dutifully thorough as my actions. And those questions are still there. This restlessness may well contribute to my famed faculties, famous only in the sense that I still have them at seventy-four, much to the astonishment of anyone under fifty.

Now it would seem that someone else is asking questions, or jumping to conclusions. I have done nothing of which I might be ashamed. But there are things I remember when I cannot sleep. These packages are strange, but not unduly alarming in themselves. There is something unpleasant ahead, I've known that for months, and it's coming closer. Maybe it's the obvious (but I don't worry about death in that way any more), maybe it's a loss of faculties, maybe a loss of respect.

In any case, this approach of the massed ranks of family is somehow unsettling.

It was as if she had summoned Jad with the twist of the gin bottle's cap. He loped up on to the veranda, tucking a dull lock of hair behind his ear, where it lay against the shaved vulnerability of the sides. Even she could tell that the hairstyle was some kind of tribal loyalty.

'All right?' he enquired.

'Yes, yes. And you?'

'Yeah. Grass looks like it needs a cut. Shall I do it now?'

'Why not?' She was pleasantly distracted by the thought. 'It would be very, well, appropriate. I have visitors today. They'd be impressed.'

'Would they? Who is it then?'

'Both my sons, the grandchildren, my daughter-in-law, my son's girlfriend . . . And my husband, of course.'

'Of course.' There was a pause. She smiled.

'He's a good man, you know,' she met his flat gaze with her pale eyes. 'He's been very ill, it's robbed him of a great deal. It's very cruel.' She felt suddenly uncomfortable, stifled, and looked around her. 'Anyway, I don't know what state the mower's in. Do you want a drink before you start? It's very hot.'

'All right. Whatever.'

She busied herself, half-wondering why he deserved the Plymouth dry or what effect it might have on the mowing.

'Your sons,' he said, tumbler in hand, 'Richard's the older, right?'

'That's right. He's a very *busy* person. He pushes away at life – this multi-media business, I expect you understand that better than I do. It seems to work. He has a senior position in quite a big company. They're doing well, I think. Richard worries, but I think he's doing well.' She paused. 'And he, they, have two children – nice children. They always seem a bit frantic, poor things, rather under pressure. It's hard being a child these days.'

'And what's the younger one called?' His directness was a relief.

'Oliver. He's in television, although he calls it film-making. It is, I suppose. He's more complicated. Richard's the organiser; Oliver thinks.'

'How old is he then, Oliver? Thirty or so?' She saw that he felt this to be very old.

'A little more, not much. He has a new, well newish, girlfriend. She's younger, but quite well known, I believe. She actually, you know, appears. *I* scarcely know her.'

'So why are they all down today? Special occasion?'

'No, not particularly,' but she did sense an agenda. 'We all get together from time to time. It's not so easy to find a Saturday when everyone's free. Oliver's away so much.'

'Just family then,' he gazed at her.

'Yes,' she said, gulping her gin. 'Although it's true that they think I'm mad to live here on my own. Richard worries, of course. He'd like me stowed away in some little "convenient" abode, close to hand, under his eye. It's possible,' it occurred to her, 'that he may launch a campaign to that effect. Perhaps even today.'

'That's pretty heavy,' said Jad.

'No, it's quite the opposite. It's ludicrous and it's insulting. Now can you help me move some of these chairs out of the sun lounge and put them round the table?'

8

BEFORE LUNCH there was an incident. Richard arrived first, turning his vehicle in a great bounce into the driveway, then braking sharply to avoid the garden tools spread out across it. As he got out of the car, Daphne observed anger in the way he adjusted his shirt on his shoulders. The back was dark with sweat.

Jad, lost in his mowing, was doubly insulated by the Walkman earphones. Richard stood with his hands on his hips for a moment, then turned back to the car to help his father out. From her vantage point, Daphne saw him mutter.

The children rushed in, followed slowly by Joanna and Kenneth, who staggered slightly as he negotiated his way around the bicycle she'd abandoned near the steps up to the veranda. What a fool, she thought, what a fool I am to leave that there. She turned away from his painful progress on the stairs, Joanna's solid hand under his elbow. Richard had gone back outside to watch Jad, who continued, oblivious. Daphne felt a sudden creak of concern. Where's Daddy, she said to Sam and Arabel, go and bring him in. It's hot, he'll want a drink.

Certainly needs cooling down, said Joanna.

The second car crept along within a few minutes. It was a car Daphne did not recognise, the girl's car. Oliver was in the passenger seat. Neutered.

Richard went out to meet them. In the driveway he encountered Jad, who had put away the mower and was slowly gathering the tools that lay on the ground.

She watched the pantomime from the kitchen window. 'That was a bloody stupid thing to do,' she heard Richard challenge. She couldn't hear the response, could only see Jad staring back from under the lock of hair, but she saw that it wasn't an apology. She saw too that beside Richard, who was not small, Jad appeared bigger still.

Oliver was getting out of the car. His movements were sleepy. He seemed at a loss to grasp the exchange of hostilities in front of him. Richard half-turned, as if appealing to his younger brother. Oliver looked quizzical and ran a hand through his hair. Richard spoke to him, gesturing towards him and then at his own car. Oliver put his hands on his hips, puzzled.

Jad carried on with his task: the garden tools were almost cleared. He shouldered the last and took it to the shed. Then he walked straight past Richard, on past Oliver and away down the road. The brothers turned to watch his progress.

Richard shook his head, exasperated. Oliver shrugged. He clapped his brother gently on the shoulder and smiled.

At the stove, Daphne saw them come slowly into the dark of the kitchen. As their eyes adjusted, they hesitated for a moment together, uneasy partners.

'Hello, you two,' she said crisply, barely looking up from the clouds of steam. 'Out of the way now, I'm coming across.' She bent stiffly into the oven and hauled out the shallow sizzling pan.

'Boiling oil to repel intruders,' observed Oliver.

'For God's sake, Mother,' exclaimed Richard, rocking back as if on starting blocks, 'let me do that.'

It was a squeeze to fit all eight around the table. Kenneth seemed to take up very little room. Arabel, by contrast, spread her knife and fork some two feet apart and colonised the space before her with glass and spoon. The food was served; the business of distributing meat and vegetables to three generations took ten minutes or so, setting up a merry-go-round of enquiry and action.

Eventually, as the sun streamed through the salty windows, everyone was eating, made hungry by the journey and a gulp of sea air, enervated by a glass or two of cheap wine. It would take several mouthfuls before they would spot that the food had little flavour. Daphne took comfort from this. She could still produce the family spread. She was not losing control.

Richard was first to speak above the clatter of cutlery and glasses. It had been a hectic week. Preparations for the stock-market launch were in hand. He had to do everything, of course. And no thanks probably at the end, only some sniping press.

Oliver was shut-down, private; exposure to family trigger-ed in him a mixture of lethargy and annoyance. He heard his brother banging on about his job, something about going public. He saw their father take notice, heard their mother quiz him on the implications.

Sliding between home and abroad, Oliver felt neglected.

'Pleased with your programme, then?' Richard eventually challenged Oliver. 'I missed the first part, but caught most of the rest. Well, until someone rang, that is.'

Oliver took the insult and disarmed it. 'I'm grateful for even your minimal attention. In any case, I don't know that "pleased" is ever a term you can apply to these things. There are always aspects you feel you could have done better, with more money and more time.'

'I found it all a bit contrived, though, I'm afraid. And I don't think she was nearly as liberal as you made out, your schoolteacher.'

'I didn't make anything out. That's what she said.' Oliver was pleased for some reaction at least. 'You saw it, Ma.'

'Yes, it was fine. Were you pleased with it?'

Oliver laughed.

More talk, more wine, more heat in the sun-filled room. A certain irritability flushed along the table. Daphne sat at the head, weary from the cooking. Even the children seemed intoxicated and quarrelsome.

Richard was again holding the floor – this time on the information revolution. He declared himself a believer in the moral function – the democratic function – of letting as many people have access to as much information as possible. He also knew its commercial potential. Oliver had heard this argument a hundred times before. He could barely raise the enthusiasm to suggest that the whole idea was a con, an excuse for pumping out low-grade rubbish. The argument about the market spun back and forth between the brothers – Richard lobbing, Oliver patting it down on to the court. The children were scraping their bowls of ice-cream. Oliver believed people did not really want more choice; they wanted to feel that they had made the right choice. Richard dismissed this as parochial, a return to monolithic steam-radio and the Thunderer days. Apparently lost in his own ruminations, Kenneth suddenly chortled and waved a hand cheerfully in recognition. They all laughed, at first nervously, then with relief. Oh God, thought Daphne, ten years ago, even five, what might he have said?

'What do you reckon, Ma?' Richard turned to Daphne who sat, pack of cigarettes to hand, at the end of the table.

'What, as a consumer? I reckon all this talk of choice is an illusion. People like me are fundamentally lazy and we like to stay with something whose choice we trust.'

'Exactly,' Oliver stole a cigarette.

'Both of you,' said Richard, 'are of the old school. It's no longer good enough for the media monoliths to hand down their view of events to a grateful peasantry. People today are happy to – no, they *want* to receive more than one source of information. They can live with the idea that there are several different views. They deserve unlimited access.'

'But this isn't about samizdats, this is about entertainment. "People" don't want to plough through hours of tedious recording by some camcorder bandit, they want Bruce Willis blowing up Manhattan.' Oliver stretched and yawned.

'I suppose it's true,' Joanna made her first entrance to the conversation now the children's ice-cream frenzy was over. 'No point in having sixty-eight channels if you can't discuss last night's television over the back fence.'

'But you *can*,' Richard was becoming exasperated. 'You can choose to discuss it with people whose interests coincide exactly with yours, not just by some accident of neighbour-hood. You might have a better conversation with someone who lives on the other side of the world.'

'I imagine . . .' There was a silence and heads turned to Kenneth, eager to encourage him in the struggle to form sentences. '. . . I . . . imagine that much of the fun lies in having interests that don't coincide exactly.'

'In what sense, Kenneth?' Oliver leant forward solicitously.

'Common experience is something . . . like a catchphrase, that only rings a bell – not much more really. Don't believe in it.' He passed a thin, veined hand across his forehead, exhausted by his contribution. The others searched helpfully for meaning, nodding thoughtfully. Kenneth's hand grasped for a further thought, a clarification, then fell to the table where it distracted itself with the cutlery. Daphne was seized with an intense irritation.

Rachel, who had hardly spoken, interested herself in the design on Sam's sweatshirt.

Oliver turned to his father. 'How are you, Dad?' He began to tell Rachel stories of fishing trips and cricketing Sundays, joshing the old man gently, trying to rekindle the memories. Kenneth obliged weakly, nodding and laughing in the right places.

'This summer,' said Oliver, 'we'll go out, maybe to Lord's or . . . You'd like that.'

'You're never here,' burst in Richard, red with wine and indignation. 'How would you know?'

'He knows,' said Daphne sharply. 'Shut up, Richard.'

The conversation fragmented, lost to the clatter of cutlery and scuffling children. As Daphne began to clear the plates, Rachel stood up to help her. Daphne shook her head and gestured Rachel to her chair beside Oliver. Oliver slipped his arm about the girl's hips as he listened to his father's attempts to speak. She disentangled herself and followed Daphne into the galley kitchen.

'There's no need,' Daphne was peering into the fridge. She was relieved that the assault had not materialised: neither of the boys had asked if it wasn't time to move from the Hut. They were too wrapped up in their own business. Everything was still okay. She felt less hostile to this outsider in her kitchen. She wasn't so bad, just short on charm.

'It was about something else, actually,' said the girl, breaking into her thoughts. 'I wondered if, not now, but maybe if you had some time later, I could ask you about your work in the war.'

'Good heavens,' said Daphne levelly. 'You must be short of material. What are you after, anything in particular or war in general?'

'No,' Rachel laughed, briefly. 'It is something in particular. It's about the internment of Italians in 1940. Did your whatever – department – have anything to do with that?'

That was a surprise; but she'd always known how to hide surprise. 'A bit, yes. It was all over very quickly, really. It's quite well documented. I'm sure you've tried the usual places, Public Record Office and so on.'

'Of course. I was really wondering if I could just talk to you more about your own experience of it. The procedural stuff I can get elsewhere.'

'Well, we can talk, of course – but you should know that it *was* all procedural stuff; that was the way we worked.' Daphne looked around the kitchen with a disciplined smile. 'But let's get all this out of the way first. Then we can sit in the sun and have some coffee.'

After lunch, Richard took the children down on to the beach to throw pebbles into the breakers. The warmth had gone from the day and the wind was fresh. Joanna followed, her waxed jacket flapping around. Oliver sat with his father in the big window, overseeing the action. From time to time Kenneth managed a question, its nonchalance undermined by the effort. Oliver would frown and start on a detailed reply, but after a few sentences lose interest and round off with some casual observation. After ten minutes, Daphne saw him slip on his coat and strike out towards the headland along the track. Kenneth sat in his chair gazing straight ahead. When she looked again he was asleep.

'Could you face the veranda?' Daphne eyed Rachel's clothes.

'Certainly.' Rachel tucked her feet beneath her in an old Lloyd Loom chair.

'What do you want to know?'

'What the thinking was, I suppose.'

'It wasn't a question of thinking. There weren't Green Papers and White Papers and discussion documents. It was a war. Mussolini's declaration of war against the Allies was a sudden development.'

Rachel studied the old boards on the floor of the veranda. 'I was wondering who made the decision to round up the Italians and how they were chosen. Did you ever know about any of that? Or do you know someone who might?'

'Times and dates of decisions, I couldn't possibly recall now. As I said, it'll be in the records. Most of the more senior figures are dead. The chain of command was rather complex – a rather unhappy strong-arm contest between the War Office, the Foreign Office, the Home Office and the intelligence people. Perhaps it would help if you could tell me what your thesis is likely to be?'

'Well, you know how it is, I'm not sure yet. We want to present both sides; talk to some of the Italians, examine the events leading up to the inquiry. Were you involved with the inquiry?'

'Which inquiry?' asked Daphne, coolly, and something acute in her tone made the girl flustered.

'Well, the one that happened after the Italians, er, changed sides in the war. Whenever that was – 1942, I suppose.'

Daphne shook her head, waving back to Sam who had draped himself in bladderwrack. 'No help there, I'm afraid. I'd moved on by then.'

'But if I came to you with some of the names, some of the specific incidents, you might be able to throw some light on them for me?'

'I might. But you should realise that the curious thing about all that time is that we didn't really talk to one another about what we did, our work. We did it, and it was absorbing and exhausting. And then we stopped. Discussions weren't encouraged, in any case. It really was quite the opposite of today, when work seems to sustain the rest of your life – not just the money, but everything you are, everything you talk about. In the war, everyone's job was important and bizarre and often secret, but always separate. When you weren't doing it, you tried to pack a whole life into the hours off. It was quite simple, really.'

'I can understand that,' said Rachel, gazing out along the

track that Oliver had taken.

'Of course you can't,' Daphne laughed. 'Of course you can't.'

For an instant Rachel looked sideways, a little lapse of petulance. 'I *would* be grateful for your help. When we've progressed a little further, I'll call if I may to run some names and dates past you.'

Daphne nodded. They watched Arabel and Sam run back towards them.

'Just one last thing,' said Rachel as the children clattered up the steps, 'and you might like to think about this. Do you think now, with hindsight, that it – the detention, the deportations – that all this was fair, that it was right?'

9

NOBODY HAS told the cherry tree that it's war. From my window I can see it, about the size of my thumb, dancing about against the dusty brick of the school wall. At least it's not in flower, God forbid, but the jauntiness of the leaves, the slight burden of the branches – I think I can just see the green dots of tiny fruit – are so recklessly normal. Nothing can stop it, not proclamations or regulations or special orders.

And inside the school are maybe a hundred tired and frightened people. In front of me on the desk, *The Times* has a short column alongside the account of Mussolini's declaration of war. 'Soho Demonstrations' is the headline.

The round-up began within an hour of the start of the Duce's speech. Gerald would call it a precision operation; I expect that's exactly what he will call it at the morning briefing. A hundred uniformed and plain-clothes police officers descended on the Italian Club in Charing Cross Road. Even *The Times* says many of the detainees were informed of Italy's entry into the war only as they were arrested. The police moved down into Soho, sweeping up the restaurant people, and that's where the trouble started. Running scraps between Italians and Greeks, bottles thrown, windows smashed. It's begun.

Since I first met Gerald, he's always stressed the importance of the work. Sensitive, he said, and I came with a recommendation for sensitivity, which is apparently unusual. I find that surprising; the haphazard collection of academics and aristocrats and general geniuses and misfits who make up our team seems to me to have sensitivities in spades – and all of them conflicting.

I can't say that I am happy in my work, but I am tremendously responsible. I am also organised. My card-index system is the wonder of the corridor. It's common sense of course, but most of my colleagues are too in-bred or over-educated to retain that sense. It is both incredible and perfectly natural that someone like me, with decent secretarial skills and a certain – what does Gerald call it? – composure, air of command even, should assume so much responsibility so swiftly. It helps that I am tall, though not freakish. In my heels, I can look most men in the eye. So although I was not brought up among the lilacs of Ascot or the downs of Wiltshire, I pass easily for the kind of steady, clear-eyed girl they need for this kind of work. For this, I should give thanks to the precision of my mother's enunciation and the gentility of Herne Hill.

I have stamina, too. I am constantly amazed at the fatigue that hangs around these clever men. They sit in their little green-painted cells under their single light fittings, surrounded by piles of reports, smoking and sighing. The skin around their eyes is grey, their hair is dusty and they are distracted. From time to time, to relieve the pressure (or break the tedium, whichever comes first), they devise pranks and japes to prove something to fellow competitors in other branches of the special services. A break-in or a spoof committee report, some little irritation that is intended to yield the pearl of perfect intelligence.

For to tell the truth, morale is very low – and with each day that passes without finding secret enemies in our midst, the more it seems that they must be very clever and very cunning indeed. Our department, to put it bluntly, is not delivering the goods.

It has got much worse in the past few weeks. I was drafted in from the secretarial pool at the beginning of April and it was bad enough then. I don't know what to say about everything that's happened, Holland and all that. But since Norway, the atmosphere has become quite horrible, really.

Everyone's like a cat on hot bricks.

Gerald has just come in with the rest of the morning papers. Most carry reports of the first detentions of Italians. Some remind all Italian nationals that they are now subject to articles 6a and 9a of the 1920 Aliens Order and must report to their local police station – A-F on Thursday, G-M on Friday, and so on. They must surrender cameras, motor cars and wireless sets. Their movements will be restricted. But not as restricted as their compatriots in the school over there. This, as I suspected, is the real reason for Gerald's visit. In the plan that Gerald laid out some weeks ago he would conduct the examining interviews, with me taking notes. But from his agitation I gather that the arrangements are already in a bit of a muddle. More detainees are expected as the day goes on; the police are already in the City, seeking out the Italians working in shipping offices and business houses.

Gerald sits beside me at my desk. We both look out across the open ground to the school. Daphne, he says, Daphne, diva of the rotary index, we are in for some very hard work. Yes, Gerald, I reply, thinking 'sir' too formal. He turns and looks at me. At this short range, his brown eyes are hugely magnified by the spectacles, their pupils seem the size of florins. He grins that boyish grimace that goes with the lock of hair that has fallen down towards one eye – since prep school, I suspect. Many of these people, he says, will be out of sympathy with Fascism. Yes, I reply in a measured way, knowing that something more important is to follow. But our task, he announces, is to weed out those who are unfriendly to Britain, be they Fascists, Communists or Anarchists, to intern them and, if necessary, to deport them.

I know all this of course, but it is part of Gerald's method to lay out the status quo before exploring the options. I wait. In London, he continues, there are some 7,000 Italians. I know this too; each has a card on my system. We will not, he laughs – though I can tell this is not a joke and I am not expected to join in – arrest them all, but we know from our intelligence that there are some 1,500 dangerous individuals. It is necessary to 'comb out' the 'desperate characters'. We have identified 300 who might very well aid any attempt to mobilise attacks on this country.

Now I know, and he knows, that we do not know this for sure. My card index is the extent of our knowledge of the Italian community. Over the past few weeks, we have assembled some information on the membership of the Fascio and the social structure of the various communities. All we do know is that we seem to know more than anyone else – and on that basis, we put in an order for certain arrests under Regulation 18b of the Defence (General) Regulations. I typed the order myself.

I should add that, up to this moment, the exercise has seemed just that. Now it is becoming apparent to Gerald that war – real war – is edging closer. It's been here in the air around us for months of course, in the emergency and the preparations and the dreadful news, building up like great clouds. So the mood of conflict in Europe is everywhere, but it hasn't been war as I thought it would be. Now we do have real conflict in the streets of Soho and Clerkenwell and Glasgow and Cardiff, and other places where Italians live in this country. That school over there represents our first real engagement.

Technically, things have been handed over to the Home Office. They're in charge, says Gerald with a monkey grimace that almost hides his bitterness, but for a few days we will be on hand to deal with the unforeseen. He allows himself a smile; it is obviously a relief to him that this first part has gone so swimmingly. The key thing, he adds confidentially, is that he knows he can rely on me. I know my stuff and I have the intelligence to apply it with – and he pauses, as if finding this word for the first time – sensitivity. Whitehall is always at Gerald's heels. Sensitivity, he hints, is not much prized there.

Armed with files and the relevant cards from my index, we walk across in the sunshine to the school. Three classrooms have been set aside for us to deal with the 'problems', which I suspect will be those who refuse to go quietly, who shout and demand attention. Gerald and I will take one classroom; his number two, Tom, will take the second; and it's not yet clear what we're doing with the third.

I am expecting some chaos, but somehow not the barrage

of irritability and suspicion that meets us in the hall. Functionaries from the Italian embassy rush forward, as does the police inspector in charge of the detainees' welfare – one complaining, the other anxious lest he be complained against. Gerald brushes them both aside and we head off down the corridor. On the other side, in the classrooms, are dozens of men in various states of dress, from evening wear to labouring clothes. All look tired and unshaven. They stand or sit. Some chat in groups. Others keep apart, gazing from a window or at the floor. There's a funny smell – airless and nervy.

In our classroom we are assigned a young police officer, who makes calf's eyes at me while Gerald strides about. There will be no tribunals at this stage, although when the internees get to the holding centre they'll have a chance to plead their case. This news is a blow for Gerald. If I've understood it correctly, he has always seen the summit of the exercise as his cross-examination of the most 'dangerous' of the characters. What's happened instead is that we are like fire-fighters, attending only to the most obvious or most influential cases – already we have notes of a number of lawyers' complaints – but the great machinery is out of our hands now and pulled behind the engine of the Home Office.

Arnolfini, Piero, claims he is sixty-two, which puts him outside the sixteen to sixty range. His white hair is wiry. He looks very, very tired. He is the proprietor of the Grotto Blu café-restaurant in Brewer Street and was arrested just after dawn. Gerald frowns; the card in front of him indicates that Arnolfini is fifty-nine. He has managed his own premises for ten years. Apart from family, he employs two people. We have him listed as being a member of the London Fascio but he denies it. Gerald sends the constable out for the records that were seized from the Italian Club last night. Gerald asks about his grandson, who is being held separately. The man looks alarmed and concedes that the boy has received violin lessons under the auspices of the Fascio at the Casa del Littorio in Charing Cross Road, but that this means nothing. Most of the young people of the Italian community attend social events there from time to time.

The constable returns and whispers to Gerald, who looks stern. The records show, Gerald informs Arnolfini, that he supports a militaristic organisation dedicated to furthering the international ambitions of Benito Mussolini. Arnolfini stares at the constable, and then at me and his expression changes. He begins to speak in Italian – very fast and very emotional. Gerald leans forward and raps out something or other. The man takes control of himself and slowly enunciates in English his record of honesty and hard work, his distaste for the Duce and his complete loyalty to, indeed love for, Britain. After further exchanges, Gerald asks him to name names. Arnolfini says he cannot. Or will not, adds Gerald.

There is silence and Gerald motions to me. I ask my first question: is Arnolfini aware of anyone who is a member of a militaristic organisation, if he is not himself. He shrugs; there are always such people, no one takes them seriously. But we do, I insist. He is too busy with his business to waste time on such idiocies, he says. Ask someone at the Casa del Littorio. He has suddenly lost energy and become truculent; then I remember that he has had no sleep. Gerald suggests a break, more for himself than out of compassion.

Now Gerald and I are standing by the open window, smoking, looking back across at the Scrubs and our HQ. I ask him about the records and he makes that monkey grimace. When the police reached the offices of the Club, all the documentation of any significance had been removed. Already this morning the Italian Hospital has been searched; again, all records were already destroyed. This is what we are up against. Tom McManners comes in, all tweed and bluff as usual in spite of the summer sun. He has despatched a teacher and storekeeper from Clerkenwell. Nothing there, he says, pipe clenched between his teeth; the teacher has a son in the Forces. The two men stand on either side of me, grinning grimly. Gerald, I can tell, is contemplating a change of tactics. He is obviously annoyed that his fine classical mind has so far failed to steer Arnolfini into the Scylla and Charybdis of his argument. Let him stew for a while, he says, and then I think you, Daphne, can have another go.

For now, we have to attend to something more urgent. These incidents unfold with the absurd regularity of a dream. Out in the corridor, a lawyer for the Maroni brothers is demanding to see Gerald. Well, well, says Gerald, rubbing his hands in anticipation of a real set-to, let him in. The lawyer is forceful and direct. His clients are the most eminent of popular entertainers, at the top of their profession for a decade and a half. It is simply preposterous that they, who enjoy the patronage of lords, ladies and (here he directs a meaningful glance at Gerald) princes, should be under any suspicion. And why not? rejoins Gerald. Are they not ideally placed to pass the most sensitive of information? Does not their way of life allow them contact with all types of people, from all strata of society? The lawyer demands that they are released within the day or he will seek recourse to (another glance) the highest authority. The brothers are shown in.

Like those masks of tragedy and comedy, Guido and Umberto Maroni sit side by side. Guido, the younger, is immaculate in evening dress; dark circles of fatigue only add to his elegance. Berto was roused from the marital bed while his six children slept and has dressed hurriedly. There is grey in his hair and his jowls sag. Only the eyes, like great tea-plates, give the slightest clue that here in this classroom we have Britain's most famous circus clowns.

Gerald is scrupulously polite. He is grateful for the brothers' time. Guido nods, curtly. Berto gives just the beginnings of a slow smile. A smile is not what Gerald is expecting and he rushes on to explain that the outbreak of hostilities between our two countries has made it necessary to investigate the links between organised Fascism and Italians in Britain. He looks at their passports. Each has been altered from 'emigrant' to 'Italian working abroad', in line with Mussolini's attempts to strengthen bonds with expatriates. The brothers have been travelling recently – to Italy, Switzerland, America even. Gerald asks who their contacts are in these countries. Berto takes a deep, judicious breath. Impresarios, he says, impresarios and artists, tightrope walkers and elephant trainers and fire-eaters and bareback riders and small children – oh yes, many of them – and city mayors and customs officials and bankers and beautiful women (his eyes flick politely at me) and ugly ones too, and Christians and Jews and Lutherans and unbelievers . . . The lawyer clears his throat; Berto's smile is now very broad indeed, although it leaves his eyes untouched.

Gerald turns to Guido, who is clearly uncomfortable. Mr Maroni, he says, you have been a regular visitor to the headquarters of the Italian Fascio in London. Guido blinks. Do you subscribe to the views of the dictator Benito Mussolini? Guido looks pained and shakes his head. What then, persists Gerald, is your association with the following, and he lists a number of suspected Fascist sympathisers. Guido looks at the floor. When he speaks, his voice has no obvious trace of accent, just a certain precision and a pattern of phrasing – like a waltz – that is not quite English. There is, he explains, a club for children that enjoys the hospitality of the Fascio. It has, as far as he is aware, no political links. Sometimes, on Sunday afternoons, he teaches the children a few simple skills – something with plates, a little juggling, he smiles at the absurdity – and these children have parents. Some of the people you have mentioned, at last he looks up to Gerald, are among them.

Do you consider, Gerald extends the enquiry to both brothers, that you put the interests of the British Isles or Italy at the forefront of your concerns? Guido responds that he has lived here all his adult life; this is where his life is. He seems very agitated, although quiet. Berto leans forward, a forearm on his solid thigh. He squares his face to Gerald. There is very little smile left on that face now. The interrogation has turned topsy-turvy. What are you trying to prove, he asks, that I was not born in my village, that I have no past? What is the reason for treating decent people, who have worked hard for this country, like cattle? We are proud of being Italian – despite the jokes and the insults and the hatred that some of your newspapers try to breed in British people. But already, out there, he gestures behind him to the door, they are becoming scared. Nobody will tell you anything. Everybody will lie. I am already lying myself and I have nothing to fear.

Haven't you? Gerald wonders, looking distracted. But he

knows, as I do by now, that the brothers cannot be held, even if they were the cousins of the Duce himself. For some minutes ago an envelope arrived bearing a very important seal indeed. The letter requests that they be treated with the utmost courtesy and released at the earliest opportunity. As it arrived, their lawyer relaxed from the edge of his chair and began to leaf through the documents in front of him. He proffers one now to Gerald. It is a statement, signed by his clients, to the effect that they swear allegiance to Britain and undertake to uphold its efforts in the war. There is no way out. Gerald is furious.

When they have gone, Gerald begins to pace again. At the far end of the classroom, he turns and looks at me. Daphne, he says, strictly speaking it is too early for you to be carrying out this kind of work on your own. However, we must appreciate that there is tremendous pressure on our time. I want you to bear in mind that you may be dealing with clever and devious people. We have to be sure that they are not slipping through the net. I want you to talk to the chief inspector and to Tom and then you may begin your first interview.

And so I have risen from filing clerk to secretary to intelligence officer. I am relieved by the promotion, if only because it means that I no longer have to pretend not to see Gerald's humiliation as his theory knocks against people. I rap on the door of the chief inspector's office.

Amongst the men eating potato-and-leek soup in the school canteen, there are apparently a number of known racketeers. Several of the restaurateurs are known to subscribe to a bootleg liquor syndicate. At least two rounded up last night are suspected of murder. The officer has waited many years to put these men under arrest. He knows that within these cream-painted walls are the fragments of an extortion racket. The excitement makes him jovial. He warns me of the criminal element and asks me to notify him of any mention of smuggling or vice. We have them now, he says.

Tom is, as ever, tremendously sympathetic. It's very tricky indeed, he says, rubbing his eyes. Those who know won't say, those who don't are too frightened to speak. Can we tell the difference? I ask. He raises his eyebrows and explains that he makes it a rule of thumb to watch their hands. He pauses and we giggle at the absurdity of what he has just said. Oh hell, Daphne, he says, this is serious. We're at war.

It is only this dreadful cliff hanging over us that allows us the shelter of a few moments of silliness. In what is now my own designated classroom, I create new files for my initial batch of interviewees. I transfer what information we have from the cards: age, family circumstances, any note of meetings with embassy officials, visits to Italy. The first is shown in and I become an intelligence officer, all crisp questions and note-taking. After a few minutes, it occurs to me that I play the part rather better than Gerald, for all his Homer and Horace. As the morning wears on, I have to deal with a difficult character; the chief inspector has warned me that he is suspected of the murder of a young man in Leather Lane. He's certainly close and shifty, and I'm ready to believe he is entirely in sympathy with the Duce's views. I have to say in all honesty that we would be better off if he were not on the streets. I recommend internment.

The afternoon passes at a brisker pace. In the chairs in front of me appear various figures – the shy schoolmaster, ebullient hotel manager, obsequious tailor – with their personalities amplified by nervousness. Most deny any sympathy for their country's Fascism, but I am getting to recognise signs that suggest that their first loyalty lies to Italy and not Britain. The names of their children, sending money back to the old country and membership of organisations, often still with strong regional, even village, allegiances; these must all be clues.

I walk with Gerald back to the offices. It has been a difficult day, he concedes. It concerns him that I am being forced to take on too much responsibility. I must, he stresses, refer to all matters of which I am uncertain to him or Tom. And what, I wonder, could they do about it?

10

13 June 1940

THERE IS something so wonderfully cool about the south side of Walton Street in the mornings. Barely after five, but the sun is already tickling the doorsteps of the houses opposite. Last night I had a bath – well, more of a lick and make-do really – just about five hours ago, in fact. I feel I could go on for ever.

Lydia sat on my bed and for the first time in days we talked. She's as nervy as I was, I suppose, back in those early days. Mixing with the most curious types – everything to play for, nothing according to the old rules.

Now I'm in a position of remarkable responsibility and of course I can't speak to a soul about it. Lydia thinks it sounds dreadful. But it's both dreadful and wonderful at the same time, as everything is. It's all spinning round, and at night, like this, it buzzes in my head. When I'm there, concentrating on the task in hand, it seems quite simple, linear. Like the card index, I follow one thing after another. But when I stop, when I come away from it, I feel as if there were a gas balloon pushing on the inside of my ribcage. I can barely breathe and can scarcely accomplish tasks fast enough. Which first? Climb the stairs, let my hair down, light the gas? Around my room are a dozen unfinished little tasks. A stocking half-darned, a plate unwashed, the first few lines of a letter. I was so tired last night that I had the distinct impression that Lydia perched on my bed, painting her toenails, was a dream. My own voice seemed to be coming from somewhere out on the landing. I suddenly noticed that both our voices made the same pattern – not the words so much, but the sounds. I sound like Lydia. I wonder what Mother would say.

I suppose she would laugh, but allow herself a little grudging pride. Here I am, a stone's throw from Belgravia, living in a lady's house. To be straight, it's not terribly clean, but Lydia says that's to be expected of her aunt and I should see the place in the country. I should indeed. Lydia is Tom's second cousin, so it's Tom I have to thank for this perch. Working these extraordinary hours, it's been a godsend. I haven't been home for three weeks now. I've managed the odd note to Mother, but it is like being in another country.

This Sunday I will, definitely, get back to Herne Hill for lunch. The uncles will be there. If I can get away early I might get a lift down to Clapham from one of the boys in time to scrub the vegetables. There'll be a bit of mutton. Mother has yet to fail the uncles in her supply of scrag-end. She'll want to know everything, although she'll be fierce and very critical. Funny sort of work – well, I suppose so, Mother, but it has to be done.

My mother has a way of looking at you with her head on one side. She observes and judges all at once and, whilst her eyes glisten with amusement, her tongue is always sharp. I suppose there's something quite manly about her features, especially since she shuns the Marcel in favour of a severe cut from Mrs Taylor next door. She's done it for donkey's years now; ten minutes with the kitchen scissors and Mother's hair falls like a heavy steel curtain across her forehead, held back behind one ear with a kirby grip. Her eyes are grey and her skin is tanned and tough. She is no fool.

My father died some five years ago, when I was nineteen. There were complications following a particularly bad attack of influenza. Up until then, although he always said there was something wrong with him and was forever finding more peculiar symptoms, he looked the picture of health – all ruddy, if a bit nervous. But I wasn't surprised when he died, although I miss him still. He was somehow always on the edge of the room, charming or infuriating us. He was also always on the edge of his work, adding up columns into infinity while humming a tune from some light opera and often, or so we found out later, producing the wrong total.

Mrs Taylor would say that we have done well, all of us. Mother snorts at this, although photographs of the boys in uniforms take pride of place on the sideboard. Alice has married into money, despite her larking about in the theatre. Alice of all of us can manage Mother; there are rows and confrontations, but Alice's great skill at times of deadlock is to fling back her head and laugh like a fishwife or break into song with that great, deep voice of hers. Mother cannot possibly, in her heart, approve of Eddie, Alice's husband, with his gold rings and his divorce, yet she accepts the black-market gifts and the invitations to their Marylebone flat. By comparison, the rest of us must labour for her approval. The boys have all gone into selling of some kind – either as reps or on the clerical side. They will do well, once this war allows them to get back to it, since they are pleasant and handsome and hard-working. Just as well, as they have four children between them already.

And me, the little one, the afterthought – I think what I am doing is the most extraordinary of all. They can tease all they like; I really am in the front line. They've got every excuse to tease anyway. Since I don't and can't talk about my work, it must seem even more bizarre than it does to me. I can hardly explain that we seem to make up the rules as we go along, because there are no rules. It is so different from anything in our upbringing. That was all rules for the five of us, six if you include Father. Tasks and duties, meat on Sunday, cold on Monday, cottage pie on Tuesday, every night half an hour of reading, followed by twenty minutes of reciting some passage to improve the memory. Relentless improvement – that is Mother's creed.

Great lumps of Dickens or Jane Austen or Lewis Carroll run in my head sometimes, at three o'clock in the morning, when I'm buzzing beyond exhaustion. Tom and Gerald as the Walrus and Carpenter, that's the sort of thing – and useless it is too. It's the same when I open my files in the morning. There is a kind of excitement that only a blank page, fine-ruled, makes. My head hums so loudly, I am sure someone will hear it through the walls. A shiver runs down from my ribs to my knees. And then the satisfaction at the end of a page to see the notes full up, each word a worker-bee buzzing around the task in hand.

I don't mind this part – the putting together, the careful collection of information. Detail is what I like. What I can't bear is that grand argument stuff, Gerald's department – people who start sentences with a pull on their pipe and a reedy 'Could it not be said . . .?' It automatically gives me the feeling that I am going to fail, even though common sense tells me I won't. I never stop caring about the possibility of failing. That's the curse of having done so well for myself, I suppose. Mother knows that, although it doesn't win me any sympathy with her. She knows that I've got myself on a merry-go-round that won't stop. I wanted to do better, to be better, and self-improvement is hard. She makes out she despises it, but she doesn't. She sits in the parlour by the sideboard with that cruel picture staring out with its wall eye. I've always hated that picture. It used to scare me and now I just loathe it for being so ugly. It's embarrassing too; no one in Walton Street would have a black-and-white copy of some Bible picture in their parlour. Or if they did, it would be amusing or quaint. But this is plain grim. The Scapegoat. Mother got it as a girl. It was one of her Sunday-school trophies. She loves it.

I've had so little time to put together so much. The chief sources of information, the horses' mouths, were hardly likely to co-operate. Of course, from the earliest signs of trouble, they became slippery and mysterious. Changing stories, changing records, changing tack. My saviour in all this has without doubt been the Italian community's talent for publicity. The Book has been my mainstay. When Gerald first gave me my orders – compile a list of the most dangerous, big responsibility, Daphne – I floundered for a day or so until the Book came into my hands. What a find it has proved, not just for the names and addresses listed in it, but for the opera-glass view into their world.

This book, which has been locked in the lower drawer of my desk every night for some six weeks now, is a directory of the Italian businesses in London. But it's more than that, says Gerald; it's a clear statement of where their true loyalties lie. If someone's listed in here, then they must approve in their heart of hearts of what Mussolini is doing.

I can't read Italian of course; Mother never quite got me round to that, for all her ambitions. So for me it isn't so clear. *I* would have said that this is just some kind of trade directory, with a few photographs and some grand addresses from dignitaries with great flourishes on their shoulders. But as Gerald says, I have no comprehension of the *undercurrents*. So after a few days I was assigned Miss Eddington, a tetchy old duck from Bayswater. Together we made painful progress through various publications, but our chief work was this guide to Italians living in London.

Now it is true that some of the information there is seven or eight years old, but in many ways that is the great advantage. Their pride in their country, their pride in Mussolini and, no beating about the bush, in Fascism shines through. If you know how to look for it. Just opening the covers, you are almost pushed backwards in your chair by the confidence and success of the advertisements. For me, it provides a glimpse of a world I might never otherwise see, but hear of from people who work here, or perhaps from Alice and Eddie, or rather Anna and Eddie, since that's what she's known as amongst theatre friends.

You can tell from the outside, just from the Book's cover, that you are entering dangerously unknown territory. There's a sort of frieze of people engaged in various kinds of heroic and industrious activity – athletes, farmworkers, scientists – and running between them are aeroplanes and great liners and trains. But in the middle is what Gerald tells me is the great symbol of Rome, a shield and an eagle and the letters SPQR. And – and this is the chilling part – there is a map of Britain and the Continent with Italy shaded dark and two bits of Africa coloured in the same way. Then there's a great angel carrying a bundle of sticks, the *fasces*, and he or she is throwing a rope – as if to encircle Britain. Underneath this tableau, a squad of blackshirts march diagonally, with their poisonous salute.

Fernet Branca!, shouts the frontispiece inside, has ALWAYS BEEN and ALWAYS will BE King of Bitters. It is almost impossible to open the Book when you are hungry, which in my case is at almost any hour, for the advertised menus from hotels in Queensway and Regent Street are laid out with five and six courses. Soup, hors d'oeuvres, entrée and dessert, and so much more. Evelyn Laye opines, 'Leoni! – I know of no better place in the world to dine or lunch than "Quo Vadis" Restaurant.' No better indeed. Opening the covers of this book, a bustle of noises and smells, all wonderful and plentiful and *continental*, is released into my tiny room. Men bow low over the white hands of women who dress for dinner. Laughter fights with the band and the sound of knives and forks. I have never been there but I can see it. Most of the advertising notices are in English, which saves Miss Eddington's limited energies. Ladies' hairdressers, all with an identical drawing of an elegant wave poised on a long neck, wine importers, mechanics, purveyors of ice-cream cones – the Italian community in the bloom of its prosperity, even in the hard times we've just been through.

It is sometimes difficult to resist the enthusiasm and industry that swells out of these pages, but Miss Eddington manages it as she launches into her translation of the text, the dozen or so chapters that lie between the classified advertising and the directory. Italians, it seems, are impatient of their subservient role within Britain. No longer happy to be regarded as 'Macaronis' or mandolin players, they feel angry that much of their ingenuity and endeavour is credited to someone else. And, of course, we the British are that greedy someone else. We do not, it seems, value their efforts, although if you look at these pages, you couldn't argue with their success. But, they say, the Italian state still loves them, even though its children have wandered far from home. Fascism is looking anew at their talents. It alone recognises that the nation, however far dispersed its children might be, is buttressed by history and destiny.

After all this flowery stuff comes a list of instructions. Italians must obey laws, keep out of British politics, and so on, but then comes the nub of the whole thing. Italians must respect their compatriots above all others; they must defend Italian-ness in the past and present; and they must remember that any favour paid to another Italian will repay generous dividends throughout the whole community. If there is a test, as Gerald rightly says there must be, this is it. The first loyalty of these people is not to Britain.

Over and over the pages were turned by Miss Eddington, making pale notes in pencil on her pad. There is a description of the Fascio of London with a list of achievements of the Young Fascists' Organisation, the magnificent initiative of the annual holidays in Italy, the celebrations marking the anniversary of Mussolini's advance on Rome and the splendid record of the gymnastic and music squads. The violin group stands, about twenty of them, staring ahead in full white blouses and dark shorts, hair parted from left to right. Some 600 pupils attend Italian schools in Clerkenwell, Oxford Street, Southwark, and so on. There is a photograph of the new Co-operative Club built in Soho, with its svelte black marble-and-glass façade and its electric lights that look like those same little bundles, *fasces*, here on our streets.

When Miss Eddington slipped outside, I turned the book around and gazed at the pictures of the women. Many are formidable, fur-trimmed and portly, challenging the reader from under dramatic brows. Their eyes are heavily lined, like screen goddesses. In many pictures a Princess of what Miss Eddington says is a northern Italian region is seen accepting flowers or visiting the sick. She is always wearing a new outfit, sometimes a two-piece, sometimes a gown with three-quarter-length coat. Unlike most of the ladies, she is tall, like a gracious insect, appearing doubly so beside the bowed heads of anyone she meets. In one photograph, a sad child in striped pyjamas waits in bed with a teddy bear. Beside her a nursing sister is obscured by a huge coif. The Princess is smiling, congratulating the expert medical staff of the Italian Hospital. It is all so strange – a world within our familiar London – but glamorous too, as if it were a film of real life.

There are lists of trade organisations and a mutual society, churches and religious festivals and, best of all for me, a comprehensive directory of the Italians who live in London. From Streatham to Colindale, from Shepherd's Bush to Barking, they're all here. Agostini, Allegri, Amato down to Zambardi and Zucconi.

Gaetano and Vittorio and Cesare, Loreto, Andrea and Ugo. Ettore and Luigi. I sat for days, simply making a card for each name and address as it appeared here. My first selection was to pick out those who were members of the Fascio or had attended functions there, although I'm still not entirely clear what that means in practice. And if they did have these connections – did that mean they were Fascists, like Mussolini's Fascists? Well, that was up to Gerald and Tom and people who knew more than me. Miss Eddington had gone by then, leaving a trail of Attar of Roses and dissatisfaction. From time to time, Gerald popped by. Just popping by, he'd say, smiling that monkey smile and glancing at my desk.

Gerald's interest in my work has become almost frightening. It appears we have already advised the Home Office that we have custody of the most dangerous individuals. I know this because Tom told me with a nervous laugh, which I couldn't altogether understand. What I do know is that there are reported incidents, relayed to us from various contacts in these places, of espionage and even attempted sabotage by local Fascist groups in Canada and near the Suez Canal. Why not here? We cannot afford them the benefit of the doubt.

The Casa del Littorio in the Charing Cross Road is known to everyone. The Book even contains photographs of a concert given by a famous Italian tenor while he was in town to sing at the Opera House in Covent Garden. In the front row, those women are there again, their shiny hair pulled back, pale shawls about their shoulders, gleaming beads at their necks and ears. The concert itself was infamous, not for the arias but for what our contacts tell us were inflammatory speeches between the music. The respectable crowd sitting on the gilt chairs had, just seconds before that flashbulb exploded, been listening to exhortations to support Mussolini in his global ambitions. Now they sit, serene and sophisticated, listening to the music, hardly seeming to have subversion on their minds. But that is what is so very dangerous. When you look hard, it's not so difficult to see that these people are not like us.

I know all these names on the cards so well and yet I have

never met them. I receive reports and I debrief our contacts, of course. We have a number of people who mix in these circles, although rather more at the concert end of things than down amongst the grocery shops of Clerkenwell. There has never been time for me to go out to collect information myself. It's now far too late and we are under so much pressure. We've had just six weeks to gather what we have already. Goodness knows how things will develop from here.

Gerald's list, which is essentially my list, was delivered ten days ago. Gerald was pressing for Whitehall to act upon it immediately, but nobody seems quite to know how to go about things. What a business! It is clear that this is a very dangerous time and yet no one seems to know what to do. I cannot say I am happy with the list, but events have shown how unpredictable Italy can be and Gerald says something must be done, now.

What is also becoming abundantly clear is that our great scheme is close to collapse. We are not going to be given the time to interrogate the detainees to discover the more sinister organisation. Things are moving too fast. Everything is now buzzing outside as well as inside my head.

Two things, above all, I remember from the Book. One is a publisher's advertisement for the memoirs of Mussolini and also, in smaller type, for Hitler's *Mein Kampf*. The other is a photograph. Three old women stand in line before a portrait of Mussolini in profile. Gerald says what he abhors most about the Duce is his coarseness, his peasantry, his rejection of what Gerald calls the classic liberal values.

The photograph is quite dark but in their hands I can just make out a chain and some rings, perhaps a small box. A man is taking the chain from the first grandmother. The caption below explains, apparently, that these loyal daughters of Italy are giving their jewellery for the Duce. Here in London, they are giving their gold so that he can wage war against us.

11

14 June 1940

I MUST have spent a good five minutes on this collar; you have to be so careful – the water's barely warm and there's only a fragment of soap. The cuffs are already out drying on the sill. Under the circumstances, the mirror reports back quite kindly. I suppose I dropped off around two and it's barely six now. As usual my shoulder is giving me gyp – the bones squeak across each other, you can almost hear them – and the blotter has left an indentation the length of my cheek. Thank God for my own little office. These dawn repairs can't go on; I must try to get back to my rooms tonight.

Yesterday I saw eleven detainees. Today I must deal with what Gerald describes as the more 'challenging' cases. More sorting and re-sorting. They are all challenges, of course, even more so when they can hardly speak the language. We are each approaching this in our own way. Gerald is searching for the sophisticated spy, the fine-tuned mind that seeks to subvert. The chief inspector wants the troublemakers, undesirables who disturb the peace of law-abiding people. Tom loathes Fascism in all its forms – from street-corner bullies to dictators. And I want to do what's right, which is the most confusing of all. I want to do right so that no one can say I did wrong.

Before half-past seven I must finish writing up my notes and prepare for the morning's list. At seven a cup of tea appears, thanks to the filing auxiliary, and my collar and cuffs are dry enough to be reunited with the blouse. Before me are what details we have on the fifty or so we hope to deal with

78

today. Replaced in the card index are summaries of the notes made yesterday and cross-references to the files. So far, five have been released and thirty sent to the Ascot camp. Those held will be examined again later. The doubtful cases will be deported. At least that's the system in theory. Nothing has actually gone according to the system so far.

There's pressure too. Fifteen hundred. Someone, some-where – although I could make a pretty good guess as to who that might be – fixed on this figure and now that's what the Cabinet are expecting. Six hundred persons of 'hostile origin or associations', around half of them here in London. That's our job. Find the dangerous ones, the 'desperate characters', as someone described it.

Many of these people do look desperate, but not des-perately dangerous. But that could be their skill. The one certainty we must hang on to is that their leader *is* both desperate and dangerous and, if their first loyalty is to him, then they are dangerous too. And the fact is I have to find at least another twenty today; even then, we're hardly above 150 all told, with all three of us working flat out.

Alessandro Delle Rose is first on the list for this morning. I have noted only that he is a publisher, or possibly a publisher's agent, who has been in London for two years, staying with his aunt, that he is thirty-four and has a wife and family who travelled to America six weeks ago. He is known to associate with officials at the Italian embassy and to have organised cultural events at the Casa del Littorio. Between us on the team we do not speak of individual cases, but as Gerald picks up his files he taps his pen beside Delle Rose's name. Caution, he says.

Mr Delle Rose is a surprise. He is tall and slightly built. Like all of them, he looks tired, but although his clothes are weary, they are mustered to some kind of order. His skin is pale and so are his eyes, but his brows, his lashes, the shadow of his beard are all bluish-black. To start with, all I notice is his energy. My mother would call it jumpiness. That pale skin can barely contain the force of him. Reason enough for suspicion. Unlike his predecessors in this room, he leans for-ward resting his elbows on the table, his long fingers together as if praying. He looks expectant and excited, but very concentrated, like a child at a theatre. I run through with him the formalities and he answers almost before I have finished speaking, confirming date and place of birth, and so on. His voice, like so much else about him, is not what I am expecting. It's quite gruff, quite old, to come from a young person.

'So,' he says, 'we wait.'

Wait for what? I ask, taken aback by the firmness of his tone.

His eyes widen and his voice has a sarcastic edge, 'For the inquisition, of course. Who will carry out the inquisition?'

I shuffle my papers and clear my throat. We'll begin at once, I declare. I'm sure he can't make out the tremor in my voice. He thinks I'm the secretary. It hasn't crossed his mind that I could be the examiner. A few weeks ago I was the secretary.

He looks at me carefully and smiles a little. 'So,' he says slowly, slyly. 'It is you.'

So. It is me. I'm caught on the defensive. I have to justify my position to someone who doesn't even belong in this country.

Why, I ask, has he chosen to come to England at this particular time? If his wife and children have recently arrived in America? It is not, he replies, a question of choice. His work is to represent artists and the imperative of art cannot be resisted. He is terribly serious. Why is he here now? I repeat. He is the sole representative outside Italy of a late master of Italian letters, a Great Poet, whose death twenty-six months ago still causes him intense pain.

Well, no one has come up with that one so far. His hair is oiled back; behind his ears the little curls gather in rebellious groups. After the initial surprise, he is looking at me directly but the drooping eyelids give the impression that he is squinting into the sun. He looks at once shy and familiar, as if he were my best friend when I was eight, meeting suddenly on the street corner.

I check my notes and continue. His appearance here at the beginning of the year was noted by the intelligence people. He has been spotted consorting with many known Fascist sympathisers in diplomatic circles. He is bound to fall into the second file, the dangerous one.

Why England, why did you choose England?

'The Poet has admirers throughout the world. Here in London there are many who admire his aesthetic. At his home in Italy we are already classifying his manuscripts. The task is monumental and we have only just started. So I am here for some business. Then I go to New York to talk to publishers about the presentation of his works to the American public.'

I have never heard anyone speak like this before. It would be funny, under different circumstances. It's as if he were making a little speech, but in that soft, hoarse voice. He clearly thinks what he has to say is extremely important; I feel that each word is dropped carefully on me. But none of it means anything and I press on, hoping to return to safe ground.

What duties are these?

He still insists on talking about his poet, as if he's not concerned by the seriousness of the charge he faces. It's like another language. His hands are resting on the table, the long fingers lift in emphasis. He mentions various ladies, the Honourable This and That, the Countess of something, all admirers apparently of his poet. He talks of their grief and quotes something – it could be Italian, it could be Latin even – looking at me intently. *Post mortem nulla voluptas.*

This is all beyond me. My hands and legs are shaking. Something like a giggle forces its way up. The whole conversation has run out of control. I take a gulp of air.

'Our understanding is that you are here to further the work of this poet, an associate of the dictator Benito Mussolini.' My voice sounds nasal and sharp.

'Associate?' He pushes back from the table, looking at me now with his chin tilted up. 'He was his inspiration, his guide. Just a short time before his death, the Poet wrote to the Duce that the best of the "so-called Fascist movement" was generated from his own spirit. Mussolini has betrayed that spirit.'

All this nonsense goes on a bit more. It might be nothing, it might be an admission of sorts. I make a couple of attempts to interrupt, but he waves his hand in a gesture of dismissal, as if I have misunderstood. As if he is just about to impart some really important information. He leans back in towards me and, despite myself, despite my annoyance and apprehension, I lean forward too.

'When I was thirteen, my father took me to the Adriatic port of Fiume. That was the birthplace of Fascism in its noblest and truest sense – not this marching to order and shouting. You may remember, Miss, that the Yankee President Wilson threw Fiume away as a lure to the Yugoslavs. It had been promised to Italy, although no promises were needed, for it is indeed Italian. At that time, September of 1919, the Poet gathered his men about him, led a few hundred grenadiers and marched from Ronchi. When he reached the city, his courage and audacity led him to confront the General commanding the Italian troops. These troops, chickens who had no idea of what they were doing, were waiting with English and French forces for orders from the damned Peace Conference in Paris. When they saw the fervour and determination of the Poet, the Italian troops cheered him and pledged themselves to him. That was the beginning of a perfect time.'

No, I am shocked to hear myself interrupt. Shocked and relieved. His concentration almost had me in a trance. But he waves away my interruption with a smile. A smile, for heaven's sake. I try to break in again, but this time it sounds more like a squeak.

'It was not an idyll, you understand,' he continues. And I do not. 'It was the most perfect expression of patriotism, a brave experiment in a new Regency that would reinvent Italy's great glories. But the tragedy was that, if the Poet lacked anything, it was the resolve to act. His sentiments were noble, but he did not act. That hesitation left the opportunity for betrayal. And – over Christmas, of all times – the betrayal came. Italian troops were sent to fight against their own brothers; the Poet was in torment. Twenty-three of his legionaries surrendered their souls in the struggle at the gates of Fiume. Ten of the government troops also fell. His last act as *Comandante* of the city, on the bitter day when he had no option but to leave, was to speak over the coffins in the cemetery. He saw their souls rising from the caskets to weep and embrace one another, to drown the quarrel in their greater love of Italy. The women of the town came, one by one, to place sprigs of laurel on the coffins. I was barely fourteen.'

When he takes a breath, I jump in so quickly that I am almost shouting. Do you have links with the intelligence network of Mussolini's government?

'But you,' he insists, 'you must understand the nature of our patriotism. In the Poet, the sentiment for country is as warm and as thick as blood. It cannot be corrupted by politics.'

I still have no idea what he is talking about, but even so, in the midst of my anxiety, I am just a little impressed. Like Gerald, he is obviously a man of ideas, but unlike him, he is proud to be emotional about them, even if it makes him seem mad. Gerald uses ideas simply to demonstrate his cleverness.

But is this what they mean by dangerous? He is still talking about his country and he doesn't seem threatening, but he is loyal to an enemy power. I take a deep breath and ask the question I have to ask – are you a Fascist?

He closes his eyes. 'No, no. I am a patriot; I do not subscribe to the games of politicians.'

They are hardly games. In any case, your country is at war with Britain.

'Technically, yes, but am I going to place a bomb outside Buckingham Palace; will I assassinate your King, Miss . . .?' He searches for a response, but I frown at my notes. 'I belong to an artistic fraternity that transcends these manoeuvres.' He's very haughty, that's for sure.

I push on. But during your time here, you have aided and abetted the cause of Fascism, you have organised rallies that were intended to inflame the expatriate community against its host. These are phrases I have heard over and over, from Gerald and Tom; they are lodged in my head too by now. If he asks me for proof, I shall be in a mess. But he doesn't. In all honesty, he doesn't seem interested in what I have to say. The lopsided discussion staggers on.

'No, not against. People may burn with love for Italy, but

that does not lead them to hate others. We have much to be proud of; the Italians living here have achieved much and it is always to the glory of Italy.'

But we are at war. I press this point since it seems the one certainty. I remind him of the provisions of Regulation 18b. I question him on his allegiances. Would he be prepared to fight for Britain against Italian forces? Would he work on our behalf?

To my amazement, he bursts out laughing. Work for a country that has held him in a, he searches for a description, donkey shed for two days? And what kind of work did we have in mind? Espionage? Or waiting at tables? Hospital orderly? No, he would not be prepared to work for this government.

Well, that's all there is to it. Makes life simple. I inform him that, if that is his attitude, he will be taken to the clearing centre within a day or so and his case will be decided within a few weeks.

Now he is not smiling. He chews the inside of his cheek. Why should I waste any more time on him when there are other cases waiting in the corridor? But I cannot fathom him. Is he mad? Or do I simply not understand? How can I know? It's uncharted territory.

'Listen,' he takes a breath and begins slowly to count off the points on his fingers, 'you are very young. I am not old myself, but I have some experience of great men and their politics, and so on. The danger for you, now, lies in the threat of invasion – not from us in Italy, but from Germany.'

This sudden change is alarming. He seems reasonable, as though we understand one another. But we don't.

'For your island, invasion is a terrible violation. The fear of it bites deep. You fear, in fact, that it has already happened; that the enemy has penetrated your shores, secretly. And if you can't find it, then the more you believe that this enemy is very very clever, working silently, invisibly, to destroy you. But if I am the enemy, then I am not silent – or invisible.' He gives a triumphant grin.

This is annoying. It really is nonsense and I begin to pack away his notes. 'That is for us to judge,' I remind him, and I sound stern, even to myself.

'It's no good,' he says suddenly, leaning back in his chair and looking round him at the classroom. 'It's no good that you do this. Outside there, what do you have? You have many people. How long is it going to take you to work through them? Do you know what you are looking for?' ('Oh, we know, believe me,' I try to cut across him, but he doesn't hear.) 'Maybe you believe my case is simple,' he is saying, 'but – what am I? I can tell you that outside there are true Fascists and also anti-Fascists, criminals and priests sitting side by side. Sitting on these little benches made for children. But what am I? How can you know? The only thing you can be sure of is that maybe I might be more Italian than English.'

They will try to test you, these people. It's all splitting hairs and making you feel foolish over nothing. I've had enough experience of this with Gerald.

I tell Mr Delle Rose that the interview is at an end; only the administrative formalities will be left. Any money he has in this country must be held frozen in deposit. His relatives must report regularly to their local police station.

'No,' he shakes his head and the tentative smile returns. 'Maybe we shall talk again? I am entitled,' he adds.

I doubt it, I tell him, but I will do my best. I suggest he tries to make a representation from the holding centre. There will be procedures for such things, most certainly, procedures that end in triplicate forms and telephones ringing in empty offices. My recommendation – and I have almost eliminated the tremor from my voice – is that he is to be deported and held at an internment centre in one of the colonies.

He sits back with a slight sigh.

I should move on to the next on the list, but I cannot hold back a last question. It seems natural. We have been having, however crazy, a conversation. He may be a Fascist, but he didn't issue orders or try to flatter me. Maybe he just wants to find out what is happening. Why, I ask, do you want to stay?

'Because I am looking for my country. For now I do not find it in Italy. Certainly it's not here, maybe in America.' He takes a breath. 'Please, I need for someone to take a message to my aunt in Clerkenwell to inform her of my health, and so on.'

I take all the details and, for now, I really do intend to follow it up. Even now, we have to do the right thing. His request reminds me of all the women, waiting out there to find out what will happen to their men. For a moment I can see them, sitting patiently on a chair by the shop counter or mending in the evenings, gathering together to reassure or comfort. I barely see another woman all day long here. But I should think first of our women too, excited and frightened for lovers, sons and brothers. At least these men here are safe. The worst we can do to them is shut them in for a while.

When I look down, his card from the file is now black with my notes. I feel that I have somehow failed; I've certainly fallen behind in my own schedule. I can't let this happen again. Gerald will be furious.

During the rest of the morning I question an almost silent waiter from one of the more fashionable Soho eateries. Esposito, Gaetano. Since he does not deny membership of the Fascio, or indeed say anything, he will surely be deported. He seems resigned, but perhaps stunned might be a more precise term, since his grasp of what is going on is at best patchy. After him comes a shipping clerk from the City who, by contrast, is full of emotional outrage. Fiori, Olimpio. But we have to detain, there's no question and no exception. Few exceptions, perhaps, for the Maroni brothers were an early casualty in our record. That already seems a long time ago. More have been brought in. Arrigoni, Beschizza, Caldèra, Farnese, Gallati, Lucchese; I search for their cards.

Then there is one very puzzling one, a lawyer. He is thick-set and balding. His face is dotted with gold – in the rims of his spectacles, on his tiepin and among his teeth. That apart, the face is plump and tanned, although for now it is furrowed with worry. Everything I say he takes down in a small notebook with a gold-coloured pen, frowning with the effort of keeping up. His own responses he notes down too, as if he is surprised by them. From the conspicuous gold I suspect he must be a racketeer, even though his suit is rather shabby and was never, I imagine, quite the thing even when it was new. When I ask him about his association with various individuals he thinks hard, hang-dog, before answering. He denies membership of any Fascist or Fascist-sympathising organisation. Most violently in fact. I think he's rather overdoing it.

Later I see him in conversation with Delle Rose in the classroom. The lawyer, Trentino, is squatting on a low bench. His shoulders are bowed forward and his arms fall in the space between his legs. The plump hands are clasped together, but one index finger traces something in the dust on the floor. He gazes down as if unaware of Delle Rose, who is sitting astride the bench with one thin arm across the shoulders of his compatriot. Delle Rose's whole body is twisting with energy; his left hand, the free one, makes circular gestures as though he were flinging something on the ground, as he whispers into Trentino's ear. It's as if the thin man is pumping some of his energy into the fat one. The lawyer never looks up. As he talks, Delle Rose spins the occasional look around. He seems to ask a series of questions, yet never waits for a response. One of these looks fixes on me as I stand across the corridor, watching through the open door, caught in a tiny gap between the names on my endless list.

He stops speaking. The other man continues with his patterns in the dust, but Delle Rose looks only at me. The look isn't familiar, or aggressive, it's just a look; yet I feel at once an excitement and a sadness. It's a view into another place that I cannot understand, but which promises – what? A mystery that could be enchanting like stories. But could be evil. And must, surely, be wrong. This is not what I am here for. I have a job to do and this kind of sympathy – it's almost fascination – is just what Gerald and the others would expect from a woman. It's what I have to guard against. It would be a betrayal of the trust placed in me.

Suddenly the knot of energy that the two men form erupts into laughter, although I saw no one speak. For a moment I feel anger. Have I provided them with their joke? Delle Rose was direct. I took that for a conversation between equals; perhaps I was wrong. Now I feel scrutinised and captured in the door frame, so I move quickly on. These people seem so forlorn one minute, so full of themselves the next. It's impossible to trust them.

Just before noon, just after Fontebello, Girolamo – the cheese importer from Dean Street – has gone to the detention queue, Tom's large outline appears at the door. He lights his pipe and motions me outside through the side-door. The sun is again putting on a fearsome display.

'Sorry about the stink,' he says ruefully. 'Better outside.'

I can truthfully say that we're all so soiled and tired, interrogators and interviewees, that I scarcely notice. It is bad luck on the men that they have to wear such heavy clothes. I think of Delle Rose, strangely cool in his crumpled suit. How's Gerald? I wonder. Heat dare not touch Gerald. He frowns; Gerald is under tremendous strain. And you? His eyes are so very tired and so very sad. I am as strong as an ox, he says, and as stupid, don't you worry about me.

12

IT IS all falling about our heads. Or at least about their heads, since mine is so far below the parapet that most of the botheration doesn't reach me. All I can tell is that the System, the Order, the Work that Gerald has engaged us all in for months now is unravelling, whether from direct sabotage or carelessness it's hard to say.

Gerald seems in no doubt. Since the order came about an hour ago, he has shut himself in the end classroom. He made just one trip down the corridor, taking small steps, leading with his left shoulder and looking purposeful. His neck is a strange deep red, but otherwise he doesn't seem angry, just excited. He came in to me and gestured the carpenter, Mori, Cesare, to leave the room. We'll need the full list, with annotations, he said sharply, they're moving them all out. Where? I asked, startled into a direct question, something we avoid if at all possible. Lancashire, he said, disused mill. Bloody disaster, letting all this slip through our fingers. Bloody disaster, he repeated, it's all out there, and if we don't get at it now, we'll pay later. They're moving fast, you know. We're getting so close, Daphne. The monkey smile never leaves his face now.

Then he went out, turning sharp right and taking those same short, fast steps back to the end. I heard the door close and slipped out to find Tom.

Tom explained that the Home Office and Foreign Office have between them decided to take control of the detainees. In some ways this is no surprise. Everything we've done this spring has resulted in a battle with the Forces of Darkness, as

Gerald describes the co-ordinating committee. What I hadn't realised until just now was that this fight had given our work so much purpose. It was because of them and their constant complaining that Gerald came up with the idea of finding the most dangerous Italians and rounding them up. That way we could eradicate the Fifth Column problem at a stroke. Collar the lot, as someone rather more eminent put it. Now the whole thing has been taken out of his hands. Tom said we have to submit our reports on the individual cases, and a separate committee will consider what's to be done when they all get to this place in Lancashire.

That was two hours ago. I've been sitting here, compiling and listing and putting together, running through my entire repertoire of skills in alphabetical order. Tom said I should put reason for detention, details of known activity and recommendation for action beside each name. It seemed simple enough, but now that I've started, it's not at all easy. My job is to list, but somehow I've run out of things to list. I really can't be sure any longer quite what it is I have been doing. I am so tired and I have been staring for weeks now at the same slips of paper.

I did believe we had got somewhere. Out of the detail, I could have sworn that there was a pattern, a chain linking several families who share membership of the Fascio. There has to be. We have established that they all attended the same events and we know that they make donations, that they attend church, that their children travel together to summer camps on the shores of Lake Garda. This was the network, surely, that would allow Fascism to spread. What those youths learnt in the summer they could now take the opportunity to put into practice. Time and time again, the smokescreen is fanned out in front of us. Membership of the Fascio does not imply support of Fascism in the strict political sense, but it most certainly does mean support of the Duce. I cannot see how it could be otherwise. And yet, looking at what I have written, you would have to understand the code to see the message.

Tom comes to collect my files. I try to explain a little of this – that the notes to my notes can be found overleaf – but he raises his hand slightly to stop me. Don't worry, he says, this will do fine. Outside we hear the jangling of police keys and scuffling that indicates that more have been brought in. Suddenly I know that my notes are of no use whatsoever and that Tom knows that too. After all our efforts of the past week, my card index will stand on a table at the back of an office in Whitehall or Lancashire. Occasionally it will be spun briefly, but mostly it will gather dust.

It seems stupid that after all this time, our intelligence will lie unused. If Gerald seems even stranger than usual, Tom has become slower and more melancholy at this latest development. He is clearly preoccupied with the strange electrical phenomenon that is occurring in the end classroom. At a stroke Gerald has changed from leader to problem child. The humiliation of having every piece of his advice ignored has burnt straight through him like a great flat-iron on muslin. Until now he had seemed strong, but there it is – a kind of collapse in him that leaves a great hole at the centre of our team and no means of repair. Tom starts to apologise to let me know that this is just a temporary setback, that the old order will be restored as soon as possible. Until now I would have agreed, nodded and made supportive noises, but I simply do not have the energy. I am just staring at the desk in front of me, pulling pins from my hair and replacing them half an inch higher or lower, rearranging my disarray.

I'm not quite sure, Tom's full voice tails away until he clears his throat. I'm not quite sure what all this means for the team. He means me, of course. Talking of the Home Office, he says they intend to clear all of this up pretty quickly; many of our detainees will be straight on a boat for Canada within days. He and Gerald will have to clear up all this mess left behind. Of course. I will be re-routed in due course. Someone of my ability must be used; there are plenty of units that could do with me right now, he smiles weakly. And weak is how they look, these men who bothered me and badgered me for what seems like months. And I did perform for them; not just competent but bloody marvellous really.

And yet, even in his strange grinning distress, Gerald is still running the show. Tom feels deeply for his humiliation, but I don't feel that way at all. Nobody will ever ask me, but I don't feel that way.

13

IT'S A good thing Tom's aunt let me stay on, even though I'm posted to another department. Otherwise they wouldn't have known where to find me at four o'clock in the morning. Lydia heard the phone and crept down, still tipsy from the night before. Tom said a car was on its way and ten minutes later I was heading back to the old office.

Gerald was standing with his back to the door, but he swung around as Tom let me in. Daphne, we need your list, he said, avoiding my eyes and staring at the desk. We need to know. I looked to Tom for help. It's all gone, I said, trying to work out what Gerald was really after; it went to Lancashire. I need to know the categories, he insisted, close now to a shout. His eyes were fixed on a point about six inches above my head. We decided the categories, I began; you have the details. Your categories, he barked, we need to know why you decided as you did. The same way as we all did, I said, still looking to Tom.

After what seemed ages, Tom answered my look. Daphne, there's been something of – he shuffled and looked down – an organisational mishap. An accident. I can't tell you much more at present, but we need as much detail as you have on the people who left here. What is not altogether clear is which individuals have been involved in this accident. There's some confusion from the people in charge up there. So we have to be as clear as we can.

What kind of accident? I asked. As people always do.

Tom looked across at Gerald, who was staring at the picture rail with a slight grin of concentration. Torpedo, he said. Torpedo, I repeated blankly, wonderingly. Where? Boatload, he said, mixed bag bound for Canada.

I'm sorry, I said, but I don't altogether follow. How mixed? Mixed who?

Tom sighed. Germans, Austrians, POWs, and some of our Italians, he said.

How many? I asked.

Don't really know. Around a thousand on board, it seems, maybe six or seven hundred Italians.

All dead?

No. Well. Most lost, I believe. The problem, you see, Daphne, is that it's not entirely clear who they are.

They haven't found the bodies?

No chance of that, broke in Gerald, with a grim guffaw.

They don't actually know who is – was – on the boat, Tom explained. It's confused. The detainees have been swapping papers. When they gave out the list of those due to sail, some kind of bargaining began. Nobody, it appears, is quite who they seem. You're probably the only one who knows what's what.

After all these weeks, this came as a rotten sort of joke.

Two hours later, it doesn't feel much better. I've been through what remains of my filing system in Tom's office. I've got lists certainly, but not much detail to go with them. I can barely remember them all, or if I can remember it's from my research, not from meeting them face to face.

In the meantime, the telegrams keep coming. The survivors have been taken to the west coast of Scotland. Preparations are already in hand to put them on another ship, for Australia this time. Perhaps four hundred are missing; most of them were asleep way below when the torpedo hit. They never got anywhere near the lifeboats. Gerald says there are reports of an unholy panic, with hysterical screamers jamming the passageways. Not difficult to imagine, he repeats, with what seems like disgust. Bloody pandemonium. Poor bastards who had to deal with that. Seems they'd had some trouble with the German merchant seamen on board earlier. What a combination – Germans and hysterical Italians. Those who managed to find a life-preserver and get a seat in one of the boats don't seem to have much to say about it all.

I don't suppose they do.

At about ten, I left. There was no official car to take me away. I wasn't really even dismissed. Tom and I agreed, as Gerald went pacing, that there really was not much more I could do. I got on a bus and headed for Marylebone. Alice's girl said they weren't up yet, so I sat in the lounge, pretending to look at the magazines but really just playing with the gold fringe on the arms of the big chair. After a few minutes, Alice came in wearing an eau-de-Nil wrap with her great hair lying in a fat rope over one shoulder.

Hello, Baby, she said. What're you doing?

I never cry; so I don't know why I started just then. There have been enough awful things already, even disasters with ships; this one isn't really so bad. It's just so stupid, such a mess and a waste. And the whole thing has hardly started yet. I told Alice the bare bones of it. Didn't sound much really. She listened with her head on one side and her feet up on some Oriental stool thing. Very exotic in a Hollywood way, is Alice's décor. The girl brought in some tea and biscuits. Alice and Eddie never want for those little extras.

I explained about the rush and the pressure to make the list, how difficult it's been, how we've had to be so careful, they were so slippery. Then somehow all that got jumbled up with thinking about the water, cold and black and greasy. There were so many of them, I kept saying to her, so many all trying to get out. I bet none of them could swim. I think of the young frightened ones and the old ones, too.

'I shouldn't think they could,' added Alice helpfully, as she fixed a cigarette in her holder and lit up.

'Somehow,' I said, 'and I know this sounds daft, I keep seeing myself pushing them back down.'

'It is daft,' said Alice. 'It's not your fault. It's just an accident. Like Dad getting the influenza. It's awful, and it's strange and you might look at it and think it had some meaning. But it just happens.'

'But they were only there because I wrote reports saying they should be.'

'Why did you write those reports?'

'Because we had to find the dangerous ones, the ones who were prepared to back Fascism.'

'And did you find them?'

'Yes. At least I think so. It seems very muddled now.'

'Well, you've been up since four. I expect it does.'

'They gave money to Mussolini, you know. They sent their children to summer camps to learn about Fascism. They held meetings and rallies in London. They . . . they loved Italy; they didn't love Britain first.'

'There you are then. You were doing your job, Baby. It's not an easy job.' Alice looked at me and her air of weariness was reassuring. That's what gives her the knack for comedy, Mother says, that look that says 'I've seen it all – and more impressive'. I felt such a fool, but a lot better.

'Drink your tea,' said Alice. 'I'd better wake him. The way he was going last night, the Savoy Orpheans couldn't keep up.' She hauled her long self out of the chair and went through the mirrored doors to the bedroom.

Looking after her, I caught my own reflection. When I'm tired my nose looks about six inches long and my shoulders creep forward. I suddenly remembered I hadn't told my new division at the War Office where I was. I called to Alice to ask if I could use their phone.

The office understood; they even seemed to know something about it. Alice lent me a blouse and I went into work; it was reassuring to have those large jolly girls and boys around.

And that was that.

14

THERE WAS an inquiry of course, but that was years later. After Italy came on to the side of the Allies, it all looked so different. The inquiry questioned the method of selecting those who should be detained. I was far too unimportant to merit a question, but Gerald got it in the neck. When I saw Tom, from time to time, he told me about the way the inquiry was going. He knew someone on it; he was probably related to them. It was clear from the start that blame had to land somewhere and it landed squarely on Gerald. Sloppy research, over-zealous interpretation of the legislation, insensitive handling of the subjects – just words of course, but words that must have stung Gerald hugely.

Although I think they stung Tom more. Gerald always had a capacity for turning anything unpleasant into fuel for his outrage. He and Tom were still working as a team, but Gerald's bitterness at the obvious direction of the inquiry drove a barrier between them. Tom seemed very hurt whenever we met, his eyes duller and more wary. Once he was a little brighter; I remember a mustard-and-green tie, quite shocking, and a certain forced jauntiness. He was determined to have a good time and we giggled and drank a lot. But just the once.

I don't know when I realised. I suppose I had always known, but in those days nobody talked much about those things. In fact, nobody talked much about anything to do with how we felt, and in truth, in that great kaleidoscope of work and excitement, I'm not sure how much we wanted to stop and feel. I knew Tom was somehow protective of Gerald, but so was I, that's the team thing. I remember being impatient sometimes, thinking that's just wrong, but knowing I could never speak out, that it wasn't worth it. But Tom kept silent as an act of love.

I realise now why he sat so late into the night, shuffling his papers, in the hope of a little time alone with Gerald. At first I felt a complete fool not to have spotted it earlier, but unrequited love is slippery. Other people's passion has been something strange and baffling to me. And in this case it was odd, because it did give me a greater feeling of exclusion than any of the barriers of class or education – or the whole business of me being a woman doing men's work – had done. This lack of recognition above all was proof of my stupidity, my naïvety, my ignorance. And I felt something a little like jealousy. It did all help to explain Tom's great sadness, but I envied him the certainty. As for Gerald, nothing really seemed to make any impact on Gerald. He was so absorbed with the whirring of his own schemes and prejudices that King Kong might have presented himself at the Scrubs window and declared undying passion, and Gerald would simply have shaken his head and said, not now, not now. He would have been horrified, fiddling and twitching, if Tom had declared.

At least, I suppose he would. My only clue came after the war, at the funeral. Tom's family was there in battalions – tall horsey women, some of them quite lovely, broad older men, pale young ones – and then Gerald arrived. He was wearing a rather grubby mackintosh, belted too tightly and carrying a briefcase. He looked like a schoolmaster and it turned out he was teaching Latin at a prep school in Hampshire. He slid into the church at the back, but from across the aisle I could hear the rustle of his mac. He nodded at me on the way out and we stood together awkwardly in the cold porch as the family took the coffin to the grave.

He seemed oblivious to the occasion, as if we had met on the Tube. We exchanged light news – very light on my part, as I was still holding down the tears. Glad you've done well, he kept repeating. I think he was genuinely pleased. In a strange way I was his protégée; it was his decision to take me off filing duties that got me promoted. He would always feel as though he had taught me – perhaps not all I know, but the classical principles that pass for a trained mind in Britain. That would be his view, anyway. He did teach me, but things I wish I didn't know how to do, because I do them so well.

Nobody spoke of the cause of death. The cliché of an accident, shotguns and country houses, it happens amongst the landed classes. Where I came from, gas and rivers are more the style. I can't remember quite how I tried to refer to Tom. I must have muttered something or gestured in the direction of the grave. Gerald looked truly foxed for a moment, then seemed to slip into a professional mode, as if schoolmasterly duties had just dropped on to his shoulders. I felt as though I might be a parent whose child was somehow failing. Tragic, he said, inclining his head at the requisite angle. Young and very able, a great loss. He tried an expression of regret, but that damned monkey grin came back.

So I don't believe he ever suspected, let alone guessed. I'm sure, too, that Tom didn't kill himself for love of Gerald. I'm sure there were other chapters in that particular sentimental education. Now *I* sound like Gerald. There must have been some less convenient reason for his despair.

The funeral was just a few weeks before my own marriage.

I met Kenneth at one of those great gatherings that occupied weekends when everyone celebrated peacetime and made a feint of prosperity. Putting enough people together in one house felt like opulence. Kenneth was tall, with a slight stoop. At first he seemed reserved, although clever, but when he spoke he was surprising – offbeat we'd call it a decade or two later. I didn't think much of all of this until a group of us went dancing in town a fortnight later. Kenneth could jive like an airman. It was the most extraordinary thing – quite outside his class and experience. And there was something bizarre – offbeat, literally – about the way he jived. He would hold you just a little too long, until you felt the beat racing away and the whole step falling into fragments around you. Then he would propel you into the turn so fast you couldn't believe the light grip on your hand would be restraint enough. You would surely go spinning across the floor, sliding off your heels and bouncing into the doors. But it never happened. Suddenly, you were back on the beat and reunited. Every time that happened you felt ridiculously grateful.

We danced quite a few times over the next few weeks, interspersed with dinner and the occasional show. Alice could usually get tickets, although she and Eddie never came with us. We did meet her for cocktails once. She was late of course, but funny with it and Kenneth responded at once to her. She was very obviously checking him over in a chummy way, like another man, and he loved it. It was a dry run for Mother.

Despite my worries, Mother was fine. I collected her and took her up to an hotel by Hyde Park one Saturday lunchtime. She was not in the slightest inhibited by her old coat and hat, which were needless to say both spotless. She challenged Kenneth on every particular of his work. He took it in good part, explaining the American theories of marketing that his company employed. She looked sceptical, but was impressed by his energy and commitment. She could never be accused of giving anyone an easy ride.

Our engagement followed shortly after. Kenneth had style and charm. He was great fun and kind, he always was. I suppose even then you could sense a little regret in him, a suspicion that he was underestimated by the world, playing middle of the road – good-looking, good-mannered, good prospects – when he yearned to be devastating. It was that assumption that made him so amusing. It's what England expects, he'd say. There was plenty of laughter, then; we fancied ourselves as one of those wisecracking screen partnerships, of course. Who didn't?

Since it was what I wanted, Kenneth was happy for me to continue to work, although we both knew it was little more than a gesture. I had had a great run right through the war and after. I was nearly thirty. Even allowing for the interruptions of world conflict, it was probably time to settle down.

Whatever it was, that strange time, it wasn't the moment to look back. The weekend after the funeral, I stayed in London while Kenneth went to see his parents in Lincolnshire. I was conscious that something, freedom I suppose, was about to be squeezed from my life. It was July and hot. I met a girlfriend on Saturday and we lunched in Piccadilly and afterwards walked in Green Park. We sat in the sun as a small band played. Lulled by the heat, we had given up on chat. A middle-aged woman and a young man walked along the path, handing out pamphlets. They had the pallor and formality of religious officers. My friend and I instinctively turned towards one another, preparing to ward them off, but they glided past, leaving just the pamphlet and tired smiles.

I turned the pages. The whole thing was presented under the guise of a survey of world events. It found patterns in the various settlements between countries, Molotov-Ribbentrop, Potsdam, Yalta, Brussels. None of it made much sense and I wasn't prepared to give it more than a quick glance. On the back cover was an announcement by some ecumenical organisation of the various church services in the city that weekend. At first I was intrigued by the various blends of Christianity and how exotic they seemed. Then I noticed that tomorrow, Sunday, there was to be some sort of festival (I had never got very far with the language) at the Italian church in Clerkenwell. The procession would start at half-past two. I wondered how many had returned to Clerkenwell. It was just a thought.

In fact Sunday woke as grey and wet as Saturday had been glorious. I spent the morning making a final inventory of my things for either packing case or thrift shop. In the afternoon I intended to go through my wardrobe, checking everything, and then call on a friend for tea. But just after one, the steamy heat became too much and I had to walk. I went up to Hyde Park and wandered north. It was lunchtime, still quiet, but gradually the paths filled with promenaders. I seemed to be walking against the flow, which was appropriate since I found myself for the first time in months without any clear plan. I was truly taking an afternoon off.

By Marble Arch I took a bus east, gazing at the Oxford Street windows, clear now of their blackouts and reinforcement. The drizzle had dried up but the pavements were still shiny. I clung on to the rail and lurched down from the top

deck at the broad sweep of Holborn. From there I set off
north into the little streets. Within a couple of minutes, the
quiet was cut through with the sound of a large crowd, close
by but out of sight. People overtook me, chattering in Italian.
The buildings were three and four storeys high, packed in
tight, squeezing the curving street between them. Up above
they were ordinary enough, but at ground level the shops
were mysterious – closed now, but their contents visible
through the grills. I glimpsed jars of pale cheeses and bright
vegetables in oil, packets and tins in orange and yellow and
silver. Now and again there was a workshop of sorts, a
watchmaker's perhaps, or a café painted cream and red.

As I turned the corner, the road was solid with people
across Farringdon Road and up the hill beyond. A network of
wires from first-floor windows supported paper garlands
strung across the street and gathered into soggy rosettes.
What had seemed at first a mass of people packed tightly now
resolved itself into the spectators who were spilling out over
the pavements and the procession, which was as yet idle,
waiting, chattering and smoking. Between them was a scant
line of policemen suffering the heat in caps and helmets and
long, steaming raincoats.

Across the road from where I stood was the Italian church,
a slice of marble and pillars squeezed between two town
houses. On its steps milled priests and altar boys with a small
copse of crosses and flags and saintly effigies on long poles.
The crowd heaved as a priest made his way down, preceded
by the largest cross. More flags, many small boys, some girls
in white tulle dresses and old soldiers with blue-black feathers
in their hats all fell into line, passing before the people three
deep in front of me. Slowly, slowly, the procession moved on
up the hill. Apart from two old ladies standing up on an old
cart behind me, everyone was speaking Italian. Then came the
walking tableaux, Christ and the Apostles at various stages,
the Agony in the Garden, the Crucifixion, the Resurrection.
The depiction was simple – a piece of greenery for the garden,
a theatrical-prop stone for the tomb – with simple costumes.
Most were attended by a figure of the Virgin Mary. Finally
came the climax of the whole parade, a huge plaster statue of

the Virgin, festooned with pink and red paper roses, carried on a gold plinth.

The crowd was noisy but attentive; it was a little like being at the circus. I stood there in the damp for perhaps forty minutes.

Gradually, the procession ran out. People milled into the street, forming their own loose squad, five or six abreast. Behind them, I could see that the first statues and flags had completed a tour of the block and were making their way down Farringdon Road towards Ludgate Circus. The people surrounding me began to move towards the church, where the steps were now clear. I was half-carried along with them, but also curious. I had never seen the inside of a Catholic church, let alone an Italian Catholic church. Would I be discovered and cast out? But as I looked around, I saw that many of the young women were wearing similar two-pieces. My hair was dark; I wasn't so very extraordinary.

Like me, many of the crowd were stopping to look at the inscriptions around the church door. I hung back a little, taking in the height and the light of the building. I followed two women in as they crossed themselves with water from a stone basin and bobbed down, genuflecting towards the altar. I did the same, barely looking up as I did so in case someone spotted my clumsy mime.

It was at that moment that I acknowledged something that must have been on my mind since I'd seen the leaflet in Green Park. It was just possible in this world of coincidences that someone would recognise me. It was unlikely; after all, I had come in direct contact with no more than a few dozen detainees. It was six years ago; I had changed, if not beyond all recognition then at least substantially. But there was a tiny risk and I could be sure that anyone who recognised me would not be pleased. The feeling stole over me like a draught on my shoulders as I kept my head down and followed the women along the aisle. It was so obvious: I could not understand how I came to be there, how I had got myself into this situation, but I took a deep breath to calm myself. After all, my home town was just a few feet away, just outside the door.

In ones and twos and threes people were filing through the benches and sitting and kneeling to pray. Off to one side I glimpsed an open doorway and a short corridor. At the end was a functional little room, possibly a cleaner's den. On the wall by the door was a stark framed print. Something about it was familiar from my childhood. It was familiar, but ugly.

About halfway down the aisle, I turned off and sat, still with my head down, and clasped my hands together. After a few seconds I raised my eyes sufficiently to take in a high-domed ceiling supported by great pillars. Plain white paint and stone were adorned here and there with the luscious torches of Latin faith – rolling eyes, lips ruby red and gold-dusted limbs. Ahead on the altar was a high, slim crucifix. Around the base were laid sprays of lilies and carnations in yellows and pinks and reds. To the left in a small painted alcove stood a large statue of the Madonna holding a masterful, straight-backed baby whose hands were cupped in a benediction of the world. The Virgin's robes were glossy. The dress was a blood-red damask overlaid with gold and behind her fell a gold satin train. Around her shoulders was a short white cape edged in lace. Her plaster hand seemed to offer one of the carnations that lay close to it. The whole was set off by a backdrop sheet of a slate blue so powerful I seemed to feel it at the back of my nose. Conscious that this might be sacrilege, I stared at the effigy until the excess of it brought on a slight giddiness.

I bowed my head again. To my right I caught sight of an old woman feeding the beads of her rosary through her fingers. Beside her an elderly man gazed down into the distance. In front a young woman with two immaculately dressed little boys slipped into the pew. The boys immediately adopted an attitude of prayer so intense that the knuckles stood out from their fat little hands. The woman took time to arrange herself, slowly adjusting the lace veil she had just placed on her head and crossing herself thoughtfully. Another woman, stout and with a fierce expression, slid in to my left. She looked quizzically at me, then set about her devotions.

I was surrounded. I could hardly leave now without drawing attention to myself and yet I was unclear what would happen next. Much was familiar: I saw a hat of a type I had seen in Derry & Toms about three rows in front. Yet I felt I stood out. I felt more keenly that my hair was dark chestnut, not black. I felt that I was tall, and angular, sharp rather than curvaceous. I felt that my eyes were grey, not brown.

A priest in an elaborate robe had appeared by the altar. The rhythmic murmuring that gently rocked the church died down a little as he made his way to the top of the steps. He began to call out – half-prayer, half-chant. This was not the Mass, for even I could tell that it wasn't Latin. From time to time the congregation would respond, sometimes crossing themselves. I followed as best I could, in deeds if not words. The woman on my left looked across constantly. At last everyone sat back to listen to some kind of address. I resumed my study of the herringbone wood floor.

A foreign language tumbles over you according to its own current. After a while, your thoughts fall into its pattern. Unable to understand, I felt suddenly relaxed and emotional, uplifted even. My thoughts strayed, filing, cataloguing, to the house we were hoping to rent and the final preparations for the wedding; then thoughts of churches led back to Tom's funeral. But who knew where the thoughts of my neighbours had gone? For them, this half-hour might have had spiritual significance but, ritual apart, it might have been no more than a chance to sit and remember, or sit and plan. I felt the threat of being among strangers lose its edge.

The priest continued with his address, dispensing phrases into the cavernous air of the nave. Sometimes I saw his listeners nod, or sigh, or shift position. At one point, the elderly man slowly placed his veined hand over that of his wife. She held a handkerchief to her eye. The voice persisted in the same nasal tone but I could make out a long list of names and now suddenly, clearly, I heard it. Olympia. *Olympia*. The ship that took the German torpedo in its belly. At the sound I expected somehow a sudden roar from the congregation, but there was nothing except coughs and occasional sniffs as before. The roar was in my head.

All around me heads were drooping, weighed down with the communal grief. I sat in the middle, too tall suddenly, too broad-shouldered and Anglo-Saxon. Sympathy was not enough. We had griefs in our family; there were cousins who didn't return and houses flattened in the Blitz. I had felt desolate when Father died, but as much from the shock as the loss. What surrounded me now was the leaden sorrow of lives disrupted or cut short. It was amputation. Even with so many friends now widows, and so many lives tossed up in the air, I had never felt a wound in the way these people did now, together.

It was dangerous to travel like this, without scars. You couldn't tell your own strength. Disaster came to everybody at least once in a lifetime. These people had survived. I had yet to be tested.

15

July 1990

OLIVER WAS addicted to other people's telephone conversations. He loved the puzzle of filling in the gaps, of visualising the unseen caller. When he was staying at her flat, Rachel took very few calls in front of him. She was not a gracious telephone artist; she scowled and fiddled with the ends of her hair.

This evening, however, she didn't cut the caller short. The phone had purred its interruption as he was pouring himself a drink and catching up with the op-ed pages of last Sunday's decaying mammoth of newsprint. Rachel had answered in an offhand way, but he saw from the sudden frown of concentration that this was important. She had reached for a large pad of paper and was already scribbling, leaning across the hardwood work surface in the kitchen.

She had swung her back to him and her arm formed a protective fence around her notes. Her right foot entwined itself about the leg of a chair in childlike defensiveness. And then there was the voice.

The voice blended querulous and sharp. He was sure that when he'd first met her, the voice hadn't been like that. He wasn't sure that it was strictly necessary, this nasal insistence that ran through her professional speech and found its way increasingly into every little corner of their life together. She could whine and be aggressive at the same time, as if she found herself constantly boxed in. Develop a thicker skin, he said, learn the skills of evasion that go with success. If she was getting a hard time at the office, it wasn't his fault.

He could see a flush creeping up the back of her neck. He could tell from the deep breaths that she was bluffing about something, trying to persuade or convince. He was curious. She angled her body, writing all the time, and ventured a look his way – not at his face, but, accusingly, at his hands as they lay on the newspaper. He made a pantomime of getting up and leaving the room. He thought he caught a nod in return.

The spare room was strewn with his packages and books. He sighed at the effort to gather them all up again to leave in the morning. Filming began the day after. After a few limp attempts to order his possessions, he reached for the phone on the second line and dialled his father's number. It was engaged.

He pressed the interrupter while searching for his contacts book. In the silence that followed he could hear Rachel's conversation, in miniature, bleeding across from the other line. Tiny voices, but distinct. Another touch on the button and they would be gone.

He let himself listen, partly from ennui and partly from curiosity to see how she was shaping up. Oliver never interfered in Rachel's career. She hardly needed it, did she? He might offer the odd piece of advice here and there, an occasional nudge or encouraging wink, but these days she rarely asked. On the whole, she was moving further and further away from the areas he knew anything about, wandering into the fairyland of showbiz. And where he might have helped, with this latest project, she had become almost obsessively secretive. He suspected it wasn't going well.

He was eavesdropping – but everything about this call seemed dislocated. The actual delay between speaker and listener was barely perceptible, little more than a faint embarrassment, but the time and circumstance were a hemisphere apart. Rachel's caller was clearly very long-distance. He had a slight Australian accent. He could be in a beach shack or backyard orange grove or luxurious office lined with blond suede. Caught in her kitchen, she sounded hesitant and grudging – but he was measured and trenchant as though in the midst of a day's work. Technically the questioner, she seemed at a disadvantage.

Oliver realised it must be a great advance to find, at last, a relative of a survivor who was prepared to talk. But it was hard work. The voice at the other end of the line was of indeterminate age – anything from twenty-five to fifty. It was non-committal and frankly sceptical. Each of Rachel's comments was greeted with a guarded exhalation.

Oliver gathered that the survivor in question was the caller's grandfather. The old man must be some kind of retired academic – Rachel referred to him as Professor. He suspected the grandson was a lawyer; he mentioned his practice, where she'd apparently left a message, and he had sharp questions about the line the programme might take.

'We would need complete control over any material relating to my grandfather's story. We would require undertakings about the content and context of the programme. We need to know more about you and what you're trying to do. I must say at this point that I'm not over-impressed by your grasp of the history or the issues.'

'Television is bound to simplify.' Oliver heard her attempt at authority. 'You should be clear about that. What I'm doing is offering your grandfather the chance to present his view of a much-neglected chapter of the Second World War.' It had bought her a little time, but she was grasping for words now.

'How are you going to deal with the complexities of 18b? How are you going to deal with the legal side – with the wrangling over what does, or does not, constitute a dangerous alien? The whole question of detention without trial?'

'It is, as you say, complex,' she began, slowly. 'Essentially, for our purposes, this is a human story. Your grandfather, who posed no threat to the security of Britain, was treated like a war criminal, bundled into jail, shipped out, nearly drowned and redirected like a package to Australia.'

'What do you say to the other side?' There was something that sounded like irony in his voice.

'What other side?' she was puzzled and couldn't hide it.

'The people who did the detaining, who decided who would stay and who would go. Who will you be talking to there?'

'Well, you will appreciate that most of them are dead.

We're still firming up on that one.'

'Ah, firming up.' A dry laugh. 'Well, before you firm up on anyone this end, we need to know how exactly you'll be presenting this. I am not bothering my grandfather with some half-baked researcher's proposal. These events have painful significance for the Italian community. It's not like a college reunion.'

'No, of course.'

'There's only one way to present this with any credibility and that's to reveal just how chaotic the whole detention process was. Do you have enough information to do that?'

'We're clear on the timetable, I think.'

'That's irrelevant,' he interrupted across the miles. 'Do you know who these people were? Did the British authorities know when they lumped together casual Communists with civil-rights workers with the handful of dyed-in-the-wool Fascists?'

'That's why I've come to you. For that kind of clarity.'

'Is that right?'

'Yes, it is. I'm sorry if you think otherwise.'

'Look.' The tone became a touch more conciliatory. 'My grandfather speaks very little about this time. His contemporaries are all the same. You must understand that it's very delicate – to get them to talk you must convince them that it will be worth the pain of dragging it all up. That you are worth it. My generation also takes an ambivalent view of that period of history. Some of us believe that it is crucial to reclaim that time – to try to understand the loss and humiliation our relatives suffered. Others find it too confusing; they can't reconcile the stark truth with their comfortable life here or with the white-haired grandpas they see on Sundays.' He paused. 'I believe we owe it to the next generation, the one that won't ever know my grandfather, to talk about this now.'

'Is your grandfather fit enough to travel to Britain?'

'Sure, he's fit enough. Whether he'll want to is something else.'

'Well, if he does decide he'd like to take part, we could do some of the filming out there, but I would very much like to bring him to London.'

'I'll put it to him; that's all I can do.'

Oliver laid the receiver gently on the cradle, hoping the click wouldn't carry through to the other line.

16

THE HAM sat sullen on the plate. The tomato and lettuce eyed one another and the sentinel bottle of salad cream. In the smeared glass dish, floury potatoes sagged beneath dark, boiled mint leaves. Go ahead, said Daphne, briskly.

Rachel had proposed a restaurant, but Daphne had insisted. It was better to eat at home – less time, less fuss, fewer obligations. This way she could freeze her intruder out after a couple of hours.

She could see Rachel was not happy with the choice. Daphne knew she had wanted to cocoon her with an expense account, to put the interview on a formal footing. For what little she would get of use, a phone call would have been sufficient. But since Daphne was Oliver's mother, etiquette was complicated.

The girl's mouth seemed more pinched than usual. She was certainly resentful, but she couldn't surely be scared? Oliver had told her that Rachel found them daunting when they were gathered together as a family. Together, Oliver had confided, gleeful at the absurdity, they exuded a sense of ease. They might not be well off, but they knew their way around. Their orientation derived from the certainty that their family was the centre of the universe. They might ridicule it; they might complain; but their relationship to each other was the kernel. Other people were entertained but never admitted.

As an idea, it was hilarious, but Daphne saw that the girl believed it. She was so careful, rehearsing her words to impress, wanting to get it right. By contrast all sorts of old nonsense came tumbling out of their family, dissonant disputatious nonsense. It was preposterous to suggest that they exuded any kind of harmony, let alone an exclusive kind. The girl's nervousness came across as boredom, but then she was spending a damp July day on the south coast with a woman who was at best a bit-player in this drama. And probably not even that.

Daphne watched her guest. She would be glad when she was gone.

So. They began the awkward preamble to take their discussion from social to serious.

I cannot fathom why he continues to spend so much time with her, thought Daphne. There is no spark there, nothing beyond the reflexes of ambition. She's not particularly bright either, just dogged. Once, Oliver would have wanted more.

'Tell me how you came to work for intelligence.'

How tedious, she thought, but mustered a distancing sigh for the response. 'In those days, you understand, there was no advertisement in the *Telegraph* or *Guardian*, no equal opportunities or psychologists or graphologists. I was there, I was reasonably competent.' Self-deprecating smile. 'I suppose my face fitted.' This girl would never understand the great leap across the gorge that her appointment had been. They don't understand because she and others like her all come from some amorphous ranch of ambitious youngsters. Everyone has the right to succeed today. Everyone has the same voice too; a touch of Estuary in the vowels and a little Americana in the phrasing.

'What was the brief for the internment of Italians?'

Brief. Find the enemy before he kills you, perhaps. Root out the poison that could destroy your nation. What shall I tell her? Some anodyne stuff about uncertainty in the phoney-war period. Some background about the work of the War Office. A little history about Mussolini and Hitler. She's like a little red squirrel taking notes, taking it all down, no sorting, no reaction. How could she know that the one thing that made me feel that I belonged in this new world, the world of Gerald and Tom, was the certainty that we faced a common threat? The shorthand we developed in that office replaced the arcane dialect of public school that they spoke between themselves. I was important to them. I was important to everyone. There was something alien in the midst of London, something hard and unforgiving like a tumour. We had to find it and eradicate it before it caused damage.

'How was the list of those to be interned compiled?'

It's so quick, that question that changes the order, that edits the responses. We're on another tack now. She may have been talking to someone, but who? She may have seen the report, but I'd be surprised if after all these years she could decipher it. What I could say is that, as far as I can see, which is a long way, everyone did their job to the best of their ability at a difficult time. It wasn't easy for anyone. We didn't have the luxury of late-night television debates or questions in Parliament to guide us to some soft-edged consensus. Was it the best possible way? Undoubtedly not. Were there other options open at the time? Hardly.

But Daphne did not say this. She delivered vague recollections about briefings, membership of the Fascio and donations sent back to the Duce. She trotted out more about the blanket treatment of all Italians to avoid the suggestion of persecution. She had selected her recollections, edited for taste and decency. And Rachel took them, without response. The tiny tape recorder turned while she scribbled in her big black book.

So little humour, thought Daphne. I could be wooed with humour. But all I'm offered is dull persistence. Her gloss is superficial. Oliver was never dull, although he's tired and preoccupied now. The schedule he follows wrings him out, extinguishes his curiosity, dampens down that strange perception he used to have. She's not the answer.

'Wasn't it inevitable that many innocent Italians who opposed Fascism would be unfairly treated?'

No one, Daphne told her, was unfairly treated *by the standard of the hour*. How naïve she is; the school syllabus obviously stopped at 1939. What she probably means is that it was a sometimes arbitrary selection. We had to draw the line somewhere; no one was detained without any cause at all. But there had to be a moment when a decision was taken between yes and no.

And decisions have unforeseeable consequences. The ship, of course, is a clear example. It was simply a dreadful accident of war. There's no moral issue there, none at all. What was striking about it was not the rights and wrongs; it was the cruelty of chance and the strangeness of life. Not her business today, I imagine, thought Daphne.

'Who was responsible for the decision to intern and then deport?'

Another shuffle of the facts. Daphne explained the Byzantine chain of command, qualifying it with the observation that few of these senior people were available for consultation when they were needed. She seems to be getting slower with her notes, Daphne thought; you might think she was bored if there'd been any sign of engagement to start with.

'Did you ever come across a man called Alessandro Delle Rose?'

Daphne counted herself lucky in having a face that gave little away, although there was nothing specific to show. She had forgotten few, if any, of the names. It was both a blessing and a curse to have that kind of memory. Now she made a feint of a search. Any clue as to the context? Was he an internee? A diplomat?

Rachel shook her head. She didn't know a great deal herself, apparently, only that he was a survivor of the *Olympia*. Was? Is he dead? Has he written about the time? No, he's simply been recommended as someone with an excellent recall of the period. She hadn't yet spoken to him.

Alive – but no longer that face peering into the photographer's lens from under black brows, for sure. What was he now, if she had become this, a creaking grandmother? That must be it then, the link. Did this girl know more, after all?

If not, how strange that this particular individual should emerge into her life again with a curious pincer movement – anonymous parcels through the post and now these leaden questions?

'Do you believe the whole fiasco could have been avoided?'

Daphne lit another cigarette and smiled. 'You've read the report, of course,' she said to Rachel, shifting position to ease the stiffness in her back. She knew from her over-eager nod that she had not. 'Well, you'll know the shortcomings that were identified then. In their defence' (the 'their' was fielded by her listener) 'you should remember that there was tremendous pressure from other government departments and a widespread, even popular, belief that the Italians were "planning something". If you look at the newspapers of the time, you'll find some pretty unpleasant innuendo. The official response was, by comparison, muted. It was a precaution that senior figures felt they had to take for the general safety. It was not,' she concluded as she replaced the coffee mugs on the tray, 'a triumph of organisation but, given the circumstances, it was, I fear, inevitable.'

She saw Rachel to the car. They must all get together soon, offered the girl, with the enthusiasm of a stewardess despatching passengers from her plane. Was Daphne ever in London? They so rarely had the time to get out of town. She would get Oliver to fix something up when he got back.

Daphne waved once, briefly, to dismiss herself from the rear-view mirror. The dog appeared at the window-sill above her, leaping up, inquisitive to see what she was up to. He was impatient for his afternoon walk. In the sink the dishes were waiting. They could wait a little longer.

What was a decision anyway? Something you did or something that happened? Even in the middle of that fevered May and June fifty years ago, she had worried about the speed with which lists were compiled. But she knew they had to be made. Did she ever consciously decide that someone should be included or not? It didn't seem like a decision; some people fell into the category, that was it. It was just categorisation.

Marriage had been a similar decision. Kenneth fell into the category of marriageable men. No one before him had. She had known right from the beginning that he would ask and she knew it was unlikely she would not accept. All previous offers had been impossible; they had just fallen outside the category. Richard was born after a short interval and as a team they had dealt with parenthood. As well as good humour, Kenneth had brought patience to the exercise, which she never had.

He was just a delight; he took the weight out of life. When she frowned with concentration over a page or a stove, he would wrap his arms around her from behind – not interrupting her industry, but soothing the tension from her shoulders with his warmth. He could spring strange, enchanting surprises. Books and little poems for her, enigmas to lasso the children's imagination. Even when they had reached the silent sullen stage, the boys would still gurgle with delight at the eccentric forts and castles he made for them out of driftwood.

At first it was a wonder that a busy executive could be so lively and creative at home. Other women complained of the exhausted wraiths that returned in the evenings to homes whose routine was dominated by The Office. Gradually, she came to see that Kenneth would do anything to keep from talking about his work, that his feigned nonchalance about his ambition was no fake, after all. While she fretted at home, eager to rearrange the world, he danced sideways through the senior management of his company with a smile as melancholy as Fred Astaire's.

While he'd been nimble on his feet, they could get by. More than that, life had been enjoyable, enhanced. But over the years Kenneth's insouciance was overtaken by lassitude, a soft-shoe shuffle that had already lost its rhythm when the stroke came. And then she began to panic.

She did more and more, trying by her activity to massage the movement back. Surely, if she worked hard enough, organising life around him, it might restore his vitality. If she could only do the right thing. But there no longer was any right thing. Kenneth was defeated and she was, in some way, to blame. It was unbearable. Eventually, she could no longer live with her failure; she spent more time on her own, down by the sea.

Now, of course, by comparison, the early years of their marriage appeared an idyll. It had surely been a successful union – but she found the obligations of domesticity at once challenging and devastating. Sometimes she sensed that all her restlessness, all her bite and anger, was an attempt to be free. Perhaps without children and the tender debt to Kenneth, she might have cast it aside and rediscovered something – she wasn't sure what, some early promise. Something she had mislaid.

Only occasionally did she wake with her throat aching with sadness – although never for an event or face that she knew. In dreams she might, just once in a while, find something like the completeness and oblivion of great passion. In her thirties, she'd dismissed it as a trick of the hormones, but it persisted. Sometimes, even now, dawn would find her with wet cheeks, enveloped in nostalgia and regret for something she had never discovered. It was both ridiculous and embarrassing. She was always so self-sufficient. The only time she could recall when she had, quite literally, forgotten herself was in those first few weeks with Oliver. Then she had felt the visceral certainty that she would lay down her life, or better still someone else's, for this tiny child. Nothing beyond that mattered. She was able, a rare enough event, to live in the moment, without responsibility for future or past.

The dog ran ahead on the path, turning now and again to encourage her on. She wished Oliver a little more of his own early promise. But not with Rachel. He had the freedom to pursue his ideals and he was choosing to spend his time in a hinterland with this second-rate girl. What was the point of freedom if not to experiment? Wild, intense, excessive, intellectual – any of these she could have coped with, Daphne reckoned. But Marie-Antoinette domesticity would deaden him. They played at food shopping in Knightsbridge, they took weekends at country-house hotels, they bought designer furniture – that was what Oliver's childhood singularity had come to. The solemn blue eyes were fading.

As soon as she opened the front door she knew there was someone in the house. A second later, Jad's voice came from the kitchen.

'I've made a cup of tea,' he called. 'Want one?'

'Make yourself at home,' she said, surveying the pillage of her biscuit tin.

He grinned, 'Shouldn't leave your back door open then. Who's been visiting?' He gestured at the sink.

'Oliver's girlfriend. She was trying to find out about the war – something I worked on. Didn't have much to tell her really.'

'Her off the telly?'

'That's the one.' They both smiled. A conspiracy.

'What was this thing you worked on then? Special Operations?'

'Nothing so glamorous. I've told you, desk job. This was about the internment of Italians in 1940.'

'Oh yeah. Collar the lot.' Jad's knowledge of the course of the Second World War was detailed and partisan. It was inculcated by his father, a collector of memorabilia who passed himself off as the local television engineer. More recently it had been augmented by magazine series and videos or the Sunday afternoon film. By happy chance, Jad's job at the local adventure park brought him into contact with a retired soldier. He worked shifts as stationmaster on the miniature railway that carried children and parents from Jungle World to the Old English Village and Farm. The train driver had been a Para.

In the quarter of an hour between journeys, before Jad worked his way down the platform clanging shut the low iron gates of the carriages, enclosing nervy, excited brats and glazed parents, he and the Para talked military matters. In their matching overalls, with their regulation red rags tied around their necks and their caps pushed on the back of their heads, they stood in the shade and swapped pieces of knowledge. The management did not permit sitting. Smoking was a sackable offence.

In his spare time, Jad studied war novels with jagged silver titles. Holidays were visits to the Normandy beaches or battle sites further east. She wouldn't presume to challenge him on any date or fact.

'She wanted to know whether it was fair,' said Daphne.

'Oh,' Jad shrugged his huge shoulders. 'All's fair in love and war, isn't it?' He moved to the sink, 'I'll wash, you dry.'

'It's a deal,' she took up the grey tea towel.

'What's she like then?' he said, rolling up his sleeves and turning the taps on full.

'I don't like her,' she found herself saying, 'it's as simple as that. Nothing wrong with her, I suppose.'

'Not good enough for him then? Typical mother.'

'Yes, yes. Oh, I don't know. I suppose I'm afraid she might be good enough for him, after all.'

He didn't react but heaved a platter on to the draining board. They worked in silence.

'Do you enjoy this job at the park?' she asked eventually.

'It'll do until I've had enough. Beats hanging around at home. Shift work means I can do odd jobs or have time off.' He wiped the sink and draining surfaces, slowly, carefully. 'Any gardening this week?'

'Just the grass, I suppose, but it can wait till the weekend.'

'No, I'll do it now. I keep weekends free. Time to sleep. What's this girl going to do with all this stuff you told her?'

'I didn't tell her much. I don't know exactly. I think it's some kind of revisionist view. Picking over the old bones, looking for a bit of scandal, someone to kick.'

'And is there?'

'I don't think so. It was all so long ago.' She sighed and looked at him. 'Who can tell?'

17

FIFTEEN DAYS. It felt to Oliver like fifteen days of mud lapping up over the lens. Only five more to go. Did he have enough? Would it make any sense? Forty-five tapes so far – just reviewing them would be a short lifetime. Another eight or ten to add by the end of the trip – two at least for the President.

The weather had not been kind, or even offhand. It had been malevolent: mist and steady grey rain had drenched everything in this glorious dramatic landscape with gentle curves and semi-tones. It might have been the Scottish Borders.

He sat in the white transporter van, wedged between the aluminium camera boxes. The cameraman stood outside, frowning and smoking. Ahead at the checkpoint, Niki was discussing their entry with the soldier in charge. So much time spent waiting. Eventually she turned and walked back towards them. She still wore the gabardine mac and dark suit. The coat and worn court shoes were heavily splashed with grey mud.

She swung herself up on to the bench seat in the front beside the driver. 'It's okay,' she nodded and reached in her bag for cigarettes. The cameraman clambered aboard. Ahead of him Oliver saw three pairs of shoulders – the wide leather jacket, the narrow dark suit and the driver's donkey jacket.

They were headed back into the war-zone for the third successive day; it promised to be just as miserable. So far, they had travelled around the perimeter, almost as far as the Russian border. There they saw conscripts in long coats the colour of the mud, backed up by heavy vehicles. In the countryside they had come across skirmishes between government troops and the Russians. Nothing serious, just a few shots and a great deal of revving of wheels in the mud, but enough. Today, they were headed for a small town that was a rebel stronghold, although a few villagers loyal to the government lived just outside. Oliver's protection from Mekhusla's troops ran out at this point.

The white van crawled along. Oliver scanned the skies for some improvement in the light. The cameraman had taken it personally and was sunk in gloom. Much had been riding on these few days after the interviews and general filming in the capital. At last, something that moves, he would repeat. Except that it moved only very slowly, if at all. It was all Oliver's fault.

Niki, in turn, displayed professional defensiveness. In time, back in London, it would all be her fault. The edginess Oliver had glimpsed at their first meeting had been sharpened. She could bite, he had discovered, and she could be obstructive to great effect. Overall, however, she had been supremely efficient. Between them, she and Mekhusla had engineered five meetings with the President – sometimes no more than a few words, but on a couple of occasions a good twenty minutes of discussion. It would all help for the last act, the set-piece interview. Day 20.

The President was still a puzzle. His moods were notorious, although Oliver had seen only melancholy jump-started by righteous anger. He was urbane, able to drop names from the international literary 'A' list and illustrate his argument with slightly troubling metaphors. He was very tall. Critics continued to pop up but their arguments were fragmented. Oliver would include a couple, but these people did themselves no favours. They rattled on about obscure pieces of legislation and slights against unknown protesters years ago. It would be a struggle to make anything of it.

This little war bore all the signs of ethnic conflict. Nobody could quite pinpoint when it had begun; both sides were supported, albeit discreetly, by greater powers; it was vicious and bloody. It was also sporadic.

At the approach to the town they were met by a pick-up

truck with two men and a feather-tailed dog on board. They scanned the van without enthusiasm for weapons and motioned them on.

The town square was surprisingly full. A couple of decrepit old cars, which had once aspired to be cheap copies of limousines, were parked on the diagonal. From out of the boot, two men were selling the bits and pieces of everyday life – soap, cassettes, medical remedies and mop-heads, candy bars and string. Men and women, bundled up against the damp, had crowded round. Their faces were chapped and shining. Dogs and children wove between them. The driver of the pick-up flashed his lights for the van to stop.

With a sigh, Oliver slid open the van door. Already a few curious heads had turned. One or two of the men were drifting their way. Oliver looked towards Niki huddled in the front of the van. She was eyeing the crowd warily. It was never going to be easy for her in the rebel area, even if she was travelling with a foreign crew, but she hadn't complained or passed comment. Only now did he sense her reluctance.

She jumped down, still clutching her bag as if on the way to a meeting with the bank manager. The men, she translated, wanted to show Oliver and his team how these people had been suffering. By now they were surrounded by about thirty onlookers. A small woman with frizzy hair, dyed red but pushing through grey at the hairline, was making herself heard above the others. At first she addressed herself to the driver of the pick-up, then she began to throw comments directly at Oliver. Come to the school, said Niki, she says come to the school and see what they have done.

'In a moment,' said Oliver shortly. 'I want to know what else there is.'

A large man in a thick charcoal coat elbowed his way in. His face was florid and pock-marked. Over here, reported Niki, they say they have kept some records of the government's atrocities. The man pointed behind them to a three-storey building in the old, baroque style. The plaster decoration was cracked or missing in places. It had once been painted a muddy terracotta.

Oliver signalled to the cameraman and they unloaded the equipment. The cameraman asked what they were going to do. Fuck you, thought Oliver. We'll have to see when we get there, he said, trying to short-circuit the groans with a grimace. Sorry.

Burdened with camera, boxes, tripod and lights, they made their way slowly towards the building. The crowd swarmed around, talking across them and becoming more excited. Some steps led up to the doorway. He says, said Niki in her flat translator's tone, that you can see the bullet marks from the battle with the army. Up there. The man was pointing to shattered stucco on the first and second storeys. He was becoming more agitated; his face drew closer to Oliver's. Turn over, muttered Oliver to the cameraman. Jesus, came the response, thanks for the warning.

Now the woman reappeared. She had burrowed her way to the front row again. She is complaining about the government, reported Niki, she says they are treacherous . . . that they are practising genocide. She glanced sideways at Oliver. The woman was waving her finger at Niki and edging forward until the two of them stood face to face in the centre of the group. She began to jab her finger at Niki at the base of her throat. Startled, Niki took a step back and trod on Oliver's foot. There was laughter from the crowd and then some jeers.

'What are they saying?' hissed Oliver into Niki's ear.

She seemed confused. 'They – it's because I am from the capital. They want to make it difficult. They say I am a government spy.'

'That's ridiculous.'

'Yes, of course, but they just want to threaten.' She broke off as hands began to grab at her raincoat.

From behind Oliver placed his hands protectively on her upper arms. He could feel her trembling. Conscious of the camera on him, he talked steadily into her ear while keeping his eyes on the big red-faced man. Gallantry like this was cheap: even this bovine mass wouldn't go for him in front of the camera.

'Ask him what exactly happened here, and when. Ask him to show us the building. We want to follow him in. Then tell the woman we'll go to the school afterwards.'

Niki took a gulp of air and began to speak. There was silence and then a series of grunts of assent. An argument broke out between the woman and a young man.

'What's that?' asked Oliver.

'I can't tell: it's some kind of pig dialect,' Niki replied tersely.

Together they spilled through the broken doors and up the steps of what had once been an official building, perhaps a theatre. There was rubbish in the hall and a dew of broken glass on the steps. Even in the mid-morning light, it was cold and dark inside. The crowd with them had thinned to about a dozen.

They walked along a dirty corridor and came into a small gloomy room. Gradually they made out more empty and broken bottles and graffiti on the wall in red paint. Over a wooden chair by the window lay a uniform, with a swastika daubed on the sleeve. The large man swung his arm in the direction of the scrawls on the wall. He spat on the ground and began to speak.

'This,' Niki appeared to be having some difficulty following him, 'is the mess that the government troops left behind. They tried to take the building, but after a big struggle, the people of the town managed to get it back. They have put,' she paused wearily, 'dreadful obscenities on the wall. This is one of their uniforms.'

The man held the army tunic up against him and pointed to the swastika. Flecks of white had appeared at the corners of his mouth. He was almost shouting.

Oliver nodded, shifting from one foot to the other with impatience and cold. They moved into a second room. A foul smell – part mildew, part shit – hit them. Niki took a paper handkerchief from her coat and masked her nose. An over-turned table had shed the mouldy remnants of food. Empty bottles of sweet, gassy local champagne lay against the wall amongst piles of excrement.

Niki was gagging into her handkerchief. When she got control of herself she muttered, 'While they were here, he says that they had a feast. They brought local women here and raped them. He says they are barbarians.' Her eyes were running.

'Okay,' said Oliver, who was queasy himself. 'It's enough now. Let's get outside.'

Twenty or so people were still waiting by the steps. The woman with the gold teeth was there, flanked now by two dark-haired younger women. As Oliver and the crew came down, one of the younger women stepped forward.

'Please,' she said in a curious Americanised tone like a Japanese car, 'please come with us.'

'What do you want to show us?' asked Oliver, glad to be back in the driving seat, if only linguistically.

'We will show you evidence of the massacre at the school. We must drive. You follow us.'

She seemed to glide. Her head was large for her body. It was crowned by glossy black hair pushed under an Alice band. In a sea of dirty grey wool, she wore a bright blue coat. Her companion wore a sheepskin jacket.

'Fucking Lady Penelope,' murmured the cameraman. Oliver heard his own nervous snigger.

The school was less than a kilometre away, but the road was a mire. It was a low white building, demure, like a thousand other schoolhouses. Except for the playground. Here the basketball net had been pushed back and the ground turned over to make way for a score of rough graves, piles of earth with wooden crosses. Some had photographs in plastic bags swinging from the crosses. The earth was fresh; some of the flowers were only just beginning to wilt.

'This is where we have had to make our graveyard,' intoned the animatronic guide. 'We cannot get to our cemetery. The people have had to drag the dead from the street where they fell and make what ceremony they could. They are buried like animals. You can talk to this woman. Her husband is here.' She shouted across to a pale woman waiting by one of the graves. The woman approached, hesitantly.

Oliver listened as Niki unlaced the story for him. It was as brutal and poignant as he was expecting. In the cutting-room it might be effective, but for now he felt only fatigue and distance. There was something wrong here. The mud, the squalor and the lumpen people were beginning to unsettle him.

The cameraman changed tapes. How much more of this do you want? Better do the graves, said Oliver, and inside the school, and then we'll have to pull out. Light's going anyway. They all nodded, relieved.

Inside the school, a makeshift chapel had been set up in one of the classrooms. The light from the windows was blue. As they moved around, lining up shots, they were followed by a knot of locals, men and women, who sat and stood, smoking.

The pair of sinister young women volunteered pieces of information. This is where they laid the coffins out. The government troops advanced as far as that farmhouse you can see from the window, here. It was a very bad situation. Always they spoke of the people in the town in the third person.

Their guides accompanied them back to the centre of town. We can show you more, they said, not quite in unison. Do you have to go so soon? They inclined their heads together in enquiry.

'I'm afraid our schedule doesn't allow it,' explained Oliver lamely. There was just the catch of panic in his stomach. Was this a trap? Would they be held by the rebels? How stupid to get themselves into this situation. Out there, with Mekhusla and his brigand troops, you could understand the rules, but in here was Looking-Glass country. Nothing was what it seemed, not least these bizarre Vestal Virgins.

It's a shame, they remarked to one another. We could show you much more. Maybe you could return on another day.

'Yes,' said Oliver, too quickly. The crew had packed all the equipment into the van. They shook hands and exchanged cards. The women both had Russian names.

The van lurched across the ruts towards the government's checkpoint. Oliver lay back in his seat and gave a loud groan.

'Got what you wanted?' enquired the cameraman, mischievously.

What he wanted. Yes, and a whole lot more that he didn't. There were three possibilities: the President's troops were running out of control; or, worse still, they were under orders; or, just possibly, all they had seen today had been staged for their benefit. The problem with the second scenario, although it felt in his gut as though it might be horribly correct, was that he could find no motive.

'What was that all about?' he asked in exasperation. 'Who *were* they? What was that – some kind of Cook's tour of misery? That stuff with the uniforms – it was bizarre, unreal, like someone had been watching war films end to end. Niki, what was the deal behind the Museum of Atrocities? Was it real?' His voice was rising to a whine.

Niki was lighting up, frowning in concentration as the van bumped over the road. She looked across at him and leant back against the seat. 'They are brutal people. They have a brutal way of showing how they feel.' She looked out of the window. He could sense she was still shaky.

'But I want some guidance here.' He persisted, a touch petulant. 'I want you to help me make a judgement. Have we just been sold a load of shite?'

'No,' her voice came back, low and surprisingly strong. 'You make the judgement; that's for you. I arrange for you to see all you can. The rest is up to you.'

It was anger. He was startled. Behind Niki's back, he caught the cameraman's eye. The cameraman waggled his shoulders in a mime of petulance. Oliver looked away.

Great. She was genuinely upset. That was helpful. He sighed and watched the bushes scurrying past the windows. It was difficult to gauge not just this, but where he was with the whole country. Mekhusla, the Interior Minister, had said to him on about the second day that there were many contradictions, but he had discarded the cliché. Now he was forced back to it. A President who was both a liberal icon and authoritarian; an ethnic war that seemed generations old and, right now, politically expedient; a critical stand-off with Moscow that was also a stalemate; a beautiful chaos of a country – peopled by artists in film and books and music – that was in some respects ruthlessly efficient and detached. Mekhusla had shown him a selection of the arsenal of weapons seized from the rebels. The minister had picked up the semi-automatics and rifles, looked through their sights and joked with the sergeant detailed to display them. It had seemed like a pleasant amateur show, until Oliver asked what had happened to the rebels who had been holding them. Nothing much happens to them now, Mekhusla smiled boyishly, though some are still in prison.

Sometimes Oliver felt they welcomed him and his film; sometimes he felt they lost patience, as if they were suddenly bored with the game.

But it would still make a good story. The President's English was excellent and he had a certain tragic dignity. Oliver had heard for himself how far he was prepared to go to defy Moscow. And it must be an impossible country to govern, even without the Moscow-backed insurrection in the war-zone, which was taking men and resources that the country could ill afford. He knew the President sometimes likened himself to one of the ancient kings; he wondered if there were a way to utilise this.

Small wonder that Niki felt bruised, forced to contemplate all the problems that beset her country. They were all tired. He looked with a new sympathy at the back of her head resting on her hands as she, too, gazed out. He saw her thoughtful eyes reflected in the glass, fixed on something he knew nothing about. He looked at his watch: 7 p.m. and three hours' drive at least.

'We'll try to stop, at least for something to drink,' he nudged her shoulder.

She nodded. She needed to telephone home and make arrangements for someone to be with her son later in the evening. Who? he wondered. He knew the father was an engineer and working abroad. They had separated a long time ago.

They reached the hotel well past midnight. The crew peeled off to their rooms for showers with duty-free Scotch and Pot Noodles. Oliver collected his messages and faxes.

Niki was sitting on the low, brown plastic sofa that stretched into the middle of the hotel atrium. She had tucked her feet up beside her; her head was resting on her hand. In the greenish light she looked paler than ever. Dark circles stood under her eyes.

'What will you do?' he asked. 'Do you want me to get you a room here? We could meet early in the morning to sort out what still needs to be sorted.'

She shook her head. 'I have more numbers and my revised schedule at home. It's easier if I have my things.'

'Fine, we'll call you a car.' The van had left without warning as soon as they had unloaded the equipment.

The solitary receptionist put in the call. There would be a delay.

'Oh Christ,' said Oliver, conscious he ought to wait with her. 'I tell you what. Let's have a drink and try to do what we can now. You get your car home and you can work from there in the morning. You needn't come back in until eleven or so.'

'Fine.' She didn't seem grateful. He looked across at the bar. It was dark.

'We'll have to go to my room. Sorry.'

Only when she stood up did he see quite how pathetic she looked. Her dark suit, the brave attempt at efficiency, was creased and splashed with mud. Her mac had greasy marks on the sleeves. Her hair lay loose and limp.

They went up to the room in silence.

He poured the drinks. She sat with her eyes closed, sipping, her hands cupped around the glass. 'I'm sorry,' he began, 'it's been a ghastly day. Probably worse for you.'

She smiled slightly, still with her eyes shut.

'Shall I see if I can get something to eat from room service?' She shook her head. 'Really, isn't there anything you want?'

She opened her eyes, but looked down at the table. 'This will sound strange – but what I would really like is a bath. I would have taken you up on the offer of a room just for that. My apartment, well, the water is not so hot, the boiler is broken. It's stupid, I know.' He saw that she knew it wasn't. She glanced covetously at the bathroom door.

'Not at all stupid.' He was relieved that somehow – this easily – he could dispense generosity. 'Help yourself. There are plenty of towels; the bathrooms are something this hotel does rather well. This time of night at least there always seems to be plenty of hot water. Go ahead. I'll begin running through my list here.'

Slowly, she took off her jacket and put it on the back of the chair, gathered up her bag and went into the bathroom. He heard her shut the door and turn on the taps. Relaxing back on one of the beds, he closed his eyes. The sullen threat of the crowd was still pressing in on him, but the whisky was a help. Desperate people in that forsaken place. A malign polyp intruding into the country. Fatigue gave his recollection a Gothic tinge. He was fascinated and horrified by the images. His thoughts ranged across the dirt and the fresh graves.

A gentle splash from the bathroom reminded him suddenly that Niki was still there. Not only there but, extraordinarily, taking a bath a few feet away. Exhaustion had forced this intimacy from her. She had been shaken today, but he was impressed by how quickly she regained her resolute expression. He thought of her lying back in the steam, eyes closed, free for a minute or two from the grinding responsibilities of money and motherhood. He hoped she had taken her whisky in there. He looked at the table. She had.

He kicked off his boots. It was a revelation, this sudden glimpse of indulgence. He felt a lick of excitement. Just behind that flimsy partition wall, in the same room.

'Is the water hot enough?' he called, gently but needlessly. He heard her start, shocked in turn out of her reverie.

'Yes. Yes, thank you.'

'Do you want another drink?' There was a pause.

'No,' and then, a few seconds later, 'thank you, yes.' Her voice came back more firmly.

'If you leave the glass by the door, I'll fill it up.'

He heard her get out of the bath and pad across the floor. When he heard the splash again he gently opened the door, keeping his eyes on the glass on the marble surface by the basin. He poured another inch. As he withdrew his hand, his eyes slipped up to the steamy mirror. She was looking straight at him and he saw her eyes were startled and enormous, but excited by the absurdity of the situation. He laughed, too.

Her hair was piled up; the warmth had brought colour to

her cheeks. He could see olive shoulders sloping into the water and a little olive toe resting on the tap. She looked perfectly composed, like a little short-legged statue, challenging.

'Look,' he said, smiling apologetically, 'would it be easier if I . . .?'

He gently pushed open the door and took the glass over to her. She looked at him levelly. 'Thank you.'

He leant down to place the glass in her hand, but suddenly bent down into the steam and briefly kissed her. Abandoning the glass on the side, he squatted down and began to trace his finger down her shoulder. She gazed straight back.

'I . . . I don't want to do anything you don't want,' he said, awkwardly.

'Close the door. I feel the cold,' she said.

He lifted her to stand in the bath. She stood in the steam with rivulets running down between her breasts and into the crease of her thighs. He began to unbutton his shirt, to tear off his jeans. She watched, detached, the height of the bath putting her eyes on a level with his.

Finally naked, he embraced her. He placed his hands under her narrow buttocks and lifted her out of the bath. Her arms were tight around his neck. Suddenly he felt like an adolescent.

'I . . . is it, you know, should I . . .?' It was an idiot's stammer. Her eyes fell open and he glimpsed the old wariness.

'Yes. Please,' she whispered – or was it an order?

Grabbing a towel, he ran into the bedroom and rifled through one of his cases. Condoms, like cigarettes and luxury soap, were the currency of the briber, always carried for emergency deals, only occasionally used. When he turned round she was lying on the bed.

Her hair was wet at the ends. It stuck to his chest. The day was whirling in his head.

He tried to coax some pleasure into her. Briefly, almost dismissively, she seemed to respond, but by then he was lost in his own struggle to erase not just the grim day, but the whole confusing fortnight.

They lay listening to the plumbing and ghostly backstage

sounds of the hotel. He stroked her hair, but sleep was dragging him down. After twenty minutes or so, she swung out of bed and went into the bathroom. Once again, he heard the gurgle of water, but this time it was a long way off.

It was only when the beam of light from the door fell across his eyes that he knew she was leaving. He hauled himself up on to an elbow, blinking.

'Where are you going? What time is it?'

With practised efficiency she looked at her watch. 'It's five to two.'

'Come here. Close the door.' He beckoned her towards the bed. 'Can't you stay?' he asked half-heartedly.

She shook her head. There was an edgy silence. Now she was back in the uniform of work he felt vulnerable, like a small boy being tucked into bed.

'I must go. I'll be back in again around ten,' she said. He pulled her towards him and kissed her, briefly, on the forehead. The door clicked shut behind her.

He lay in the warmth, too tired to shower. He heard the diesel rattle of the taxi starting up in the cold.

18

THERE WAS a time when I looked forward to letters, thought Daphne. These days the prospect of a chatty missive from an old friend or a niece is eclipsed by cool notes from unmet offspring informing of death ('We were so heartened by the obituaries, which I expect you saw') or illness ('This damned heart/cancer/Parkinson's is a nuisance, but we soldier on'). Always a sting in the tail now and sometimes right up-front.

This one looked bad from the outset. She knew at once that the whole matter had taken a serious turn. The logo on the envelope indicated it was from Rachel. The tone was polite, on its best behaviour. The letter ran to two pages.

It was the most glorious day. She had been out at seven, racing along the road, keeping pace with the little clouds bouncing along the horizon. The air was already warm, with a light breeze and the denim-blue swell criss-crossed with foaming ridges. By the time she'd breakfasted, a dozen people had gone past the veranda, laden down with windbreaks and rugs and picnic bags. A young couple manoeuvred a buggy over the unmade surface. The girl was heavy, with the weariness of someone up since dawn; her broad flanks swayed with the effort of pushing the toddler. The man was smaller and slight. He'd limited his burden to a brace of plastic bags. He was handsome in a pocket-sized, Mediterranean way, a little love-god following in her exhausted milk-and-motherhood wake.

No point in putting it off, can't sit here all day staring. Read it again. She took out the letter, which had folded into an unsympathetic square in her cardigan pocket.

'Dear Daphne,' it began, with an informality that shortly

gave way to the stiff tone of a council communication.

'Thank you for your time last week. It was very useful to talk through your wartime experiences.

'As I may have explained, this research is for a programme in a series that revisits neglected parts of recent history. The series title is "Old Scores".'

What followed was a lengthy description of the genesis of the series, the awards that it had won, the illustrious producers who had been associated with it – nothing, in short, that gave Daphne any idea of what had been in the programmes.

'The core intellectual strand of the programme is a continuing discussion between two people who were involved in a particular episode of history. Through their testimonies, the viewer is drawn into a reappraisal of what really happened. There may well be differences in perception, but these will be explored.'

What did they have in mind – a kangaroo court or 'What's My Line?' Daphne snorted. What a pompous little girl Rachel was.

Two tedious paragraphs later. 'In this case, we would like to bring you together with the eminent Italian professor Alessandro Delle Rose, who was interned and then deported in June 1940. The recent fifty-year anniversary provides another reason. We do not intend the encounter to be a confrontation, but your differing experiences would illustrate the complex morality of the situation.' Then followed another paragraph with a proposed filming schedule.

Not a confrontation. Then what was the point? What was the purpose of the programme's dreadful title if not to deliver blood?

If not to lay responsibility at someone's door. Ironic, to have been promoted to a position of responsibility simply because you were the last one alive. Well, she wouldn't play, thank you. The whole notion, however camouflaged by weasel-speak, was loathsome. It was wrong. It was simply muddled and wrong. As if events had not borne out the very necessity of what they had been doing, the failure of Fascism, the need to oppose it firmly at that very moment. There was no case to answer, except for a very human tragedy, a ship that sank. An accident given greater poignancy by the circumstances of the war, an accident that otherwise would have been just that – an accident.

Complex morality. What did television know about that? Over the years she and Oliver had argued this into the ground.

And Oliver would have to hear about all this. Oliver would have to know the particulars. He couldn't know already, surely. She would have heard.

Just have to tell him, just have to tell everyone. Drag up all the memories, set it all in context. Now she was facing the prospect she realised how repetition would trivialise and distort. How ridiculous, how humiliating, how unnecessary to have to account for one's actions. What a nuisance this girl was.

She sat with the mug of instant coffee, cushioned by her annoyance. Only as the coffee grew cold did she hear the little murmur of warning. It had been there, she knew, since the first package two weeks ago.

Oliver must already know. How stupid, how stupid – they would have discussed it. Could all this even be his idea?

She took a deep breath to control the nausea. Of course not, the world does not at a stroke go haywire. He was away, out of contact, busy with his own projects. He had nothing to do with this; he would never be so crass.

Why did she feel she had to 'account for' it? The family knew about her war work. Broadly. At least, she supposed they did. There had never been much call for detail. Kenneth hadn't ever quizzed her much; so many more things had happened – five years of wartime – before they met. He knew in principle though, didn't he? One way to find out.

Ten o'clock was a good time to catch him before the day took its toll on his speech. He was slow to raise himself now, he who'd always been up at six, but by ten the marathon of breakfast was over, the cleaning lady would be around and he'd be as alert and comfortable as he'd be all day. If she'd been there in the house with him she would only have increased his agitation with her fussing and cajoling. It was better that she was here.

He would know how Oliver would react to all this. The number rang a dozen times before Kenneth slowly picked up the receiver. As soon as he answered, her desire to confide ebbed away; her usual sense of responsibility took over. No need to bother him with this. She was the strong one, the capable one. All she had to do was decline the girl's invitation. And the parcels? Were they connected? Not with Rachel perhaps, but all this was surely connected. The worm of panic grew again as she made her usual enquiries in the bright, distant voice she reserved for Kenneth.

No, nothing much to report. Yes, glorious day. Had he heard from Oliver? No, no she supposed not. Due back mid-week anyway. Of course, of course.

Good of you to call, he had said, with just the hint of a question, before he replaced the receiver.

She stood by the telephone. She could try Alice, but it would be two in the morning with her. These days any conversation with Alice felt like two in the morning. Her contralto had long slid into a growl, lubricated by the booze. Alice and Eddie had emigrated to the United States in the early Fifties, but he was only to live for another two years. Marriage number two – to a real-estate attorney – had been swift and acrimonious. Number three had taken Alice to the West Coast for the light – she'd fallen among artists now – in the early Seventies. And there she'd stayed, her thick hair striped with white and piled on her head. The artist was long gone, not dead but lost to Alzheimer's, and Alice tended the estate (bonds rather than crops). She'd had no children of her own, although a community of expectant youngsters had apparently gathered about her. In their occasional conversations, Daphne found Alice still amusing but utterly dismissive – of herself, of others, of everything. She might just remember that morning in 1940, she might even appreciate Daphne's current predicament, but it would all be a cosmic joke to her. No bloody help at all.

Old Scores. Nothing could be settled. They, the television people, didn't want it settled; they wanted old antagonisms fanned into a simple flame. They wanted to place the prism of hindsight on to an incident – any incident – and turn it into a burning moment. Look, they wanted to say, we found this thing and, strange to relate, it turns out to be the most significant event of the century, or the decade, or that week. To hell with them. Let them look somewhere else.

She had been cutting back the lilac for perhaps twenty minutes when Richard appeared around the side of the house. He looked startled above the moustache – a rat peering through a bush, as his father had once joked.

'There you are,' he was exasperated. 'Front door's open, car's unlocked – anyone could walk in.'

'And so they did.' She felt grateful for his officiousness. 'What on earth are you doing here?'

'Impulse, I suppose.' He was defensive, embarrassed. 'I've just got off the red-eye special at Gatwick. It's only forty minutes. Might as well. Jo and the kids are at her mum's. Turned left off the M25, easy.'

'Ah. Well, what a surprise. What do you feel like? Breakfast, lunch, just coffee? Seat in the sun?'

'The last two sound great. I'll get the chairs.' He dived into the garden shed, with a clatter of metal rods and flowerpots. After much cursing he emerged with two faded canvas chairs, traps to crucify the fingers.

From inside the kitchen she heard the yelp. Peering out, she saw him carefully hang his jacket on the back and sit in his shirtsleeves, sucking the wounded digit. He was pale and crumpled, slightly blotchy around the eyes. He shut his eyes in the warmth. Richard would be happy with a seat in the garden, sheltered round the back of the house. Oliver would always confront the sea.

Her coffee, he noted, was even worse than that on the plane, but he ate three biscuits to stave off the jet-lag shakes. She realised he was settling in, even for the night. It was an extraordinary detour. He'd not been expected back until Sunday, tomorrow, so Joanna had made other plans. Richard felt displaced, out of schedule, off the agenda. Perhaps his computerised organiser had suggested to him that he might make a virtue of this by a visit to his mother. Or perhaps he really did want to see her. Either way, she was glad to have him there.

She overruled his plan to keep on going through the day and sent him off for a bath. From the airing cupboard she dug out the old spare sheets, multi-coloured stripes now fluffy with age, and made up the bed. His executive luggage sat boldly on the faded carpet. On the bamboo bedside table was a lamp made decades ago from a bottle of twelve-year-old malt. Beneath it was a pile of old thrillers bought in the Fifties from the Boots Library. These had always intrigued the boys. ('How can you buy books from a chemist? Did you need a prescription?')

In the kitchen she looked at the fridge and grimaced. Slim pickings. He wasn't hungry anyway, would get two or three hours sleep and then they could go out to eat. Oh, by the way, he added, your front offside tread's nearly gone. We'll get that replaced. Bloody dangerous.

When he had shut the door, she went to the card-table and pulled the letter out of her cardigan pocket. The envelope was beginning to look lined; no longer an intruder, it was acquiring a history of its own. She pushed it on top of the others. Those earlier packages she couldn't mention. This last one, perhaps, she could try out on Richard. A controlled experiment.

She sat inside, looking out at the sunshine and the pebbled beach, staying in the gloom. She felt a little shaky at the prospect of change. All her life she'd been open to it and had even preached its virtues to those less robust. Yet, as Richard had once remarked in the midst of some tussle, the essence of her love of change had always been that she had initiated it. Now there was talking to be done, strange, unpredictable discussions – an eventuality she had not prepared for.

There was dust in the corners of the metal window frames, and sea-salt spattered diagonally across the panes. Into her thoughts came the little Eros she'd seen earlier, as he returned now along the beach road. He was wearing a tiny pair of stretch trunks and his legs were slightly bowed, accentuated by the weight of the toddler on his hip. He and the baby flirted and giggled while the mother, flushed by her day in the sun, pushed the caravan of baby paraphernalia. Every so often they would stop and turn and watch her labour towards them. See, darling, there's Mama.

Later, in the town, they ate not at the hotel that Richard favoured, but at a café. Daphne hadn't wanted to dress up. After several glasses, she broached the subject. At first, he was confused; Rachel, war work, television – had she perhaps mis-understood? What exactly had she been asked to do? He seem-ed mildly irritated, her first clue that he was taking it seriously.

She tried to explain what she believed Rachel's proposal was. He nodded.

'But what *did* you do? What was your role?'

She laid out the bones of it. Employed as an administrative assistant but drawn increasingly into the compilation of lists of those to be detained. Responsibility without power.

'Fine, that's what I've always thought, more or less, if I've thought of it at all. What I didn't know, because I could never be bothered to ask, was that stuff about the lists for the internment.' He looked curiously at the backs of his hands resting on the table. 'I suppose,' he continued, 'if they were to confront you with someone who still bore a grudge – that they had been unfairly detained, or unfairly deported – they could make an emotive case.'

She sighed and lit a cigarette. He frowned, she thought in disapproval at her smoking, until she realised it was concentration.

'It's quite simple,' he began again, 'you don't do it. There is no point in putting yourself, and us, through this. We've no idea what their real agenda is. It has to be stopped.'

'But will it all stop if I just say no?' Despite the concern, she was amused.

'It has to, they have to find someone else, or some other incident. This could just be a flier: they may not be that committed. I have contacts – so does Oliver. Obviously.' A grimace. 'We ought to be able to put the lid on this.' He thought. 'Have you told Dad?'

'No, I didn't want to worry him.' She was slightly con-temptuous. 'It's nothing to do with him, so long ago, years before I met him, even. Anyway, this makes it sound like an affair. It's nothing to be ashamed of. It was a job carried out for the government of the day, in good faith.'

'Exactly. These people were Fascist sympathisers, weren't they? There really is no more to say. I think she's . . . well, she's acting in a pretty shabby way. She might have let you know at the outset that this was what she had in mind. And she waited until Oliver was away.' He gazed at the candle. 'Joanna doesn't like her, you know.'

'I suppose she did wait,' Daphne felt the old fear return. She threw in the other option casually, 'They might have discussed it. He might know and just not have mentioned it.'

He looked at her reprovingly. 'Come on, now.'

'Don't patronise me, Richard.'

'Only if you deserve it, Ma. You should talk to Dad. He'd understand. He'd want to know. Tell him.'

Daphne wasn't so sure, but when the phone rang at eight forty-five on Sunday morning she guessed that it was already too late.

The paper, said Kenneth. Saw it in the paper. He was very purposeful, knowing each hard-fought sentence had to do the work of many. It's a silly article, he said. Don't worry, we'll get an apology. If that's what we want.

Richard pulled on jeans and raced the car to the general store perched on a crescent of grass between the retirement bungalows. He came out of the shop holding the fat bundle, scanning the front page. With great self-control he threw it on to the passenger seat and drove straight back, throwing up sandy dust on the turn into the beach road. Daphne was on the veranda, feeding toast soldiers to the Jack Russell, in a tableau of unaccustomed tenderness.

The article was buried five or six pages in. The text was laid out in a long, thin column down the side, like a postscript. She wouldn't have noticed it particularly. The headline trumpeted 'Italian rage at war wrongs', but in amongst the leukaemia clusters and child-abuse cases, it was struggling to be seen. Kenneth always had been a diligent newspaper reader. The length of their married life, before breakfast he had taken the paper and flattened it on the kitchen table. As he carefully worked through the pages, licking a finger to turn them, he would drink his first cup of tea, humming Fats Waller. Whatever excitement or chaos raged in the rest of the house, he stuck to his discipline. This, she supposed, must be the pay-off.

The rage of the headline never materialised in the paragraphs beneath. There was a plodding account of the Italian community's plans to commemorate the fiftieth anniversary of the *Olympia* disaster. Only towards the end was there mention of a forthcoming television programme, which would allow survivors to 'confront the woman who had decided their fate' and there was her name, a 'grandmother who lives in the Home Counties'.

'The problem is,' Richard said, after he had read the article for third time, 'not so much this in itself, but that this could be the beginning of hysterical, half-informed enquiries. You must let me deal with it.'

'There'll be nothing to deal with. Whatever they say, I'm not going to play. I don't care about this ridiculous rag and I care even less about this girl – she'll have to make other plans.' She got up from her chair and began to clear the breakfast things from the plastic cloth.

His voice was soft when he placed a hand gently on her arm. 'Ma, I know I said it was simple last night. It may not be that easy. This might all disappear, but it might well not. Even if you decide not to talk to Rachel – well, we know people, even people who read this,' he pushed the paper aside, 'and you may feel you have to talk to them.'

'"Even if . . ."? You think I should go on television?' She was intrigued rather than horrified.

'No. But I think you might have to do some talking. Not to me, not to me, necessarily, not if you don't want to.'

Daphne turned away into the kitchen, where she got control of the tightness in her throat. 'You're a good boy,' she barked out, attempting a joke.

'Me or him?' said Richard, scratching the Jack Russell's neck.

She wanted Oliver home. In the uncertainty that her routine was falling into, she wanted his imperturbable beauty. No one else could quite make the room complete. Richard's kindness accentuated the distance between them. Oliver wouldn't know how to be kind.

Instead, later that afternoon, after Richard had badgered her, she rang Kenneth back.

'This is a fine mess,' she said. 'I am so very sorry that you have to deal with this. You're absolutely right, it is quite preposterous. I wish I knew a quick and easy way to deal with it. Of course I compiled the damn lists, but I didn't dream up the criteria or decide what should be done with the information.'

'Stop it,' he broke in, with a mighty effort. As she paused, he continued, 'It is perfectly clear what you did, and it was right. Maybe not convenient, later on. But it was right, then – and now. That's all we have to say.'

'To each other or to them?' she tried to deflect her embarrassment. He grunted.

'Shall I come down?' He took another enormous breath. 'Do you want to come here?' There was a pause. 'Or is that ridiculous?'

'No.' She was distracted now, evasive. 'Maybe I'll come up to you. Next week. Tuesday perhaps. Or Wednesday. When Oliver's back.'

'Is he still away? Weeks now.'

'Yes. Thank you, Kenneth. Good night.'

She put the receiver down. Richard was assembling his bags in the sun-room.

'I want you to get home tomorrow,' he said as she walked with him out to the car. 'I know it's been quiet enough today. That might be all there is to it. It's not much of a story really. But just to be safe, I'd like you to be close. I wish you'd come with me tonight.' She shook her head. 'Tomorrow then, just get to the station if you don't fancy driving.' He kissed her cheek, which was cool in the sun.

After all, she supposed, she didn't mind being on her own. In the familiar quiet, gazing at the sea, she felt almost invigorated by this whiff of notoriety. She certainly had worked where it mattered. Her duty now was to protect

Kenneth. She was the one who had done extraordinary things.

And she was amused by Richard's plans to send her home. Not exactly in disgrace, but for her own safe keeping. Treated like an invalid or, if not that, like someone not entirely responsible. After all those years, there was another irony.

19

Oliver hated early calls. Often, as he brushed his teeth, he fell into a light trance of self-contemplation, checking the deepening lines around the eyes and scanning his hair-line for gaps. It was like the first descent into deepest sleep: any interruption then was the more violent.

The phone trilled from the bedroom. He hauled himself from the mirror and walked through, snatching up the lightweight handset. There was a pause and a rustle of static – long-distance – then his mother's voice.

'Did I wake you?'

'No, no. Been up for what, minutes. Nothing wrong?' What was this? He felt the clutch at his stomach.

'No. I don't think so. Just wanted to run something by you,' her voice seemed light, controlled. 'Rachel came to see me. I gather you suggested it. To ask about my war work.'

'Yes.' He was slowly, irritably, catching on. 'How did it go? Were you co-operative? Did she ask stupid questions?'

'I suppose the answer to the last two is yes. But something slightly odd happened yesterday. There was an article in one of the Sunday papers.'

'Yes.' He was already stuffing his notebooks from the table into his bag. The crew would be fidgeting down in the van.

'There's some sort of campaign being run by relatives of Italian internees. You know, wartime internees.'

'Daphne, I'm sorry but I'm in a god-awful rush. Could we talk about this when I get back? Or later tonight?' He was searching for his room key in the bedcovers.

'I know. Ridiculous. I just wondered if she had spoken to you. There was nothing directly relating it to her, except that it mentioned there would be a television programme in a few weeks' time.'

'I haven't spoken to her for days. There's been no time.' He took a deep breath. 'Look, I'm on a plane at the crack of dawn tomorrow. Why don't you ring her?'

'Yes. Well, I'm glad to have caught you.' She sounded formal, even embarrassed. There was no time to worry about that now. Only in the lift, flying down towards the jungle of reception, did he realise that in England it was five am.

In the van the crew sat, quietly resentful. Niki was outside, smoking. She threw the cigarette down when she saw him and ground it into the gravel with her clumpy shoes.

'We must hurry,' she said reproachfully.

'I know, I know,' he clambered into the van. Since their encounter three nights before, she was if anything, a touch more distant. Already it seemed little more than a short-circuit in the imagination, a preposterous memory like a teenage kiss re-run endlessly during double Geography. Occasionally, he felt the shudder of embarrassment: it was so gauche – something that might easily have been left undone. But at least it seemed discreet.

The interview was scheduled at the parliament building for ten. Oliver looked at his plan of questions. Why so many dissident prisoners? What exactly are your troops doing?

At ten past, Mekhusla rolled in. He shook the hand of everyone in the room, joshing with the crew. So Oliver, he said, the big match. Ready for it? Oliver said that he hoped the President was ready. Ya, ya, of course, the minister smiled, opening his arms wide and circling round the room, never stopping. The President would be here within an hour; he was just landing at the airport.

'Just landing?' Oliver was shocked. 'Where's he been?'

'It's no problem. He'll be here. Some coffee, have some coffee. Tell me how things went. I can stay a few minutes, why not? Did you see action?'

'You should know, I imagine,' began Oliver, glancing across at Niki, 'What did we see?'

'It's you who has it on tape,' Mekhusla was grinning, rocking from side to side on the balls of his feet, warming up. 'When you left my men, you were headed for Village Number Six, I believe. Number Six, was it Number Six?' This was the military map reference. 'Were they rough with you?'

'No, just strange. There was a rather bogus collection of souvenirs supposedly left by your boys.'

'What souvenirs? Arms?'

'No. Some uniforms, a lot of mess and oh, about two dozen graves.' The attempt at nonchalance sounded pathetic. 'What happened there? Was there some kind of incident?'

Mekhusla shrugged. 'I don't know. I don't believe so. Is that what they told you?'

Oliver nodded.

'You see, enemy forces are there, right by our border, even if you can't see their tanks. They influence everything. The region is small but it poisons everything around it. Now you have seen.'

Oliver wondered just what he did have in the four videotapes they had brought out of the war-zone. If he only knew for certain what lay under the piles of earth. And if he did, what would it prove? That the combat in these villages was more than skirmishes. That the President's troops played for real. That they'd found a way to thumb their nose at Moscow. It was such a mess.

The coffee came in. Ten twenty.

'You'll get your interview. Don't worry.' Mekhusla was behind him, but also by his side, so broad were his shoulders. Through his agitation Oliver felt the reassuring warmth. He should like to run through life, charging head down, charming and bullying his way. He should like to be careless of details. 'You know what you want.' His arm was being pummelled now. 'It's not so difficult – and then it's home, back to London – Harvey Nichols? Earl's Court?'

'What a strange view of the world you do have, Minister,' said Oliver, dredging up a smile.

'But Oliver,' and Oliver felt his collar-bone crunch from the affectionate squeeze, 'it is at least real to me.' And with a white smile Mekhusla was gone, angling his shoulders slightly to fit through the door-frame.

Ten thirty-five. Niki returned from the secretary's office. The President was in his car. Oliver let out a sigh of exasperation. The cameraman squinted at the ceiling.

'Look,' said Oliver, to the crew, who were booked on the evening flight. 'Once this bastard turns up, we're through. You can get everything packed up for the flight.' He pulled up a chair beside Niki. 'What do we still have to do, is there much?' She ran through the tasks – letters, payments, archive footage from the local television station. 'Fine,' he said, 'we'll tackle that this afternoon.' She nodded, not looking up. More gently he added, checking that they couldn't be overheard, 'Do you want to eat tonight; I'd like to thank you for all your sterling efforts.'

'I don't know,' she replied, 'Maybe it's possible.'

He couldn't pin down his motives. It was a lame attempt at gallantry, something easy and expedient. But it made him feel better to have done it.

Ten fifty. Oliver was calculating the cost of cancelling the flights and staying on another day when the secretary came in to say the President was in the building. There was a token flurry of activity: lights were adjusted.

The President's eyes were bloodshot in the glare. He sat back in the chair and crossed his legs carefully, pinching the crease in his trousers. From where Oliver was sitting his shins seemed to stretch a metre from knee to ankle.

The first few exchanges were routine. Then Oliver asked if the war was inevitable. The response came back like a battering ram.

'They were the aggressors. Our nation has the right to self-determination. The differences between our people and the rebels go back more than half a century – to Stalin and the Soviet State which put those people there.'

Wasn't it also true that his nation really only achieved a sense of cohesion this way? That the rebels had become the focus for hatred that far outweighed anything they had done. Without the war, continued Oliver, the nation was simply a collection of tribes and factions, constantly at each other's throats. Wasn't the war, in short, useful?

The President's gaze rose slowly from the contemplation of

his fingers. Oliver felt a tiny creak of apprehension at the back of his throat.

The eyes were focused on a point just above Oliver's head. The problems of the country sprang from one overwhelming threat – Moscow. It was necessary to make themselves strong against this menace. They must present a united face to the enemy. Internal squabbles were no longer important. The dissidents – the President was now close to shouting – were mad.

But all dissidents are mad, thought Oliver. You were once a dissident yourself, if the accounts are to be believed. Now you are clinging with the same lack of reason to the power of state.

The President's zealotry was icy, but the chill was offset by Mekhusla. The minister could lay his hands on the people and make them feel that the suffering was worthwhile. He could make warm sense of stubborn abstractions. If they shivered when they saw their President, cashmere coat around his shoulders, turn away from them on the podium, Mekhusla would be there to make light of it and to include them all in the people's cause as choreographed from the Presidential Residence.

Oliver smothered his doubts with a cushion of admiration for their politics. This portrait would be timely; within months, perhaps weeks, there would be confrontation between the President and Moscow. The man in front of him was already fêted in salons from Prague to Martha's Vineyard to Campden Hill. Soon he would be an international hero – or martyr.

Dinner was, after all, possible. Niki came to the hotel at seven thirty. She was wearing black and earrings. She gave the taxi-driver instructions and settled back on the plastic-covered seat.

'How is your son,' he asked and then, after a short pause, 'Does he enjoy school?'

'He wants to be a physicist like his father.' She smiled, obviously touched by an irony that was closed to him. Was that a good thing, he wondered. She smiled again, looking across at him this time. She thought so.

The restaurant was dark red and slightly greasy. Their table had wine stains on the fringed cloth. Waiters swooped between the tables arranged in a series of small rooms. He caught a roasting smell of garlic and coriander.

'You have made this trip bearable,' he said as he poured the wine into their glasses, 'More than that,' he added, with a nod. The place was busy. Thank God.

'Have you got what you wanted? Will the film work?' she seemed preoccupied.

'Yes – but it's largely down to your efforts. All those hours on the phone.'

'I'm used to it. And the President? What did you think of the interview?' The level gaze again. 'Did he give you what you wanted?'

Probably it was time to be frank. 'I was surprised how fixed he was. Obsessive, of course, they're all like that, but I was expecting him to be more discursive – with his background. You know, less dogma.'

She nodded and he saw that the corners of her mouth were tense with amusement. 'Perhaps you didn't notice it before.'

'You're not telling me, after all this, that it's true – what the unwashed dissidents say – that he's a maniac. If so, I have to ask why you didn't mention it before.' He was teasing, in a way.

'You don't want my judgments.' It was a statement, not a protestation.

'Tell me more about Mekhusla, then. I know all the stuff about his sporting career. I know he's popular, that he's the fixer, that obviously he won't shirk from a fight – but the more I see, the less I understand why he remains so cheerful, so bullish, in the face of what is – the more I contemplate it – an unwinnable situation.'

She smiled, now, directly at him, a gaze made over-steady by the wine.

'He won't be here.' A flash of triumph.

'What, dead?' ventured Oliver, startled, and then flinched at his own banality.

'No,' she snorted. 'In Vienna, or Stockholm, probably not London, but somewhere.'

'But how?' This was disturbing.

'He has money, some from his years, you know, as an athlete, but much, much more from later. He has interests.'

'What kind?'

'What the geography books leave out is that we grow many things on those fertile uplands, not just grapes. We have to pay for our guns somehow. So it's a two-way trade and there is always someone in the middle. It's not big-time, by international standards. But for here . . .'

'So he gets the money out?'

'People come and go. Joint ventures. Television companies. You know the sort of thing.' She was tracing a pattern on the shiny red cloth.

'Could we prove this?'

'We?' she put her head on one side, almost girlish. 'What can you prove?'

He was suddenly irritated. 'Why didn't you tell me any of this before?'

She stared back. 'I answered your questions. And you have had plenty of opportunity to talk to him yourself. Make judgments.'

He nodded and signalled to the waiter for the bill. He was tired and disappointed and he needed to think this through.

Niki was watching him. 'Does it make any difference?' she said, just a touch scornfully. 'Really?'

'I don't know,' he snapped, 'but I would have liked a little more time to find out.'

She shrugged and looked round for the waiter.

Back in his room, Oliver tugged aside the peacock blue curtains and looked at the lights of the town across the gorge. He had tried to conceal his annoyance with courtesy, but he was up against an expert. He had thanked Niki for her work, she him for the meal; before he paid the bill, she had run through the departure arrangements with clinical precision. Their taxi had dropped her off at her apartment. They had nodded goodnight.

In the end, though, Oliver would have to concede that it wasn't Niki who had let him down, it was Mekhusla. What made this story work was the black-belt champion of the people who could roll up his sleeves and wield an Uzi. He'd been a little in love with the minister himself. The truth was that when the planes came over, or the tanks rolled in, he would scuttle down the rat-run to his numbered deposits in Vienna – giving the Air Austria hostesses the benefit of his charisma on the way. And there was no way that Oliver could show that paradox. A line of script might hint at it – but who listened to the script when the humanity of the man dominated the pictures? It was all too human to want to escape a battle that would certainly be lost. Up until the moment that conflict became inevitable, then Mekhusla's loyalty would be to his country. Only a crazed obsessive like the President would stay longer, and then only out of a perverted bid for the history books. There they were – the two faces of patriotism, cerebral and pragmatic, deluded and clear-eyed. In his version of events they would march side by side – both equally heroic.

His plan – spread out on the round white table – still made sense. No time or money to shoot more anyway. Was it true? He'd better believe it.

20

WHEN RACHEL'S phone call came, it was not apologetic. Daphne heard that it was the newspaper's fault, entirely; they'd got it wrong. Her name had been mentioned, off the record, as someone who might take part in the programme. She must not get the impression that they were out to crucify her. She didn't have that impression, did she? They would be mortified if she did.

Daphne grew colder. The girl's voice became querulous. How could they reassure her? Would it help to meet the researcher? It would not. Rachel could understand Daphne's irritation, but the programme would surely give her an opportunity to put the record straight. Please, would she think about it?

It was some small satisfaction to hear the girl twirling around on the end of the line. Until she had replaced the receiver, Daphne felt in control.

It was only later that she realised that whatever she did was probably irrelevant to the progress of events. She sensed that Rachel was committed now. Her hopes of being able to raise a hand and halt proceedings were futile. I am afraid there has been a misunderstanding – please return to your homes.

For Oliver, landing again at Terminal 3, home was a shifting concept. Historically, it had been the house in Surrey where his father now lived alone, but which had once housed all four of them, plus the occasional au pair. From there the boys had been launched into school. The beach house in Sussex held the vivid childhood memories, however. He was grateful that it remained unchanged over the years. Technically,

Oliver owned a small terraced house in West Kensington, but had more or less abandoned that to the tenant. Much of his stuff was either in the office or, since last year, at Rachel's. On reflection, home was probably the office.

In any case, when he called that particular morning, his mother wasn't at the coast, so any fragile domestic structure he might have held in his head crumbled. As she answered the phone in Surrey, his usual fears for his father's health ground into gear.

Daphne's skills of organisation were not obvious from her surroundings. She had an offhandedness with possessions that many of his parents' generation affected. Her organisation was apparent to Oliver from the way she had managed her life. A career, two children, a marriage that had lasted one way or another for forty-five years, leaving her fit and healthy, and sharp with it – it wasn't bad going. He had always believed she was tough; it must have taken some determination to squeeze that much from post-war life. She'd been tough on both her sons: Richard particularly had suffered from her expectations. You just had to watch him beg for praise even now. Oliver hadn't had an easy ride himself: nothing was ever quite good enough for her. One thing she had handed down was her clear-sightedness; an ability to cut to the crux of an issue. No messing around with abstractions – on the rare occasions he'd taken a conundrum to her she'd steered the shortest path to a solution. It was surely her great gift; over years of repeated exposure to her technique, he'd discovered moral certainties in the fog where his work led him. Clear thinking had earned him praise. An image of the Interior Minister, cramming his muscle-bound frame into an aeroplane seat bound west, intruded uneasily into his reflections. He could scarcely admit how close a call that had been. But the programme would be out in a few weeks. That judgement might not exceed its sell-by date.

Lately Oliver had found the family house to be dark. Even at the height of summer he was tempted to turn on lights in the kitchen or in the panelled sitting room. He guessed that this sensitivity was linked to his father's increasing disability

– that the mannerisms he loved were disappearing into the shadows, that you had to peer to see the jokes now. He felt guilty each time he rang the bell, when he calculated the time since he last stood in the porch gazing down at the tan tiles.

This time, though, there was something else to unsettle. His mother opened the door and grasped his forearms firmly as she embraced him. Her pale eyes seemed to bulge slightly; she was obviously on edge. It must be sickness of some kind. He dreaded the announcement. She led him into the sitting room. He saw they had been sitting together. There was a tea tray and a fuggy intimacy he couldn't remember from before.

She brought another cup and more biscuits. She asked about the trip. He sighed and went into the usual riff about the weather and the frustrations of the job. He made them chuckle, although Daphne was ever acute, quick to jump on his laziness. Eventually, he took a gulp of tea and asked why she was there.

She looked across at Kenneth, just like someone in a television mini-series. At times like this, thought Oliver, life does indeed revert to cliché. Which one of them is it? And how long? He could barely watch his father's shaking hands for fear of the tenderness that choked his own throat.

At first he thought his mother was stalling, putting him off the scent with some story about Rachel. Her words were competing with the ticking of the clock in the hall, which was suddenly very loud. Gradually, he heard her outline the position, matter of fact, even ironic, and he felt a sudden anger. A television programme, she's worried about a television programme. She's making him worried about a television programme. Christ!

'I don't see what the problem is,' he interrupted, 'either you take part or you don't.' His annoyance was fed by a sense of being behind the race on this one and a suspicion that Rachel, arrogant in her inexperience, had somehow cocked up. He shouldn't have to apologise for her. Or was it all still a prelude by his mother, something to throw in his way before the really bad news came? But he saw from the concentration of his father's brow that this was it. They had arrived at the important item on the agenda. Oliver began to listen.

It wasn't just the television programme; that morning there had been two telephone calls from newspapers. Nothing urgent, just enquiries. Might she contribute to a feature for the fiftieth anniversary of June 1940? Could they send a photographer?

Oliver realised he was missing something, the crucial premise, in fact. His mother was worrying away at the details but not giving him the substance. Tell me from the beginning. The request was directed straight at her. He turned his shoulders away from his father, the better to look her in the eye, but the better also to protect the old man from whatever was about to rain down.

And so Daphne recounted, as she had done briskly to Richard, the events of that hot May and June. She added a postscript about the sinking of the *Olympia* in July. That was of course something that happened later, although from the media point of view, she added drily, it was obviously the attraction of the story.

He understands, she thought, he understands. None of this holds any mystery for him. It's ephemeral, so much sand kicked up in the water. But it *will* all settle.

The rehearsal of the story gave her a kind of exhilaration. This is not pleasant, but it is duty. Duty doesn't come easily, I've always known that. What I had to do all those years ago was the first task in decades of duties – all discharged.

She had not made drudgery of her duties. There were lapses and minor indiscretions – little snatches of happiness caught here and there – but the steady momentum of her life had been the discharge of duties. It was also, to be fair, the great satisfaction. What had disturbed the equilibrium was the passion unleashed by Oliver's birth.

Daphne watched her younger son as she talked. His fair hair was swept back, as it had been since he was a child, although a hint of fringe slipped forward – once artless, now cut that way. His gold hair was still long at the collar, but the gold was dusty. *He* was the reward for those years of duty. It was right that he should be back here with her now, as if she had called in a debt. He would see off these irritating demons. He and she travelled the same path. Now they could demonstrate it to the rest of the world.

Her self-obsession was total, thought Oliver. That crisp, mocking tone – always pretending to deprecate herself, but highlighting her own self-effacement – enraged him. This was not a crisis, but she was making it one. The anger he had felt for years at the injustice of it – her growing potency set beside the husk of his father – now came to rest in the airless room.

Kenneth sat there, his feet twitching occasionally, performing a tiny dance of agitation and frustration. He wanted to help, to take charge and protect, but was bound by his weakness. Years ago, he would have found some absurd joke to put the crisis in perspective. Oliver suspected he still would, but for the betrayal of the arteries. And that made it worse.

Throughout his childhood Oliver had seen his father as clever and able, lighter, wittier, better company than his mother. She'd made heavy weather of her sacrifices (in an ironic, detached way, naturally), but Kenneth had come home from his senior job with the International Corporation without a murmur and entertained them. Glorified salesman by day, he'd sold them the cultured gentleman in the evenings and at weekends. He played the piano, hit straight to the boundary and wrote (or so Oliver believed, never having asked directly) fragments of poetry. He had glued and painted their childhood like an Airfix model.

Now he sat there, constantly shrugging a whimsical apology, with the evening light shining through the edge of his ears, his white hair standing out stiffly from the oversized shirt collar. It gave him something of the bohemian at last – as he might have been when Oliver rewrote his life story for him.

Daphne was talking still, something about reports and classified information. Oliver was suddenly impatient.

'Let's clear this away, shall we?' He stood up. His father leant forward and made a clattering attempt to replace his cup on the tray. Daphne looked startled and annoyed at the interruption. Oliver took the tray out into the kitchen.

When his mother had closed the door behind her, he took a deep breath. 'I don't understand your point. What do you want the rest of us to do?'

'Do? There's nothing to do. I'm simply informing you of the facts.'

'It's all very upsetting for Father.' He knew it sounded petulant.

'Well, darling, naturally I'm sorry, but the situation is hardly of my choosing.'

Oliver laughed. 'That's a joke, I suppose. You've always been so strong on personal responsibility, rights and wrongs. You did this. It was right; you said so. Well, fine. Let's not construct a great drama from it.'

'But the issue isn't whether I did the right thing at the time, it's whether I did the right thing with the benefit of hindsight as applied by your friend, with her vast experience of these matters.'

Oliver ignored the challenge. 'Don't worry about her. Your only concern is the people who have a right to feel aggrieved. You know, the people you decided were dangerous. The people you despatched.'

'And what do you think?'

'It doesn't matter what I think,' Oliver was suddenly defensive.

Driving back through the dark green of the Surrey hills, Oliver knew he didn't want to tell his mother because he didn't know. He hated the drive, up and down and bending around. Dorking. He accelerated through the ersatz villages. With the leafy corners you could never see clearly enough to overtake.

South London, all dust and billboards, video shops and late-night stores, was a relief. Here at least the traffic forged on, in single or double file, clogged or free, but purposeful. He tried Rachel on the car phone, but the answering machine clicked in, again. He tried another number, a number that he'd never tried to memorise but that stayed with him. After just a couple of rings, his ex-wife picked up the call.

'Celia. Hi.'

'Hello.' She sounded equable enough, if a little distant.

'Have I disturbed you? Are you working?'

She indicated she was, but it was okay. What was he up to?

'I know you're working, and tell me to fuck off if you like, but can I come and see you? I mean, now.'

'Is there something the matter?' Her voice, always low, took on a note of curiosity.

'No. Well, not serious. But odd. And if it's all the same to you . . . well – you know the cast of characters better than most.'

'Now? Really now? Does it have to be now?'

'No,' he thought about it, 'I suppose not. But I'd prefer it, if you could. I won't stay long.'

'Okay. Where are you?' She was brisk.

'Vauxhall, I'll be about twenty minutes.'

Celia had a basement flat in the crotch of Tottenham Court Road. It was tucked behind the fitness clubs and electrical shops, not quite Bloomsbury and not quite Soho, in a small, grubby square a few hundred yards from the British Museum. He opened the little iron gate and stepped carefully down the worn stone steps to her front door. It opened before he could knock and Celia, tall and droll, stood in the door frame.

The flat was tiny and Celia pushed past him to get into the galley kitchen and find a bottle of Scotch. Through an open door he could see into her study with the bulging box-files and piles of paper, on the floor, on the desk, pinned to the walls. The study windows were open on to a tiny upward slope of earth, fifteen foot at most, densely planted with white and purple flowers, a miniature garden in a light-well. It was hot.

'We could go out. If you prefer,' he offered. After she had brought the glasses.

'Are you staying that long?' She didn't look up from the pouring. Her eyes were heavily pencilled, although he knew that was habit and not for his benefit.

He settled himself on the shabby leopard-skin sofa. 'It's about Daphne. Something's come up about her wartime work. Some decisions she made. There's going to be publicity.'

Celia looked intrigued, marginally less laconic. 'Good or bad? Are you in charge of it?'

'No, I . . .' He sighed. 'My problem is that I don't know how I feel about it – or her.'

'And how does she feel?'

'I don't know,' he was taken aback. 'I think she might be quite enjoying the attention for the moment, but the old man's upset for her.'

'And that upsets you.'

'Of course.' He outlined the facts, as far as he had taken them in. Celia looked impressed.

'I knew nothing about all that, but social historians don't burden themselves with that kind of thing.' She lit one of her Turkish cigarettes. 'What do you want me to do, apart from reassuring you at a time of crisis?'

'That exactly. I don't know what to think. Was she wrong? And if she was, which I suspect she was – in fact, I know she was – what does that do to my relationship to her? What does that do to all the years of her telling me to be clear about the issues?'

'Sounds like she was clear all right.'

'But she made a superficial judgement. She made a superficial judgement that was politically expedient.'

'For God's sake, Oliver.' She yawned. 'That's any judgement under pressure. Bang, and it's gone. Fifty years gone, in this case. What's different here is that your love interest has dug it up for trial by television. Plucked it from its context and put it on a slab.'

'But I have to decide where I stand. With her or not. It's what she wants. Daphne, that is.' Oliver stared at the floor.

'You bet it is.' Celia studied the top of his head. 'Don't ask me to endorse your judgement. Think for yourself on this one. Don't whinge, Oliver.'

He kicked at the tassels on the rug, flipping them over and back.

'Anyway,' she said after a pause, 'this isn't really about fifty years ago, is it? This is about now, your chance to put her through it. You know, the way you always complain she's done with you. She should understand that.'

'But she was wrong. Then. Not just wrong in an argument or wrong in an academic article, but wrong in a way that affected hundreds of lives – thousands, indirectly.'

'You're just jealous. She did something real, something that didn't evaporate into the ether. Bit frightening, is it?'

'Fuck,' he said, too tired for rancour.

Celia stood up and walked into the kitchen. She returned with a bag of designer corn chips – a queasy shade of blue. 'Eat these. Somebody brought them. You seem a bit low on salt.'

She sat down again in the low armchair. Her toenails were the same colour as the chips. Miserably he broke open the bag.

'I'm sorry. I'm knackered. I just got back and the film's got to be cut in ten days. I don't need this. Kenneth . . . it's too much for him, all this. I wish I could take him away from her. She always manages to do it, her timing is spot on.'

'He doesn't want to be taken away. He's fine. It gives them something to think about – together. And the timing you can hardly blame her for.' Celia was looking away from him, through the study door, wistfully. 'Anyway,' she went on in a preoccupied tone, 'you know what that's all about. She can't bear it . . . can't bear being around him, watching him, not able to fix it, make it better. It's her great failure.' She turned back to him. 'You don't want to understand that, do you?'

He shrugged, put down his glass and the bag of chips and slid across the floor until he was squatting in front of her chair, between her long legs. She put her head on one side. He played gently with the ends of her thick hair.

'How's the book going?' he asked.

She shrugged. 'Not great today. But only a couple of months behind schedule. In my world, that's prodigious.'

He nodded, duty done. 'Celia . . . thank you. If only . . .'

She looked down her long nose, impassive. He rested his hands on the tops of her thighs, feeling the warmth through the loose linen, and squeezed gently, nervously.

'I love you. I'm sorry for the adolescent drivel.'

She snorted. 'Run along.' She swung a leg across, pushing him out of the way, but not unkindly, and levered herself out of the chair.

At the door he glanced at the monograph on the top of the

nearest pile of books. 'Studies in future models of companionate marriage.' He looked at her wide-eyed.

She eased him out of the door. 'When I find it, I'll give you a call,' he heard her grumble as the door squeezed shut behind him.

21

'MY GRANDFATHER said you once promised him that you would review his case. I'd like to remind you of that promise.'

The letter was from a young lawyer she had never met – the grandson of a man she had met once fifty years before – but the tone of the letter was so direct she could not guard herself against it. He was shrewd to appeal to her sense of obligation. Daphne's regrets were always for the small things; on the great matters of principles she couldn't shift.

She did remember her promise to Alessandro Delle Rose and how, later that day, she had put in the call for a box of service postcards for the detainees to let their families know how they were. She left before it arrived.

Grandfather and grandson were in London and they wanted to meet her; it was nothing to do with the television programme, he stressed. They weren't in the business of traps or deals; they just wanted a chance to talk. She should consider it, not least because 'Old Scores' did not sound, the letter concluded, like the ideal medium.

After some thought, mindful of the postcards that never arrived, and because she could see no other way, she rang the hotel where they were staying.

Despite her directions, the luxury hire-car drove straight past the beach house, coming to a bouncing halt fifty yards down the dusty road. From her seat in the window she had glimpses of two silhouettes. The passenger gazed ahead, even as the car growled in reverse. The driver, by contrast, was eager to be out. A tall man, he unfolded himself from the Jaguar and stretched, grimacing, before walking around to the passenger door. He helped his grandfather out, conveying respect and solicitude in equal measures.

She raised herself from the chair, smoothed down her linen slacks, ran a hand over her hair and centred the knot on her scarf. Her sense of etiquette, her civil servant's facility, was still to hand.

The house was shabby; she saw that clearly reflected in their expressions. They manoeuvred themselves into the sun room.

Alessandro Delle Rose was stooped but elegant. His thin features had grown more pronounced with age and his pallor had long been varnished deep brown by decades of Australian sun. Veins of ebony persisted in his crinkly white hair. His jacket, confidently checked, was cashmere, and the shoes were gleaming chestnut brogues. He wore the international aura of wealth. He was courteous and quiet and distant. His grandson, Antony, was more direct in appearance and manner. Daphne couldn't yet gauge whether his confidence was aggressive or Australian. A republican, no doubt. He was altogether larger, more untidy, than his grandfather had ever been.

Antony led the conversation. Daphne was thanked for agreeing to the meeting. She nodded: she wanted to say at the outset that she wasn't sure what they wanted, or if – since courtesy was also her strong suit – she could be of any help.

'You could listen,' said Antony, not roughly. 'You could listen to what happened to my grandfather.' He looked across at the old man, who raised and turned his hands, just a couple of millimetres, but enough to express ambivalence, or anxiety, or indifference.

'You will appreciate,' Daphne replied, 'that I am very much aware of what happened, how unpleasant the entire episode must have been and,' fixing the younger man with a cool look, 'how war works, in fact.'

'But the detail,' Antony went on, 'the detail is important. Those of us who came along later, we need the detail now before it goes. The truth is in the detail.'

'Very well, I am perfectly prepared to listen to anything you've got to say – either of you. Forgive the Englishness, but would you like tea, or coffee, a cold drink?' The drinks brought, she settled back on her chair by the window, her elbow on the table, and listened.

To her surprise, it did not seem a story that was frequently rehearsed. Delle Rose seemed reluctant at first, bullied slightly by his grandson. He spoke quietly, so she had to incline towards him to hear, but she soon realised that was his technique. He was establishing his place in the trio, pulling them to attention.

The old man made a last feint of protest, looking across at Antony for reprieve. His first sentences were slow and disorganised. He described his arrival as a young publisher in Britain and the circle of writers, artists and aristocrats who had welcomed him. Names once familiar in certain salons floated up, bringing a chuckle of recognition. Daphne suddenly remembered the pride the young man had shown in his Belgravia connections; it was still there. She wondered whether this might be all there was, a stream of reminiscence. Then Delle Rose seemed to shake off the details and find the narrative.

'The men came – as they always do – in the low time of the night, two-thirty, maybe three. I was deep in sleep and they turned me out of bed. Just policemen, ordinary "coppers", but with guns. You know all this, of course; I was put in with others in a van and taken to that school somewhere in West London. At least, for me, there were no children there to be scared. My family – Antony's mother, uncle and grandmother, and Antony and his sister too, of course – had travelled to America some time before. But my aunt, she was very distressed, crying, confused. Her nephew, her brother's son, what were they going to do with me? It was hard for her; it's always hard for those left, not knowing.

'And then those hours in that school, less than two days anyway, which you know about also: you were there. You were "in charge". We could not adjust to our new status. The day before, we had been sought-after members of literary society, or valued shopkeepers or trusted waiters, or whatever. It's true that the papers, the popular papers anyway, had begun their taunts. Could the Italians be trusted? After all, we returned often to Italy for holidays; some of us had even bought land and houses there. But could you British trust anyone – the Jews, the French? It wasn't pleasant, all this innuendo, but we decided it was your problem, not ours. And then suddenly, overnight – yes, overnight – we were the enemy. And some of us, for reasons we could not understand, were "dangerous" characters, desperate individuals who were to be herded at gunpoint and interned or deported. And I was one of those.'

He smiled at her. She remembered the smile now – a mixture of coyness and stealth. Strange to see it buried in tanned wrinkles. Strange too that, fifty years on, she felt the same confusion of fascination and distrust. She knew only the brutal facts of what had happened to the detainees. It would be a grim kind of relief to hear the details. But why were these two men here? What did they want from her? And what could she do for them, then or now?

'Back there, in London, in conversations with you and amongst ourselves, we felt that it was unpleasant, certainly, but still within the realms of what we knew. War was a shock to us all; it stirred up the deepest feelings and loyalties and resentments, but it did so for everyone. You remember the time, the rush of events. I remember that I was almost excited by this latest development, by this flinging together of so many of us. Imagine, there were doctors and lawyers, shopkeepers, barbers, cooks, a film director – yes, really – and an artist. It was a little like one of your murder mysteries, we get them on Australian TV, on the cable channels, all these unlikely people all together: what might happen? At one point, someone even threw some copies of magazines – *Punch*, I think, and *Illustrated London News* – into our classroom. Nowhere to wash, but *Punch*!' He turned his palms upwards, looking towards the ceiling, playing a little to his audience. Then he seemed to lose energy and turned his eyes once again to the corner of the room, somewhere past Daphne's chair.

'But when the initial confusion wore off, when you people became more organised, then we knew what we were in for. Chaos managed by a race that prides itself on organisation. The worst kind.' He looked scornful, but his gaze seemed to brush across her without registering her presence.

'I had hopes of our conversations, however trivial; I hoped that sanity might be restored. I thought I could do what I always did, use logic and reason to win the day.'

Sanity, thought Daphne, that's rich. She recalled clutching at scraps of reason in Delle Rose's rhetoric. She remembered the overpowering sense of foreignness. She felt it still.

He was still talking. '. . . that one of you would come in with a piece of paper and a cup of tea and say, "Please, we understand that you have been entertained in some of the grandest drawing rooms of Eaton Square, that even if technically you belong to an enemy nation, you speak the same language. Please feel free to go." I was young, and I had done a great deal. I had moved amongst powerful people, been at the centre of events.

'But what's to say now?' he continued, waving a hand. 'You did what you did. There were bad things at that time. Do you know what happened next? Do you know what you were signing your pieces of paper for?'

She inclined her head, without speaking. He was still not altogether likeable.

'That next day they bundled us into the vans to the station, for a journey – north, I suppose. That was when we truly became prisoners, in a military sense.

'When we first arrived at the camp we were taken into a series of rooms in some kind of gatehouse. All the people in charge of us were in military uniform. Not high-calibre people, but the kind who stick with the discipline, you know. They made us remove our shirts and parade two abreast around the room, answering questions they shouted to us. How long had we lived here, what were our skills, and so on. When they were satisfied, of what I don't know – that we were made like other men, that we didn't have *fasces* tattooed on our chests – we were allowed to dress. For me, this part was very difficult. I felt then that I had been reduced to something less than what I was, and yet those in charge of us were lost too; they didn't know what they were looking for, and the younger ones were frightened.

'Shortly after this, we were marched through into a great

dark space. It was a disused textile mill. You know, wool, cotton, something like that. The ground was uneven, with old timbers and pieces of machinery lying about. We were shouting to each other, you know, "Be careful, watch out", but this made the soldiers angry. The older men, and many were in their fifties and sixties, they stumbled and some fell. They were tired too. We were all tired, but they were exhausted. That night we slept on straw mattresses – palliasses, that's the word – in a large room with skylights. I remember I did sleep, although I was sure I wouldn't.

'You know,' he continued, as if the thought had suddenly occurred to him, 'keeping clean was not easy. Over those days. I think for me it became something of an obsession. We had to organise teams to scrub the latrines and the WCs. And I remember the ration,' he looked across at his grandson, his narrative gathering pace as he settled into the rhythm.

Is this really the first time he has told this story? Daphne wondered. I doubt it, somehow.

'The ration,' he intoned, 'one sheet of toilet paper each for six days. And on the seventh? The day of rest, of course!' He chuckled.

'No shit on a Sunday? For real, *nonno*?' Antony leant back in his chair. This was turning into something suspiciously like a double-act.

'It loses a little something in your translation,' replied his grandfather. 'But there was another ration too. For a fortnight after we arrived, we were allowed no communication at all with anyone outside the camp. Nothing to let our relatives know what had happened to us. But then we were given each week a sheet of white paper for a letter – no, *the* letter. The paper was very thick and shiny. It was difficult to write on it and impossible, if you made a mistake, to correct. But I spent hours on that letter. You know, it was the sense of isolation that I found so hard. I was so much accustomed to being in the centre of things, where decisions and ideas were traded. All we knew there was what some of the guards might say, but they were young and naïve. It was worse to listen to them than to ignore them. Sometimes rumours began, because some boy had heard that the Italian front had moved this way or that. Then at night we would see in the sky the firebombs over Manchester and we would fear for our relatives, for the women. To my knowledge, only one of my letters ever reached its destination. Certainly none came back.

'It's curious. With all the turmoil outside the camp, and just across the sea, we didn't talk about politics between our-selves. Not once that I remember. Maybe we were afraid to be stirring up trouble with the guards, scared of being overheard. But I think too we were afraid to fall out between ourselves. There were so many differences. Some did have broad sympathies with Fascism, like children – they might carve Mussolini's face on the underside of the bed, you know the kind of stupid thing. But there were anti-Fascists too. A lawyer, a most eminent man, who was the secretary of a civil-rights movement, he was there, scrubbing the filthy kitchen. We were Catholic alongside Jew, atheists alongside agnostics, Communists and even a few anarchists. Just men. We talked about football and religion. Sometimes women. There was enough in that, more than enough. I don't remember one single conversation about politics.

'There is a photograph I have still. It came to me later from a medical student who was in the camp. It shows a group of us. We don't look thin, it's true, we seem tanned, healthy. We are wearing shorts and open-necked shirts. Everyone is smiling, not laughing, not relaxed, but a rather, you know, mixed expression. We don't look entirely English, certainly, but not Italian either. How do you account for that?'

Daphne felt weary. Where was all this leading?

'Every night they had to count us. Someone had to make a tally of the number of Italian internees, and every night they had to phone that number to London. So each evening we had to go into the mill and line up, ten abreast. So when they had counted up ten rows and so on . . .' He looked down, as if he had lost the thread. Until now, his recall had outstripped his speech. The words had rolled out, almost surprising him. Now the images seemed to have faded and he was grasping for some memory. On the arm of his chair, his tanned hand gently opened and closed.

'It was at the end of the day, not night exactly but towards the end. It was still light, that cool midsummer light you have in the north of England, when you can't sleep. I couldn't tell myself, as I could in the dark, that my loved ones were sleeping, unconscious, not worried. I knew they would be awake somewhere, my aunt adding up the figures from the shop, trying to find a way to feed herself and her cousin. And my family also in America. My wife and children. At night in England, they are only two-thirds through the day in America, the little ones having their meal. Evening is a hard time for separation.'

Antony moved in the creaking armchair and recrossed his legs. His grandfather did not look up.

'Every evening they would make us go into the old mill. It was damp, even in June. And so we would line up in our squads, like the football teams we made during the day. There was no set order, just ten by ten, and then one of the guards would run down the side of the lines, counting ten, twenty, thirty. Then he would run back, still muttering under his breath the total number, and report to an officer standing at the front: 342 Italians, sir.

'There was very little light in the mill chamber. The counting seemed to take for ever, too, and by the time it was finally settled, everyone's faces had lost their features – we were all just grey figures, either tall or short or somewhere in between . . .' He drifted into silence.

'Some evenings we were there until past lights out, until ten-thirty or so – you know, we had a type of game. The soldier would count the columns – ten by ten – but those of us at the other end of the rows would slip away and form another row or two at the back, and when he got to the end the rows at the front would have closed up to look perfect, ten by ten. Then of course the numbers were wrong and the officer would get very angry, in a British way,' he paused, smiling at the recollection. 'They would be half a kilo – no, half a pound – of Italians over.

'It was a little something of power we had in a situation where we were helpless. You know, standing together, as the soldier ran up and down checking his figures, scared his officer would be angry, it was good.

'But within a few days they would come among us with lists, more lists, and divide us. The first we heard was always rumours. Something that one of the English boys on guard had said about deportation. Some of us – either the most dangerous, or the least dangerous, no one was sure – were to be taken by ship to a colony. Where? We didn't know.

'When the lists went up, some trading in personal papers began. Sometimes it was a question of trying to alter a birthdate on your papers or shade a photograph a little to obscure the features. Sometimes the crucial page was torn, just in the right, or the wrong, place. In the end, it's almost funny, it didn't really matter. The final rounding up was so chaotic that I believe they even took some people whose names did not appear on the list, purely by mistake.

'I was myself carrying a set of papers that had been doctored. Someone, an older man, wanted to stay and, you see, I reckoned that I could end up closer to my family if the boat was bound for Canada – which was what was rumoured – than if I remained watching the Nazi bombers go over the north of England. That was my plan.'

22

'I DON'T quite know what we were expecting – the *Queen Mary* perhaps – but the first sight of the *Olympia* was a shock. She had become a battleship, decked out for war, with guns on the deck and camouflage. What I know today, it was rumoured even then, was that she was one of the most luxurious ships afloat. Romantic, you know. But not when I saw her. Up until then I was imagining something white and gleaming, neutral and non-partisan, that would glide off with us to our mysterious destination.

'When we got to Liverpool docks we were all left on the quayside, just left at the foot of the steep gangway. It was so very hot,' he continued. 'It may seem strange, I've lived in Australia off and on for fifty years now, but I remember this English day as hot – like a dream, beyond all other heat. Already the boat was lying low in the water. There were about six hundred of us on the quay – I remember looking at us all and wondering how much lower it would get.

'It was the middle of the afternoon before they began to let us on board. On the quay it seemed unbearable – no shade – but when we got aboard we realised how lucky we had been. At least outside there was a breeze. As you came off the gangway on to the deck, a great hot breath came from the body of the ship. The bulk of us – I don't know how many altogether, hundreds – were put in a series of large cabins, dormitories. When we got there, the older men, they fell through the doorways. Almost dead. Carrying their bags up those steep gangways in the heat, they were exhausted.

'We didn't get to eat anything until late in the evening. But we were quiet, still in shock and it was in any case still too hot to complain. I remember there was a very complicated system for food. We were divided into messes, and each mess could send only one representative to collect plates and then rations and tea. Along all the long corridors in the ship, the men sent by each mess got confused, they got lost. It took hours – and there were very few people in charge of us all. Aside from the sailors, just a pair of British officers who spoke some Italian, although not perfectly by any means. They seemed to know even less of what was happening than we did.

'We didn't sail that first day. We hardly got to eat before midnight, but somehow we slept, at least I don't remember much of it. But at some stage before dawn we felt her move off.'

Daphne shifted in her chair. Delle Rose looked up. 'I'm sorry,' he said, 'this takes time.'

'No, please,' she replied, 'I'm just rearranging my arthritic joints. It's not . . . it's not an expression of boredom.'

'I don't think anyone would say they had a good night's sleep. Too cramped, too hot, too noisy. We were in cabins towards the rear of the ship, but from time to time some of our number slipped out. No one, sailors or officers, seemed familiar with the boat and below deck it was like rabbit tunnels, you know. Passageways and ladders and trapdoors. Impossible to find your way about, but impossible to control people in it. The guards were worried. Not that we could escape, of course, but that we might run around – out of control. So many of us, so few of them.

'The British told us there were also Germans on the ship – merchant seamen, Nazis mainly, but also anti-Nazis and Jews. A mixed lot. We didn't see them when we came aboard. They were billeted already in the ballroom. Well, there was some trouble. A lot of noise and somehow a group of them they rigged up a Nazi flag. Now of course most of the Germans were sailors themselves and the British were worried that, in the ballroom, they were close to the control room, close to the bridge too. This was, it seems, a problem.'

His mouth was dry and he paused to sip from the glass of water his grandson handed him.

'Anyway. Someone decided that they would have to be

moved to some location less . . . risky. Which meant we too had to move. A young British officer, he had a passing knowledge of Italian – all Verdi and "I Promessi Sposi", a Robert Browning man – came to explain this operation. His suggestion was, well, badly received. Confusion, everywhere.

'In the end, some four hundred of us were squeezed into a room meant only to house two hundred. Terrible. Everyone shouting, no one wanting to give way, no one clear about what they should do, where they should be. And underneath all this – fear. Fear because we didn't know what was ahead of us; fear of attack from German planes or boats, since we were on a British ship. For their part, I don't think the officers had spoken more than a few words to the crew of the ship since coming on board. And the crew, well, I know now they had been pulled together a few hours before sailing. Nobody knew their way around the ship. We were hundreds of extra passengers – and no one could understand us.'

He paused. The three of them stared at the floor. Outside the light was low and golden; inside their expressions were blurred by dusk.

'After, I don't know, a couple of hours of this crazy squash, the young army captain who had been sent to interpret came back to the ballroom with the news that a shed (that's what he said, a shed) had been found on one of the upper decks towards the back of the boat. They had found the key only just then. Some of us could go there, if we preferred. Not many did. As uncomfortable as we all were, it was better to be together. And a ballroom must surely be better than a shed.

'But not safer. He did try to tell them – but only a few of us, maybe forty, could understand what he was saying. The shed, you see, was closer to the lifeboats. He said it over and over again, exactly the same words. He'd been practising, I think, with a dictionary.

'When we got there, I wondered if it was the right decision. It was a big place, cold and bare, but we had room at least to settle ourselves down for the night.

'I had slept some four or five hours, off and on. I was lying listening to the first noises of the morning watch when I felt –

not heard, but felt – a jolt. Nothing dramatic, the kind you get when a boat is docking. Like a mistake. The sound of breaking glass, perhaps, I'm not sure. There were two night-lights in our shed and they went out, snap, leaving us at first altogether in the dark. Someone pulled the black-out down; the morning light came in from a small, high window. I could hear running feet and then people shouting the alarm.

'The few of us threw on our coats. Our guard was already gone. On deck we could see men from the crew throwing liferafts over the side. It seemed crazy; the ship was still steaming ahead, cutting through the waves. I ran to the side and watched the rafts spinning away in her wake, no use to anyone. Was she sinking? It didn't seem so. Damaged perhaps, but not sinking. Not then.

'The strangest thing, that only then I noticed, was that there were so few people on deck. It was perhaps five minutes since the crash, which I now knew – I don't know how, some-one must have said, or maybe I just guessed – had been a torpedo. And there were perhaps a dozen of us. Then I realised that many of the sailors were already packed into one of the lifeboats, which had been lowered down on to the deck. The boat was clearly overloaded. Men were standing and lying down, holding on to the rigging and ropes.

'Just then, one of the doorways that led from the lower-decks burst open and a stream of men rushed out into the light. They were confused and stumbling, but quiet. Not panic, you know. Not panic, like they said later. Never that. Just the confusion of many people in a situation they could not possibly understand. How could they? Some were able to break through to the edge, to the rail, but many more came up against the barricades of barbed wire. It was only then that I noticed the wire. It lay between them and me.

'I am not proud that I ran then to the second lifeboat, conscious that it was the only thing to do, to live. To get there before this great crowd made escape impossible. The British officer who had translated for us was already there with a handful of officers and other ranks, also some crew and four Germans, maybe five. There was some problem getting the boat free. I remember only everyone – all of us in the lifeboat and the frightened people on the deck – staring at the ropes that held us. The ship had stopped now, she was shaking. You could tell that she was no longer straight in the water. And where were the lifeboats or the lifebelts? And the rafts, they were gone already a long time, way behind us in the sea.

'At last, one of the soldiers used his bayonet to cut through the twisted rope that was holding us to the side. It seemed we would fall into the sea – and the whole boat did – but, it was a miracle, no one lost his grip and although we had taken in a great deal of water, we still had the oars. Half a dozen of us got the oars in place and managed to row perhaps fifty metres from the ship.

'From there, maybe ten minutes later, we saw her go down. She had been listing for half an hour or more, but those last few seconds were so fast – like a child's toy, you know. Almost comedy.'

He was silent. The other two waited. Daphne shifted her elbows on the table and felt pain surge into her shoulder. Then he began, as if another story. 'I dream, still, of those little dots, all huddled at the front of the boat. They went into the air and down to the waves. Killed on impact, surely. Please God. I'm not sure sometimes that it wasn't a dream.

'Those who were not drowned at once, they had to struggle with the oil that was spreading across the heaving water. Oil and rigging and broken wood, and God knows what flung around. Someone in our boat woke first – because we were certainly all in a kind of trance – and we began to row. I don't remember much about what happened next. Perhaps we collected about a dozen survivors, but we were drifting too far to do much more.'

They sat for some minutes. Daphne could hardly see the old man now. She leant across to switch on a lamp. Delle Rose jolted in his chair, startled. He blinked at her, discomforted, as though she were an intruder. For a second or two he gazed, letting the years click over, arranging his recollections before him. Daphne felt his slight impatience, as if he'd exhausted his repertoire.

'In the end, a flying boat appeared – a Sunderland – and within two or three hours we were taken aboard a destroyer.

They took us to Greenock. We wanted to tell our families, to let them know that we were still alive. But the officers said, "But they won't even know you've been in any danger. What's the hurry? There's no need." We felt as if the world had folded up upon itself in front of our eyes. How could they not have heard?

'You know, always there was calm. There was calm now as we came off the destroyers. Even the British officers remarked on it. But for the sick or the wounded there was no help for many hours. They simply lay on the quay. If we had thought conditions were bad when we arrived at Liverpool – then how can I explain that it seemed in some ways no worse now?'

He looked down at his feet, as the memories bumped up against him.

'There is something I forgot to say. In all the rush of the hit and the chaos that followed, in the scramble for the lifeboats, in all of this, I never once thought to myself the thing that should have been in the front of my mind. I couldn't swim. I hated water – even from a child. If I had slipped or been thrown into the waves, then I would have dropped straight to the bottom of the ocean. Straight to the bottom.'

'Grandfather swims now. Every day. He's a very strong swimmer.' Daphne was surprised by the voice from the armchair. The young man sounded close to tears, but proud.

'Well, of course,' his grandfather brushed away the interruption but seemed short of breath. 'I live in Australia, in a house with a swimming pool that eats up half the garden, I have no choice. It's the culture.'

'Grandfather, are you tired?'

'Yes, and I expect our hostess is too. There's not much more to say. The next day at Greenock, we were put on a different ship. Many, of course, did not want to go back out on the ocean, but over the days, as we pulled away from British waters, they became less – agitated. And in time we arrived in Australia, where just a few of us remained after the war. The rest returned. They resumed their lives here.'

'Why did you prefer to stay in Australia?' asked Daphne, clearing her throat, as if bringing the session to a close, shuffling imaginary papers on the table in front of her.

'I suppose . . . I suppose I had few ties in this country, unlike the others.' He seemed to think the question unimportant. 'Like all decisions, the decision to settle was influenced by many things, but chance has given me a reasonable life in Australia.'

'My grandfather is Emeritus Professor, he has many publications – it's been an outstanding career. A very successful life.'

'I'm sure.' Daphne waited. For the first time, she caught the old man's gaze. He looked tired, but there was something like a challenge in it.

'He didn't want to come,' continued Antony Delle Rose. 'I persuaded him to come over here with me. It's not something he talks about, except when I bully him.' His grandfather had turned to look out over the dusty sill at the sea, no longer listening. 'I have felt such anger at what the British did. I understand that war brings constraints and imperatives – I'm not naïve, believe me. But the arbitrariness of it all. Collar the lot, round them all up together, treat them the same. Disrupt their lives, sometimes beyond repair.'

'We all had our lives disrupted. War is a great disruption.' Daphne was gentle.

'Of course, but the designation "dangerous" – no, it was worse – "desperate characters". You didn't know for sure. No, you had no idea. How could you know? How could you know anything? You all made assumptions and handed them out like the Ten Commandments.'

'That's what government is about, isn't it? Common assumptions.' She didn't want to engage, but if he carried on like this, she had no option.

'And the inquiry.' The grandson was like a steam-train. 'Still the same assumptions. That it was the panic of the Italians that caused the scale of the disaster. When the boat was overloaded already. A boat for five hundred, with fifteen hundred on board. With an odds-and-sods crew taken on that morning, with not enough lifeboats and no time for safety drill before she sailed. There is a testimony, you know, in the Public Record Office, from a British officer on the scene, who states categorically that there was no fighting, struggling for places or panic at any time. But the official report makes no mention of all this. It simply records a little limited regret that a handful of the individuals deported were in fact entirely loyal to Britain. And leaves the unspoken conclusion – and you're so good at that here – that you could lay most of the blame at the door of a racial stereotype: the hysterical Italian. That the tragedy was the inevitable result of the national tendency to hysteria. That, given a more phlegmatic temperament, lives would have been saved. Unforgivable.'

She spread her hands, but there was no chance to speak.

'And before, at the point of detention, there was no opportunity to appeal to a tribunal. Nothing to condemn but your word, which was always going to count for more than ours. And your word was simply a reaction to pressure put on you. Where's the bogeyman? Who's to blame? Here, it's the Italian. The real Fascists, because of course they did exist, they were on a boat out of there weeks before. But you had to find some, anyway. In the end, you were highly efficient in ridding Britain of a threat that wasn't there.'

'Was there, do you think, another way? When we knew the Italian record in Abyssinia? When we saw Mussolini and Hitler join forces?' She turned her pale eyes on him.

He shrugged in exasperation. He didn't know. He looked across at his grandfather, far from them in his contemplation of the rising water. She watched Antony Delle Rose; he looked back at her, the same direct gaze, the same contact – like his grandfather as she had known him, more like his grandfather than the old man himself.

They sat in silence. Daphne sighed. It was Antony Delle Rose, she presumed, who had sent the two packages, the pictures.

He grimaced. 'Yes, childish, I guess. But I was so struck by those images. I was collating information for a booklet to be published in Melbourne for the anniversary. There was no sinister intention; I guess you might have seen some, anyway, but it really wasn't my intention. I had these pictures and a copy of that newspaper cutting in front of me. I needed to do something with them, not just send them to the printer and have maybe a couple of hundred people at most look at them.

I needed someone who was at the centre of it all to see – and to feel. It was gauche. There's no other way to describe it.' He looked at her, as if in appeal.

'But how did you know who I was? Where I was, even?'

'Well, it may surprise you, but it's not so hard. My father knew your name then, although of course that was your maiden name. It's not so difficult. I'm a lawyer: I can tap into networks of research pretty easily, better than that TV company anyway, but then I have a very particular interest. I felt you should see his face again, so I sent it. Nothing more.

'The extraordinary coincidence was getting that call from the TV company a few weeks – days even – later. I gave them your name, you see, but it seems they were already in touch with you in some way. But since we've been here, it's become clear to me that there would be no purpose served by my grandfather appearing. He's seen you; I think that's as much as he wants, maybe too much at that. I can't force my sense of justice on him.'

'Or me,' she added. She was, after all, enormously relieved that there would be no television trial.

'I didn't really expect any progress there.'

'You don't really understand the change fifty years of peace makes, do you?' She was surprised to hear herself, but there was something ingenuous and open about this young man that demanded a response. She needed him to understand. 'You're a civil rights type. It's all individual liberties and freedoms to you. We're talking about another time – a more essential time, perhaps – when people believed in, *I* believed in, a common good. We did things that we didn't necessarily find pleasant, because they seemed *right*, in the national interest. We all, more or less, believed in that. Do you see?'

'I think that's patronising. But what I'd expect.' He looked away, down at the dusty beige rug.

'I don't intend to patronise. I am simply telling you how it was. As your grandfather has done.' For a minute or so, they sat together in thought, watching the old man, who shivered.

It was past eight. Daphne made a token offer of hospitality, duly refused. Grandfather and grandson were booked in at a local hotel. There was a flutter of preparations for departure, visits to the bathroom (where Daphne sensed the cracked tiles and creaking cistern were an offence) and checking for spectacles.

They were making their way to the front door when the phone rang. Daphne considered, then asked them to wait while she answered it.

The kind women who 'kept an eye' on Kenneth, who cleaned the house and cooked the odd meal, was breathless. Half an hour earlier she'd passed the house on her bicycle and the lights weren't on in the usual rooms. She called in. And that was how she had found him. The ambulance was on its way.

'I see.' Daphne's hand reached for the door frame. 'Is he dead?' she asked. Her guests were suddenly still. The woman didn't know, which Daphne took for confirmation. Richard would be at the house in a few minutes.

She put the receiver down and turned to the two men. The control came from her refuge in courtesy. 'I do apologise, but I shall have to leave, myself. Unexpectedly. There is . . . illness in the family. Please excuse me.'

They looked concerned, shocked. Could they help with transport? Would she like them to stay? No, no, her sons would take care of all that.

The phone rang again. The two men stood awkwardly on the threshold as she answered it. It was Richard, from the car. He'd been trying her number. Dad, something had happened to Dad. She was to get a cab at once – he'd take care of the bill, just get here. Have you spoken to Oliver? she asked, hearing the tremor in her voice and what, strangely, sounded like the beginning of a sob.

She had forgotten the Australians. They were still in the corridor, the old man resting against the doorway, the younger advancing to put a supporting arm under her elbow. She must sit down, he insisted on it, then she could tell him what he could do to help.

What he could do to help. She must find Oliver. She reached for the book that held the complicated co-ordinates of his various numbers and made a stab at punching the keys on the telephone. After a moment or two, Antony Delle Rose disentangled her arm from the telephone cord and took the book from her hands.

This one? He pointed to the entries by Oliver's name. She nodded and looked at him helplessly. He tried the numbers, one by one. There's an answer-machine, he said. Do you want to leave a message? She shook her head, dislodging the tear that was running down the side of her nose. It landed on his hand.

23

OLIVER WAS in the shower when he heard the news. Rachel's bathroom had television and radio sound piped through from the bedroom. The midnight bulletin of the World Service reported a coup, the rout of the President and fighting on the streets of the capital.

As soon as he was dressed, Oliver took a cab for the office. Unusually, he didn't check his answer-machine, but headed straight for the edit-suite, where he sat for four hours with the picture editor. Together they turned the structure of the film on its head.

At 6 a.m. the production secretary rang with details of his flight. He left for Heathrow at seven. At no point did Richard's calls cut across his route. It was only after nine, when he was waiting at gate 41, scribbling furiously on large sheets of lined paper, that he heard his name strained through the Tannoy.

He took the call at the desk, apprehensive for a last-minute hitch – the wrong connection, a delay for the equipment, something stupid and fatal to a three-day assignment. There was a guarded gentleness in the girl's tone. Could he call his brother? At once. It was urgent.

There was never a moment when he did not think he would get on the plane.

Richard was upset, but calm. He insisted he would collect Oliver from the airport. He'd already taken Daphne to the hospital. Then, at dawn, she'd gone back to Joanna and the children at home. There was stuff to be decided, things they – her sons – could help her with. She wanted to see Oliver as soon as possible.

But it was not possible. Not now. A screen had come down and Oliver was on the other side. The fact of the news, the sudden simple fact, was a liberation. Kenneth was gone. There was nothing else Oliver could do for him. The funeral would be in a few days; he'd be back for that. He could read a lesson or pour drinks, or walk before the hearse with a great black flag, keening like a professional. But for now there was nothing to do. He might as well be somewhere else. He would rather be somewhere else.

He heard Richard control his shock, and his anger. He heard the sigh of disappointment, tightly disciplined, that punctuated his early memories of his mother. No, he couldn't give them what they wanted, decent British grief. He no longer needed an excuse to avoid their invasive concern and affection. To hell with them.

He sat in the departure lounge, surrounded by bags, as the final calls for the flight came and went. The public phone stood sentinel opposite, but he was comfortable in his seat. It might hurt to move. After a couple of minutes, which might have been hours, a young stewardess touched his arm and spoke his name. He smiled briefly, gathered up his belongings and followed her on to the plane.

He already felt as if he were floating. The aircraft's interior was a smooth beige tunnel, not the usual inverted millipede of nervy humanity. He stowed himself into his seat, tucking his bags around him, taking comfort from the squeeze. He smiled again as the stewardess disentangled his feet from the strap of his bag and put the luggage in the overhead compartment.

As soon as they were airborne he ordered a large Scotch. In a moment, sir, she said, rather more crisply this time. Out of the window, the Home Counties receded, dull green beneath leaden clouds. Rachel didn't know. Rachel didn't know anything. To hell with her too.

It had in passing struck him as odd that they should have shared a bed for the last week. That they had had sex, three maybe four times, but that they had not discussed Rachel's approach to his mother. That he had not challenged her, nor she broached the subject – while agitation, resentment and disaster were gathering.

They had descended into a hinterland of evasion. She had seemed defensive, edgy about the project, but she was always edgy about everything. And he had no cause to raise it, to elevate its importance when it might be no more than a preliminary trawl; no wish to give her an insight into the vulnerabilities and quirks of his family. To joke about them was one thing, to lay out their entrails before her something else.

The more information he withheld, the more powerful he felt. He closed his eyes, but it was more hectic in there, in the dark. He'd spent most of the previous twelve hours in front of video editing machines. Their click and whirr, the perpetual false-starts and repetitions, the computer beeps and squeals, the lacing-up and running-back were a percussion track in his head. He felt life was moving now in the frustrating two steps forward, one back, quick-quick-slow rhythm of the edit.

He saw again the sequence of Mekhusla, dropping down from a helicopter, landing heavily on the tarmac, taking the impact in bent knees and running like the athlete he once was, until he was clear of the blades. He saw him turning towards the camera and flashing the broad smile, hands on hips, unable to resist flirtation with the lens. In the cutting-room, Oliver couldn't resist either. The man was magical. Ludicrous but magical. Over and over again, as the editor lined up the shot, Mekhusla dropped on to the airstrip. Oliver began to hear the thud of his feet and the syncopation of the helicopter's blades. Backwards into the craft sprang the Interior Minister as the tape rewound, and out again. He bounded like a great ape, muscular arms swinging, out of frame, out of sight. Then they found him, closer, in a mid-shot, just a broad expanse of pale-blue shirt filling the screen until he swung slowly round, smile burning with the turn. Frame by frame, the editor shaved the beginning of the shot until there was just the briefest suggestion of the man's bulk before the confident turn. Cut together with the run, to the urgent beat of the chopper, it was a ballet of energy. Twenty minutes of work, eight glorious seconds.

What had happened to the minister in all this? Was he

dead? The roar of the plane's engines surged in his ears. Dozing, Oliver confused them with the groan and rush of the edit-machines. The images shuttled past; sometimes they froze for a second or two before bulging towards him, exaggerated, with a wide smile or startling scarlet tie.

The cavalcade behind his eyelids made him bilious, but he welcomed it. It kept at bay the numb cavity that he could sense beside him. If he opened his eyes, he might see it; perhaps there was even a black tear in the side of the aircraft. He was terrified and also elated. The years of filial under-performing, of guilt and love neglected, would surely now slide off. His father was dead. It was over. He pushed the tray of food to one side, and asked for coffee.

Waiting for his connection in Vienna, he rang the office. Rachel was trying to reach him. More importantly, the office had made contact with Niki, who was busy on another project, naturally, but would try to make time to help him. The prospect of the task ahead, three days to gather enough material to reflect the great upheaval in the country, cleared his mind. Just three days – on his return there would be two more to go, at least, before the funeral.

Only a handful of flights were still going to the capital. Even so, that was something. As coups went, this one didn't seem so dramatic. The country had been pitched for so long in melodrama that it took more than a coup to destabilise it. He would need an interview with the new leader, when it became clear who that would be. Above all, he had to find out the fate of his principal actors.

Already, in a few weeks, the flagship hotel had lost its gleam. It was chokingly hot and the sliding glass door to his balcony was studded with dead insects. Niki would meet him not at the hotel but in her office at the local television station. Armed with dollars and the address written out for him by the concierge, he went there.

She came down to meet him in the dark lobby. There was no armed guard at the door, no sense of emergency that he could discern. In a corner, behind the dusty orange chairs, were two television screens. One showed CNN and the other the local station, which was relaying an old Michael Jackson video. He kept his eyes on the screens until she crossed his line of vision. They shook hands.

She looked somehow different. Perhaps it was the hair that seemed both shorter and more plentiful. Certainly it was the clothes. The old dark suit was gone and she wore jeans and a bright shirt, the international uniform of leisure. He felt uncomfortable with the change. Her face was the same though, tired and serious.

On the short walk to her tiny office she lit up a cigarette. It was crazy, she explained, she was already working for three people at once. Why not make it four?

Could she explain what was going on, he asked. On the way to the station he'd seen a few soldiers on the streets, but no more than he'd noticed on previous visits. Who exactly was in charge now?

It was complicated. She sighed. Put simply, there was a military-backed coup, which wanted to present stronger resistance to Moscow. The President was gone – out of the city, somewhere in the north, she believed, waiting to gather support. There was much dissatisfaction with what he had done, but he could yet return.

And Mekhusla? Had he taken the first plane out to be with his numbered accounts?

Mekhusla? She looked at him thoughtfully for a moment. No, Mekhusla hadn't done that. He was the leader of the new regime.

Oliver was hollow for a moment, incredulous, then found he wasn't surprised at all. Our man, he whooped, President? Obvious, when I think about it.

Niki nodded. She let through a smile at his excitement.

But we must arrange the interview, he said, as soon as the crew arrive. Whenever, wherever he can manage. We'll be there.

Of course. The same level gaze. I'll put in a call, she said.

He drove around the town for twenty minutes or so in the taxi she had summoned. He tried to log the evidence of military rule, but it was scarce. There was a brace of tanks in front of the Parliament building, but their guardians were out in the sun with the locals, shooting the breeze. A child scrambled across the turret of one of the great machines. He waved to his mother on the ground.

Nowhere in the streets did Oliver find the knots of protesters in washed-out denim that bobbed on the wave of democracy in Eastern Europe. There were red carnations strewn around statues of the nation's patriots, but he remembered those from last time. There was denim, but it was on its way to work or digging the road, not a uniform of refusal. If this was military tyranny, it was frustratingly subtle.

The crew would arrive at the hotel in an hour or so. The taxi driver dropped him off in the old part of town, thirty minutes' walk away. He dreaded any time alone in the chipped splendour of his room.

The act of climbing out of the taxi and paying was like a baptism into the evening. He felt liverish and shivered as he looked around. Across the road was a small area of park, no more than a rectangle of sand with a low, tattered box hedge and a couple of young plane trees. Along the centre ran a thin metal bench. Oliver sat and read his notes from the flight, as meaningless now as earlier in the day. A thin tan dog trotted across in front of him, swerving to cock its leg against the tree, keeping him in its suspicious eye.

Oliver looked up at the people drifting from office and factory. They met in twos and threes, summoned by the smells of cooking that were pouring into the air. Young men and women, solid middle-aged types and old ones – he glanced quickly over them, but returned to the elderly men and women, attended by their children and grandchildren. The pain had not yet begun: he felt the light-headedness of a survivor. The thing he had most feared since he was a small boy had happened and he was still standing.

He had not said goodbye to his father, except in a thousand ways with each little carelessness and betrayal over the years. It would have been unnatural to have had some deathbed speech, he was almost convinced of it. What he had done was not enough, surely, but it was understandable. They both understood it.

He thought briefly of his mother. Some time, not yet, he would have to speak to her. She, too, would understand his silence and would wear that understanding like a wound. He couldn't bring himself to deal with her just now. He was too vulnerable and too angry. All his memories of his father were tainted by her drive to change him, to make him more ambitious, less quirky – everything that she was. Her mask of disapproval had set in even before he was born. She judged them all, husband and sons, and found them wanting. And now it was his turn to judge.

It was her selection of facts, her editing of the truth that he had come to resent. She sliced frames off his father's achievements and magnified her own, not crudely, but with a self-deprecation that screamed the opposite. If only, Oliver heard the refrain through her life, if only I had fulfilled my early promise. If only I had not had to contend with a mediocre partner and the compromises of domesticity. But then – over and over, he had imbibed her message – but then I always did my duty, by my husband and by my children. That was my achievement, and you two boys have turned out well enough on it.

Thank you, he had never yet said. Thank you; you have my gratitude but not my devotion. Are we quits now?

And she was so wrong. The style and wit of his father, his sweetness and perception, these were the rarities, the gifts that had lifted their lives here and there into the extraordinary. Daphne was good at exams, outstanding at the tests and competitions that cropped up, unmatched in her ability to bat away the opposition and tireless in her crusade to keep them all up to scratch. When they failed, she was pitiless in her scorn.

Now, without the essential balance of his father, why should he deal with her? She would want all of him now, to pick over.

He detached himself from the mongrel's stare and stood up. The dusk was dropping down, bare lightbulbs stood out in first-floor kitchens, conversation and radio music floated above his head. He hitched his bags on to his shoulder and headed for the hotel.

24

THE SUN shone on the new President. It shone so brightly that his eyes disappeared in the shadow of his brows. Mekhusla leant back against the balustrade on the terrace of the presidential residence and dug in his pocket for sunglasses. With his shades, cobalt-blue shirt and black suit, the new President was a formidable sight. Oliver was sweating already.

They had barely been in the building ten minutes before Rambo swept through, shaking hands, shouting orders over his shoulder.

'No, no, no,' he waved briefly at the copse of camera lights, 'let's do it outside. No lights. *Au naturel*. It's faster.'

He strode out on to the terrace in the full glare. Oliver followed, lamely. 'Too much contrast, President,' he said, 'too much contrast. I'd prefer you to be inside; it would look more statesmanlike, in a formal environment.'

Mekhusla laughed and held up a broad finger. 'But this way, Oliver,' he said, 'this way is more modern. I come back in ten minutes, okay?'

If he had had more energy, Oliver would have argued, but this morning he was weak, despite the nerves. He sat in the wooden chair, dragging it into the only shade of the terrace, shifting position and profile while the cameraman adjusted the lighting.

Niki had delivered once more. She'd secured the interview, although to his regret she couldn't be on hand to smooth their way. Oliver could already see changes in the former Interior Minister. He had rejected the effete international elegance of his predecessor in favour of something more brutal and altogether more effective. The shirt was firmly disciplined; it no longer gaped as Rambo stretched his arms to yawn. His attention span had not grown with his responsibilities – if anything, it was shorter. But now he was in control; he set the pace and his sudden changes in footwork appeared dynamic, not childlike.

From time to time, an aide stepped out to check on progress. Eventually Rambo emerged, pulling down his cuffs and tightening his tie. His complexion was smooth with a veneer of make-up. He sat at a casual angle in the chair, one arm resting along the back. His sunglasses stayed in the other hand, the pose of the modern warrior-king. Oliver had wrestled with the shadows of the ethnic conflict and was left with handfuls of air. But this personality in front of him was so plausible, you could hack great chunks off it.

Mekhusla's line as President was simple. Strength through refusal. It was, in effect, more of the same, nothing original, but delivered with plenty of muscle. The deposed President had lacked the courage to see through the wishes of the people. The new regime had a truly popular mandate. And so on. Rambo's hands came together as though moulding clay. The performance was heroic. Mekhusla was good at handing out blame.

The light fell unevenly on the new President's face, adding chiaroscuro to the drama. Oliver was struck by the man's transformation: the pragmatist had apparently been eclipsed by an idealist – without an ideology.

The young men who travelled with the President, part bodyguard, part tea-boys, looked at their nails and picked invisible pieces of fluff from their jackets. Oliver hardly heard the answers. He knew the gist of them, anyway. While he surveyed his notes, Rambo began to fidget. He was looking over Oliver's shoulder, winking at one of the secretaries, putting on his sunglasses and cracking his knuckles. 'Okay,' he said. 'Let's go. Let's go.'

Oliver made one last exhausted attempt. Wasn't it true that all Mekhusla could offer the people was a new personality in charge? He had no magic policies, he had no great strategy – all he had was his populist image?

The glasses came off. An expression of troubled concentration came over the President. He sighed and fixed Oliver with dark eyes. A slight shine fought through the tanned powder.

'It is very easy for outsiders, if I can say this, to come into a country like ours and see only the shortcomings in our way of governing. If we have only a handful of solutions, it is because we have one great problem, one problem above all. This threat to our freedom and safety overshadows everything else. No question. We don't have the luxury of commissions and committees, of taking years to decide how we might proceed. If we do not act now, then our very identity – everything that we are – will be crushed. Everyone here knows that. This is our identity – to struggle against the threat from outside.'

'And afterwards,' asked Oliver, 'what will happen if you drive the threat away?'

'Then we will have the problems of democracy like everyone else – and thank God for it,' said the President, a slow smile breaking across his face.

'Thank you,' said Oliver. 'Cut.'

The President swung forward out of the chair and extended a hand to Oliver. 'Thank you, thank you,' he said, shaking hands in turn with sound and camera. His tone was brisk and his eyes were hidden once more by shades. 'When will this be shown?'

'In two weeks,' replied Oliver. The President nodded, satisfied, and charged through his office out into the day.

The stone of the parapet was warm under Oliver's forearms. He gazed out across the canopy of plane trees over the boulevard. Miniature people appeared briefly in the gaps of light and shade, proceeding along the broad pavements at the economical pace of those who work in the heat. They were the bit-players in this pantomime; Oliver's disbelief was suspended. In a fortnight he would present this confection, the world according to Rambo, to a television audience. By then, it would be stripped of its muddle, of the confusion and ambiguity that had dogged his previous visit. Audiences didn't like muddle and he would give them what they liked.

Behind him the crew packed up. He wanted to lie with the warm stone against his back. In this state of siege, it was curious how little urgency he picked up from the streets, curious too how empty the city seemed, dreamlike. The streets offered up an occasional distant shout or cry, or the drone of a two-stroke, but as he rested there the noise receded. The crew wanted to take the gear down to the car. He nodded, watching the heat-haze over the apartment blocks on the skyline. Perhaps he could stay here for a while.

In the van back to the hotel, he couldn't keep from yawning; the others made a joke of it. They set off for a sandwich in the bar, but Oliver went to his room, to find some notes or wash his face, or both. With the door safely shut behind him, he lay on the bed with his eyes on the view from the balcony, hugging his knees.

There was no way he could have closed his eyes, because they were still fixed on the blue out of the window, when there was a discreet knock at the door. The sound brought no surge of adrenaline, just puzzlement. The knock came again, louder this time. It's Niki, said a voice tight with impatience.

He rolled himself off the bed and walked in his socks to the door. She looked startled when he opened it. He mumbled something, ran his hand through his hair.

'What's going on?' she demanded.

He looked down at her. What was the matter? Had something gone wrong?

'It's nearly three o'clock. Your crew is waiting downstairs. They've been there for thirty minutes. You're late already for the next interview. Are you mad?'

He turned, harried, back into the room and searched for his shoes by the bed. The left one was stranded just out of reach. He knelt down and made exploratory sweeps to retrieve it, sprawling further on the carpet as it eluded him. Every time he made contact, it inched away. Niki stood in the doorway, watching.

'Don't you have,' she asked cautiously, 'any other shoes?'

He looked up at her in surprise. Other shoes. Why was she interested in his shoes? These shoes would do, once he got

192

hold of them. He sat in the cradle between bed and wall and rubbed his chin. It was rough with stubble.

Niki walked over to the mini-bar and opened it with the room key. The bottles lay untouched in their squadrons. She looked at him again, keenly. 'Are you ill?'

'No, no,' he replied, shaking his head repeatedly, 'I'll be fine in a moment. I just need my shoes, I just want my shoes.' He felt a tug of panic and gestured under the bed. 'It just won't work, you see. Why won't it work?' He was pleading. To his amazement, he was crying too.

She stared, weighing for a moment whether to comfort or walk away. Then she sighed, dumped her shoulder bag on the chair and fished his shoe out from under the bed.

'Here,' she said.

'Thank you,' he whimpered, 'thank you.'

He fumbled with the laces, wiping the tears with the back of his hand. They came copiously now, great sobs like gulps of air.

She crouched in front of him. 'What is it?' she asked gently, prising his fingers from the laces. In a scant second the knots were done.

He sniffed and pulled away, standing up sharply and turning to the window. He put both hands over his face and breathed deeply in an attempt to regain control. He shook his head. Niki stood up and leant against the wall.

After a few moments, she said, 'If you want, I'll go with the crew to the locations this afternoon.' He made a shrugging gesture of protest, still with his back to her, but no sound came out. 'What do you want me to ask? Do you have notes?'

He pointed vaguely to a notebook on the table. She walked over and picked it up, keeping her eyes on him.

'You'll be okay? We'll be back around seven.'

He nodded and managed a red-eyed sideways glance. 'Thank you,' he whispered, but the sobs were not far below.

'Okay.' She was brisk again. 'Get cleaned up.'

Oliver had taken a shower and was sitting by the open door to the balcony when the chamber-maids came in. At first they didn't notice him, as they burst in with clean towels and backchat. Then they came to a sudden halt, suppressing laughter. He turned and waved to them to carry on, appreciative of the noise and normality. It was something to assuage for a moment the sense of anxiety and loss that sat out there like a cloud over the city. It lurked behind the cupboard doors and was impregnated in the starched linen of the pillow. In the shower he'd felt worst of all, alone and frightened. He'd shied away from his confused expression in the steamy mirror. He felt so bruised it might hurt to touch the walls.

The women's voices retreated down the corridor. He had looked at his watch so many times that the time for expecting was past. The sun was low behind the television tower on the hill, despatching ochre contours to the old part of the city. The skills of organisation that habitually carried him through fatigue were just out of reach. He was a prisoner.

The light was quite gone from the room when she knocked. He got up slowly and opened the door. She was carrying a pile of tapes besides her usual briefcase and bag.

'You look better,' she said and walked past him and out on to the balcony. 'I'll tell you what you have here,' and she listed the contents of the tapes. Everything seemed complete and in order. He was very grateful for her efforts.

'No problem,' she said, collecting her things together.

'No, wait.' He wanted to absolve himself. 'Just a moment. Please. I should explain.'

'It's not necessary.' She looked at him directly. 'Call into my office tomorrow morning before you go to the airport and I'll have the invoice for you.'

'Yes, of course.' He took the rebuff and sank back in his chair.

Her voice softened, but she kept her eyes on the view. 'You have some kind of trouble, perhaps. It's normal. I'm sorry for it.'

He wanted to explain. He wanted very much to tell her that he was acting not in reaction to some slight in career or romance, but because the anchor of his existence, the source of sweetness and good, was gone. And in its banality, he said it.

'My father has died.'

She nodded and looked down. 'It's hard,' she said in a matter-of-fact voice.

'Yes, it is,' he managed a slight smile. They sat together in silence.

'I have to go,' she said after a while. 'You should phone your crew and tell them what the arrangements are for tomorrow.'

He nodded, reluctantly. And then he asked her, in a rush of embarrassment and confusion, if she could stay, maybe for a few minutes more.

She did have to go, she repeated, looking at him gravely. But, it was possible, she could return in an hour. They could have a drink, maybe he should eat, and finish their paperwork then. That would cut down what he had to do in the morning.

Yes, yes, he agreed. Would you? I really appreciate it. I can't tell you how much.

When she came back he had made the phone calls, with a brash apology for his absence. Some kind of virus, feeling God-awful; they probably didn't believe him anyway. But he stressed, too much, that they'd obviously done a grand job – he was viewing the rushes now.

'This is what you owe me,' she said, with a wry smile. He took the envelope and looked at the modest sum typed out inside. On other occasions he might have quibbled even with that, but not this evening. He fetched the packets of dollars from his bag and counted out the handful of notes, noting down the balance, trying not to reveal to her the wealth stashed beneath, from a desire not to offend rather than from fear of envy or theft.

Outside, on the balcony, it was dark. A round lamp, stuck casually on the plastered wall, covered them in a dull buttery light. They drank imported beer.

'Was your father an old man?' she asked.

Yes. Well, no. Not that old – late seventies, but frail, very thin. He'd been ill, a series of strokes, each one stealing away a little more. Oliver had anticipated this death for so many years since the first illness that he'd come, in a way, to believe that his father was immortal, that he'd found some way of jetting through into eternity on only one engine. What was surprising now was the violence of the loss. Even more alarming was the resentment he felt towards his mother.

Why resentment? she asked. Oliver heard the sentences stumbling out. It was as if his mother had placed all her hopes and thwarted ambitions on her relationship with her younger son. It was as if his father was the impediment to the success of this plan. He was a burden, even before he was ill. The physical weakness was just confirmation. What Oliver had never understood was why, exactly, his father had failed in his mother's eyes. Perhaps it was just a secondary symptom of what so many over-qualified, over-energetic women suffered – the chafes of domesticity. They'd expected fulfilment and some kind of secular salvation from a man: they flung all the blame back on him when they considered how far they had failed to live up to their own early promise.

Then there was the television programme. All that fuss associated with it. Oliver couldn't explain the exact circumstances, did not have the time here, but it was another mess and she looked to him to sort it out. His father would have supplied some perspective or comment that would have sprung them all from the tangles. But his mother dragged them down further.

With his father's death, kindness and felicity had been scattered to the winds. He understood his mother, but could not love her. It was a harsh, melodramatic statement, but there it was.

Niki looked saddened. Somehow he had come to be holding her hand across the table. I'm sorry, he said, I'm sorry, I should never have said all that. It's not your problem.

No, she answered simply.

With the anger gone, he had to tell her how grateful he was, how guilty that he could offer her nothing in return.

In the darkness, she laughed. He couldn't fathom the laugh: it was mocking, but not cruel. Why are you laughing? he asked. She was quiet again. It was useless to try to understand. She wasn't bothered about that, and he certainly couldn't begin to see why she acted the way she did.

Oliver thought it was good to be in the dark.

25

IT WAS kind of him, thought Daphne, a little absurd, but kind.

She sat on the plastic upholstered bench, one elbow on the window frame, as the glass-topped pleasure boat pulled away from the little jetty. It was her third revolution of the lake. As a journey, it was pleasant enough – across the man-made lake from the ersatz village to the Land of Tomorrow. And back. Jad had proposed the trip. He had a half-shift to work at the park from ten until two; he could take her in for free, if she pretended to be his nan. She'd feigned offence at the suggestion until he pointed out that his nan, at fifty-seven, was her junior by nearly two decades.

The sky was palest blue, with a film of stratospheric cloud pulled tight. The water of the lake lapped gently against the sides of the boat. It was all pleasant and intermediate, something to do for a few hours. She quite enjoyed watching the families get on and off at either end of the voyage. She hadn't wanted to stop elsewhere in the park, which seemed to her noisy and dusty and crowded, but this was bearable.

Although she had insisted on returning to the beach house before the funeral, it was no longer her haven. The extraordinary development was that she couldn't watch the sea. Too large, too fierce. This little artificial sea, on the other hand, dispensed the right amount of solace without threat.

Arrangements were proceeding fast around her. The funeral was just two days away. Oliver would return tomorrow and solve the riddle of his absence. Richard had explained that his brother was very upset, but unable to cancel his trip. Not a word, nothing. It hurt, of course, but that was the price of her devotion. When he got home she would have him all to herself.

In the meantime, Jad was filling this time with his own strange kindness and she was grateful. No, no, she replied, when a boat steward enquired if she needed some help, I'm quite all right, I'll just take another couple of turns around the lake.

At the end of his short shift, Jad was waiting for her at the Wild West railroad station. She saw him as he loomed above the crowds. In the foreground, adults administered fried chicken and lurid fizz to fractious children. The ground was perilous with greasy paper and cups.

'All right, Daphne?' he asked. 'Not bored, then?'

'Almost,' she conceded. 'I think it's probably time to go now.'

He drove her home in her own car. She'd phoned the insurance company to have him included on the policy. Richard would be incensed.

At the turn in the road, they overtook the postman cycling untidily. He gave a frantic wave and Jad swerved to avoid him. The two vehicles, six wheels, came to a halt at an acute angle.

'I found this,' gasped the postman, reaching into his pocket for a letter, 'found it in the bottom of the sack. It never happens, never happens. And if it does, well, we usually wait until the next morning. But what with your recent trouble,' his expression was briefly reminiscent of a spaniel, 'I thought you should have it.'

Daphne looked suspiciously at the envelope. It was not from abroad, not from Oliver, so it could hardly be important. Thank you, she said.

'And how are you keeping, in yourself?' the postman continued. 'It's part of our job, I suppose, what you might call the pastoral element. We do keep an eye, you know.'

'Well, this particular sheep is grazing just fine, but thank you for your enquiry.' She wished strongly that he would go away. Realising that further conversation was unlikely, he nodded and pedalled off.

Jad saw her safely inside and left her with a cup of tea and the envelope. It was handwritten and postmarked London.

Antony Delle Rose expressed his condolence easily. He wrote as he spoke – fluently and frankly. There was nothing obsequious or grudging. The circumstances of their acquaintance might be irregular, but his tone was natural.

Dear Daphne,
My grandfather and I feel for you at a dreadful time. It may hardly seem appropriate, but you know that you can count on any help from us while we remain in England. I wish we could have helped more. It was the least we could do to drive you to Surrey that evening. I know you felt awkward about it, but there was no need.

The great consolation for you must be your family. Your children will be a great support and help during these difficult days. These are times when one realises how strong the bonds of family are.

My grandfather feels that I should leave you alone with your grief, but I want you to know that, whatever I might feel about the past, these essential things transcend any national difference, or any individual differences. In the end, we are all sons and mothers and grandfathers, and so on.

I hope you understand the reason for our visit. I'm convinced that it is essential to talk about the past, but maybe in this case we were all talking about different pasts, different histories. You obviously have your own perspective. For my grandfather it is something different from the way I see it, even from the way I thought I'd heard him tell it before. But it is important that he should be allowed to tell his story. Even if that story changes.

I have never been able to understand why he didn't seem prouder of his life. I have always felt that this incident, this injustice, had tainted his memory. It skewed the past for him, for his children – my parents – even for me. It has stood in the way of me owning my own history. I couldn't be proud until he was proud.

But, in all honesty, I wonder if I had the right to stage all this with you, on my terms, for my satisfaction. It was all a long time ago. I think perhaps it happened to different people.

A simple enough sentiment, thought Daphne. All the same it hooked out so much troubling emotion that she knew she must disarm it with her usual courtesy. The letter was on the headed paper of a London hotel. Daphne rang the telephone number.

Antony Delle Rose was in his room. She thanked him for the letter and, more directly, for his help on the night of Kenneth's death. He repeated his protest from the letter and asked about the funeral.

Day after tomorrow, she said. Would it be appropriate for them to send flowers? She had not been inclined to encourage flowers, thinking donations to a medical charity more appropriate. But now, on the eve, she glimpsed the pathos of an ungarlanded coffin and relented. Yes, of course, how kind.

They would be leaving for England on the day of the funeral. It had been a strange visit. In retrospect, as he'd said in the letter, he questioned the wisdom of it. He felt no compunction about their withdrawal from the television programme, which he understood was to continue in some form or another. That was neither here nor there and, in any case, his grandfather was keen to return home.

Daphne admitted that she was taken aback by his frankness. Had he, Daphne wondered, expected her to admit that she had been wrong?

This was hardly the time to talk about that, he protested. But no, he hadn't, he had simply wanted her to acknowledge her part in the process.

She had never sought to do otherwise. She had never sought to evade her responsibility, although others around her had. Any decision is a chain of events. She had been a link in that chain. If he wanted to hand out blame, she could take it. She understood.

I know, he said, and I don't want to hand out blame, not now. My grandfather, he was also part of a chain, a chain that led at one end to Mussolini and the death-squads in Libya and Abyssinia, and at the other to decent British citizens of Italian origin who were loyal to the Queen and the Union Jack. What you did, what your team did, was to place him in the wrong part of that chain.

Maybe, she said, maybe. Probably.

He had wanted to recapture for his grandfather some lost sense of pride. He remembered being told of the brittle Utopia his grandfather had helped to build as a boy in Fiume. Once, as a student, he'd tried to visit, but found only Balkan greyness. The location was confused, he became muddled about the sequence of events. The only certainty was of old hatreds. Locals still remembered invaders and oppressors and injustices. So for him, the truth was no longer there. It could only be found in narrative; he believed in the power of ordering and retelling. But this story, his grandfather's story, was at risk of losing its conviction in the retelling. It made no more sense now than when he first heard it.

'Does my grandfather once again have a handle on those months in 1940? Does he possess them? Is he reconciled? He no longer cares and I can't make him do so. I've put in place all the components, but something's still missing.'

'What's missing,' said Daphne, 'is the man who was there.' In her mind she could see his face, just as she could hear his voice, now, on the other end of the phone.

The young man seemed upset. Everyone was so upset these days.

It was only July, but already the dusk fell a little earlier. This evening it was cool. She sat on the veranda, but her eyes were on the shingle and the path, anywhere but on the sea.

Her mother had always taught her not to dwell on things that might have been. Mostly Daphne had dismissed possibilities before they became threatening. Was hers perhaps a lifetime of evasion and rationalisation, a lifetime of denying the direct and the intuitive? Too late to think about that now.

From the kitchen, she heard a soft noise, a kind of shuffle. The dog. But then from beneath her feet came a growl and a sudden acceleration of white and tan towards the door. Her alarm quickly faded to excitement. Oliver was back, a day early; he'd come direct from the airport. He, not Richard, would drive her to the house. They would travel together.

The dog had scampered to the end of the veranda and

pushed his nose around the kitchen door by the time she was out of her chair. He ran barking into the kitchen, claws clattering on the lino. As she felt her way along the handrail, he returned, feigning nonchalance.

'Who is it?' she asked him. 'Is it Oliver? Is it Oliver? Good boy.'

But the shape in the kitchen was wrong. Daphne felt for the light switch. The fluorescent strip flared into life, etching the silhouette into her retina.

Jad stood behind the little melamine table, a strange, wary expression on his face. She gave a short laugh to hide her disappointment and busied herself with the door. As she did, the full details of the tableau leached into her mind. On the table in front of him lay her handbag, open, with her purse lying diagonally, exposed. From this little rectangle to his massive frame ran a tension.

She stared at him. He muttered something about changing the arrangement for the next day, about coming to do the lawn in the afternoon, not the morning. If that was all the same.

She nodded slowly. It was all the same. She looked down at the table.

'I'm sorry,' she said, 'I was startled by the noise. Half-expecting one of the boys . . .' She reached for her purse and pulled out the only note, a new, tightly folded twenty pounds. 'It strikes me,' she went on, gazing up at him, 'that we're a bit behind with the payments. Have this.' She held out her hand.

He protested, sweating slightly. She didn't have to. Don't.

'Oh, but I do,' she said, putting it on the table in front of him.

He stowed the note in the pocket of his large jeans.

Daphne leant back against the sink. 'In any case, there's nothing you can steal from me. That's not the nature of the deal,' she said, her heart thumping.

26

For the third time Richard had hurtled down a narrow lane towards Clerkenwell – and found it blocked by a police barrier. He ground the great vehicle into reverse; it wheezed back up the slope until he found a loading bay wide enough to allow him to turn. The route for the Italian procession in Clerkenwell was tightly bound with yellow barriers. For twenty minutes he had repeatedly misjudged the best place to leave his car.

Richard had begun his journey with a sense of righteous anger, but his crusade was fast sliding into vendetta. After a couple more attempts, he manoeuvred the car into a meter bay half a mile from the route and continued on foot. As he walked along the dusty streets, the murmur of people grew louder. A block away, the crowd was waiting in the full heat of the July afternoon.

Daphne had not wanted Richard to contact Rachel. She would have been horrified that he should do it thirty-six hours before the funeral. But Richard had found out from her office that she would be here, filming the Italian festival. It was at first no more than a piece of information, until he found himself driving into the City. He had wanted to find out if she'd heard from Oliver. But now he no longer cared.

He walked down the hill towards Farringdon Road. Advertising hoardings shielded the source of the noise until he was right on top of it. For a quarter of a mile along the road and up the hill to the west, the crowd stood five or six deep. They were a mixture: the women of Italian descent, with dark print dresses and strappy sandals, the young ones with their hair pulled back, the young men in chinos and crisply pressed shirts, their fathers with jackets, sometimes with a sash, gold wristwatches on tanned forearms, Panama hats. Dotted among them were the pallid Anglo-Saxon onlookers, who wore tired denims, bare torsos and shabby trainers. They looked untidy.

Richard stood for a moment to orient himself. Up the hill was the Italian church, the source and destination of the procession. He scanned for an eddy in the crowd that might suggest a television crew at work. Nothing.

He set off, head down, into the crowd. Around him most people were pressing on towards the front of the church, although some waited along the route. A young woman stood on a piece of raised concrete, the legacy of some unfinished roadworks, flanked by two youths with sweaters knotted around their necks. They held out copies of an Italian-language magazine and exchanged brief comments with any takers. Richard was ignored as he walked past.

Up ahead in front of the church, something elaborate and gilded lurched into the road. The crowd lurched with it and someone trod on his toe. Richard saw a holy statue, carried shoulder-high on a flower-decked dais. Behind it, giant boulders crafted from cardboard and papier mâché perched on a sea of bright blue ribbons, and a group of figures in hessian robes braced their feet against the jolts of the float. The fishermen of Galilee had model looks, punched home with eyeliner.

On the next float came the first in a series of madonnas. She was little more than twenty. Her skin was shiny with make-up and heat, the lips were pale. At her feet, their eyes sweeping across the crowds, squatted a clutch of junior angels, in gold satin and plimsolls. They waved their palm fronds enthusiastically. The Virgin adjusted her head-dress.

Richard was fascinated; it took him back to the intensity of nativity plays. He stood in the sunshine, shifting from one foot to another.

Between the Loaves and Fishes and the Sermon on the Mount he glimpsed Rachel and her crew as they worked on the other side of the road. Her red-gold hair stood out. It had not occurred to him before that the colour was artificial.

Shaken out of his fascination, he struggled to break through the ranks of spectators and cross the road. He saw the disapproval at his lack of respect.

From her expression – the slow tussle between confusion and wariness – it was clear that Rachel had not noticed him until he spoke.

'I want to talk to you,' he said, sounding like a schoolmaster.

'This isn't a good moment.' She pushed her chin up defensively.

'When is?'

'Well,' she looked around for help, 'when all this has packed up. I don't know, an hour or so. What . . . is this about?' She tailed off.

'Where? In front of the church – in an hour?' He could barely get the words out.

'I suppose so.' Irritated, she looked at him for a second, then turned back to the camera crew.

Richard moved away, uncertain what to do next. He allowed himself to drift with the crowd around the corner and up towards the church. On either side of him people were speaking Italian and English mixed. He was part of this crowd. He was wearing Italian clothes, Italian shoes. Unless he spoke, how would they know?

The procession began to thin out. The spectators broke from their files on the pavements and headed across the road to greet friends. Richard found himself buoyed along and pushed up the steps of the church. At the door, he dodged aside, cutting across the path of several stout matrons to wait in the portico. His watch gave him another twenty minutes.

Shrugging his shoulders, as if to apologise to some invisible observer, he abandoned himself to the flow and turned back into the church.

Inside it was scarcely more peaceful than on the street. There was a steady murmur of chatter and prayer. The rows of seats were filling up. He saw pale blue and grey white in Romanesque slices. The little red lights burned. The pasty plaster saints rolled their eyes. Richard took refuge by dodging into a pew.

Hands clasped, he gazed at the woodblock floor between his knees.

He had no right to be here. There were a million things to be done at home or in the office. The time-management system in his brain was grappling with the logistics of the funeral. Notices and flowers and catering, he had to be on top of it all. For a minute or two he was lost in the complexity of probate and procedure and taxis.

In my Father's house are many mansions. In my Father's house are many mansions. His secretary had photocopied the verses from John and they lay, folded and re-folded, inside his wallet. He wanted to be familiar with them so that he could address the mourners with the authority of the elder son. He had somehow imagined that the choice of reading would be personal, considered, agonised even, but the vicar had been tactful but brisk. In the case of those who do not wear their faith *publicly* – and here the clergyman had grasped an invisible rugby ball in the air before him – I find this very helpful, he had said. He had read it to Richard and his mother at a qualifying speed.

Goodness, Daphne had remarked. The vicar had smiled, sympathetically, taking her scorn for distress.

Richard kneaded his knuckles into the palm of the other hand. In his imagination his father's funeral would be perfect and precise. What Richard would in fact deliver the day after tomorrow was another drab crematorium function. The vicar would scrape together an address from jottings on the back of an envelope; there would be a couple of familiar hymns and, at best, a little hurried dignity. The old man would have laughed, but been offended.

He tried to draw a little peace, a little piety even, from his surroundings, but his agitation touched everything. The church was too ornate, or too austere; the echoing burble of voices disturbed; it was too crowded; he was too isolated. He glanced sideways at bowed heads, at fat knees on the leather rests, and at an arm lying casually along the back of the pew in front. Richard knew he shouldn't be here. In his distress and anger, he was thrashing around.

Outside, the crowd had thinned down to a few groups. His

eye was caught by a rosette of little girls in stiff white communion dresses, who tugged and flirted with one another. Some old soldiers, their dark plumed hats in their laps, sat wearily on the steps of the church. Richard felt he had woken from a bilious nap.

Rachel was standing with her colleagues a couple of blocks up the street. She had her back to him, but he could tell from her shoulders that she knew he was there. He couldn't wait and strode down the steps. Why the hell couldn't she just meet him where they'd agreed?

When she turned to look at him, it was with a look of surprise. Oh . . . right. She said goodbye to her team. Richard herded her back down towards the church.

'I don't have long,' she said, sulkily.

His anger suddenly gave him energy. Long enough, he said, and his tone made her look up at him. The arm that was fending off the pedestrians around her became a threat. She turned to face him to stop the momentum of their progress down the pavement and took a step backwards, nearly falling on to the church steps.

'I haven't spoken to Oliver, if that's what you want to know,' she said, 'not a word since he left. Is this about him, is something wrong?'

'I don't want to talk about Oliver,' he muttered.

'Look, I don't think there's any point in us talking. I really can't see any. I have to go,' she made to push past him.

Richard didn't remember taking hold of her wrist but he saw the shock in her eyes. She was too astonished to protest, but she twisted away from him back up the steps. He followed, half-curious as to what she would do next. To his surprise she made for the entrance to the church. He went after her, infuriated.

People were leaving now, mostly singly or in twos. Rachel was pushing against the flow and he was right behind her. The crowd eddied around them; an old woman tugged at her companion's sleeve and tutted disapproval. Richard pressed on, driving Rachel towards the less crowded area at the back. She went, glancing back occasionally – half-resentful, half-incredulous – not sure if it was a real chase or some kind of joke. At the back the delayed echo of the church distorted the murmur of the crowd, amplifying a few shouts and raised voices. Richard was glad of the space.

Rachel stood with her arms folded, her shoulder resting against the wall, nudging the thin edge of a picture frame. Richard didn't recognise the picture – some religious scene in a desert, most likely a temptation of sorts – but something about the colour, an engraving in flat glacial blue, had a cold fascination. It put him in mind of something from his childhood, something that prompted fear and awe that he had never understood. He couldn't remember much about his grandmother except her voice – strong like a man's, but with a nasal South London sarcasm – but in his memory her eyes would always be interchangeable with the pale eye of the goat in that dismal picture in her house. Later his mother had taken the picture to the coast. Even now it made him uneasy and, more than that, angry.

'What *is* this about?' Rachel's whisper was high, sibilant.

'What did you think you were doing? Do you know *what* you've done?' He heard himself muttering like a lunatic. After all the waiting, he didn't know where to start.

She looked alarmed. 'I realise that it's all rather unfortunate, but I genuinely didn't realise how much your mother was involved. In any case all I did was to put a simple request to her, which she turned down. That's her right. I've respected that totally.'

'What crap.' Heads turned from the pews. He nodded, acknowledging their reproach and turned his face to the wall, dropping his voice still further. 'You blundered into something you didn't understand at all in search of a little glory for yourself. You've created considerable distress – in my father's case, God knows what went through his mind—'

'I'm sorry,' she interrupted, 'what am I supposed to have done to your father?' The sneer came out in a series of little explosions.

'These are old people, who did nothing wrong. This is not like some war crime. You people look around for something that you can take some synthetic moral standpoint on.'

She exhaled sharply. 'Look, it was just a case of telling it like it was. And it was only down to your mother. I only spoke to her. It was no big deal. I never spoke to your father at all. Why should he be upset?'

He stared at her. She didn't know. 'He's dead,' he said, in a speaking voice, unable to resist melodrama.

She was very pale, but the surprise soon gave way to caution. 'I'm sorry,' she said carefully, quietly. 'I had no idea.' She paused. 'When was it?'

He told her, although he thought it irrelevant. She seemed puzzled.

'The point is,' he continued in an undertone, but he'd lost his momentum, 'the point is that all this business with my mother was a worry to him in these last weeks. All this unnecessary raking up of this and that. I just don't see . . . the point of it.

'You really don't know what you're doing,' he went on. 'You've picked on one incident – which you don't altogether understand – and you've caused upset and worry all round. Not just my mother, God knows she's sensible enough to take all this in her stride, but the old man you dragged all the way from Australia. I know about that, you know, my mother's told me. I know about him, all about him. They've met, you know, and they're both in agreement. They want nothing to do with your plans to use their history as entertainment. It's personal to them, it's not yours, not your copyright.'

'I never claimed it was,' she was flushed, but standing her ground. 'Anyway, it's not true that I've dragged anyone anywhere. Look, this thing happened. It doesn't belong to your mother, or even Professor Delle Rose, or to you. It's a fact, and a little-known one at that. Maybe it should be better known. This is a way of putting it up for discussion.'

'Discussion – what the hell does that achieve? You simply have no sense of what this does, of responsibility. You take a snapshot of time and you conveniently forget about the context of all the years that came in between, of all the circumstances that influenced it at the time. You want a persecutor and victim story. Well, tell me this. Which one is which in this case?' He was conscious of sliding into overkill, but didn't care. 'It looks to me as though you're the persecutor here.'

'That's ridiculous,' she held her arms folded against her ribcage. The words came out in a tight hiss. 'We haven't doorstepped anyone, or chased anyone or used any undercover techniques. It's copy-book stuff and, anyway, all the people you're concerned about have pulled out. This programme has been a nightmare. And I don't see why this is all my fault. I didn't do the original research anyway,' she ended lamely.

'There you are,' his voice rose as his energy returned, 'there you are. You can't take responsibility for anything. Everything is someone else's fault. If all else fails, then it must be some bloody researcher. You've made a superficial judgement about something my mother did fifty years ago – something, and here's the great irony, that she did out of a sense of responsibility to her country. Out of honour and loyalty.' He sighed and continued more quietly, trying to put the force in his expression, 'I know it sounds a joke to you – but for her it was real, and I'm not sure it isn't for me, too.'

She had half-turned towards him and was staring at the floor at his feet. 'Is this why I haven't heard from Oliver?' she asked, flatly. 'Why didn't I get this speech from him, or did he leave it up to big brother?'

'Fuck knows. We haven't heard a word since he left. I don't think he's got much to teach you about responsibility or consideration, if that's any consolation.'

'Well, *that* isn't my fault. What about the funeral? Has it happened? Won't he be there?'

'I don't know. And *you* can't imagine the pain that causes my mother.'

'I have to go now.' She ventured a glance up at him. She looked exhausted. He wanted to shake her into a consciousness of the complexity of life, wring that petulance from her, beat her, if necessary, into some kind of direct response. But he took a deep breath and looked up at the ceiling. Rachel walked away down the aisle.

It took half an hour to find his car. He couldn't remember leaving the church, although he could recall the wary expression on the priest's face at the door. He must have stayed at the back of the church for ten minutes or so after she left.

For miles into South London the air-conditioning in the car buffeted him with warm air. He didn't, for once, put on music since his head was already full of noise. The conversation ran over and over, as he edited and expanded it, giving it drama and resolution. By Crystal Palace he was feeling a little calmer and beginning to grasp a sense of achievement. In all this muddle, he had done something for his mother.

This, at least, was what he told her when he arrived at the house. He brought home the story of the afternoon like a trophy from school.

27

IN JANUARY the weather had no significance. Gales in March or snows in November advertised the variety of the passing seasons. People took comfort in reading the signs: spring's early promise, or the worse that was still to come. But in January a sudden balmy episode was equivalent to a freezing storm. No portent, just weather – and plenty more where that came from.

On the radio, commentators struggled for superlatives as winds lashed the south and west of the country. The 1987 hurricane had ensured that no meteorologist would again be caught napping. Outside her windows, Daphne saw an occasional figure, angled after a dog, defy the warnings and grimace against the hail. Her own dog showed no desire to move; after a dash into the garden at breakfast, he'd tucked his nose underneath his tail and snoozed.

It was a day for staying indoors and keeping house. Usually at this time of year she made an audit, checking addresses against Christmas cards received, noting birthdays and anniversaries in the year's new diary. She took comfort from this New Year ritual even though her own life had slipped out of gear. In front of her lay a matching set – diary and address book in heavy maroon with colour plates – courtesy of the grandchildren on Christmas morning.

So much was unchanged and yet nothing was the same. It was curious: one might spend one's whole life guarding against mishap or mediocrity, only to have disaster arrive from another unexpected direction. She'd been watching for her reputation when her husband and son slipped away. She'd girded herself against an assault from the past, when the present could deliver the knock-out blow.

Down through the As, Bs and Cs; newborns to add, names to leave out, addresses changed to sheltered housing or convenient flat. On through the busy Ss, Ts, and Ws – not bothering to transfer that silly woman or pompous man, not even remembering the faces sometimes, deleting and inserting, until the collection took on a different shape.

Safe in the furry heat while the wind raged outside, she took a subtle sleepy pleasure in this repetition. She turned the pages to and fro, checking and copying, making each entry a little project. Her writing was still clear, blue-black ink on a fine nib, and that gave her pride. The addresses completed, a new diary gave the illusion of a fresh start.

She loved that clarity but almost at once it was clouded by the thought of Oliver. As an adolescent he had loved ambiguity and muddle. Had wallowed in it – it's complex, Mum, I don't know how I feel about this – until she was driven to exasperation. Try, for God's sake, explain; don't be lazy, use your brain. In time, he had come to see that he wouldn't get far on abstractions.

The only abstraction that remained was his love, the strange hostility that she had presumed was an excess of emotion, too fierce for expression. Now Kenneth had been dead four months and so too was Oliver's hostility. Nothing had replaced it. There was nothing except a Christmas card or the occasional brief call. It was inconceivable, and yet it had happened. She wouldn't try to understand; it had to be something in his life that had caused him to shut down. It would cause her sadness she could not yet attempt to fathom. That girl had been the final evidence of his slow corruption. Poor lost Oliver.

To start with, she had felt the beginnings of grief at the loss, but now she saw that this new phase, this coldness, might yet prove interesting. It was another way of looking at what had happened. Oliver had always been puzzling – the inscrutable toddler, the dreamy child with a sudden pragmatic edge. While he could hurt like this, Oliver did not disappoint. It was a relief of sorts.

In the meantime, his absence condemned her to Richard's

filial devotion, expressed in assiduous DIY. Door frames were planed, washers tightened and creaking boards hammered into silence. Don't bother, she protested, it's not necessary, but he bent deeper over his tasks. It's no bother, he said, and it's worth doing it properly. The house by the sea hadn't looked so spruce in years. His travails were irritating, but not as irritating as her own gratitude.

There'd been some little side-shows – also irritating – as Richard sprayed his territory. There was now a flower bed, of all ridiculous things, like a great wound in the back lawn. At first Jad had attempted to mow, but had lost patience with the curves. Throughout the autumn malevolent couch grass sprouted while the rabbits polished off the pansies, but Richard persisted. He'd cleared out the shed, sweeping away the ambiguous corners. Jad had drifted away.

A couple of Sundays ago, Richard had shown her a paragraph in the paper. Oliver was up for an award for the documentary he had made in the summer. His portrait of the leader of a southern Soviet republic had been transmitted just after the surprise entry of Russian tanks. It was hailed as extraordinarily prescient. Two days before transmission, the young charismatic leader – some kind of sporting hero, she recalled – had been forced to flee the capital for the mountains. He was never found, presumed slaughtered. In this light, Oliver's portrait of the man who had led the republic's brief idyll of independence was both heroic and elegiac. It made sense of a chaotic situation, said the reviewers. It was mentioned in the Commons.

Oliver had moved on to the Balkans, where he was making a history of a town on the Dalmatian coast, which centuries of priests and generals had squabbled over. He would deliver his verdict in a month or so.

Bits of twig and dried seaweed raced along the road in front of the house. It made no sense to love anyone but the dead. They were in better order. Her relationship with Kenneth was under constant soothing revision. They were closer now than ever.

She wondered sometimes about the young man, Antony Delle Rose, or was she thinking of that other young man who looked so like him? When she tidied up the card-table drawers she found the photograph and saw a face that was neither grandfather nor grandson. She saw another person, a third maybe or a second. She saw a life that could have been lived differently and that might yet, in the retelling, take on another shape.

There was a moment when her own choices had been exposed, like bone in a flesh wound. They came into her life, grandfather and grandson, opening up the past in their search for meaning and retribution. Decades of her apprehension led to that moment – apprehension that eddied around those sinister parcels – a slow drip of premonition. Then, suddenly, the parcels were explained, the two men were gone and the wound was closing. Soon there would be no trace.

People insisted on looking at the sea and finding meaning in it. She'd been guilty of it herself. Silly buggers. People would jump to conclusions, reading signs and omens, under the mistaken impression that they'd plumbed profundity. She'd seen ripples spreading out on the water in front of her from an incident, just one incident in a long war. She'd imagined she was beyond all that, but she was an old fool.

Richard's efforts might spur her to a little spring cleaning. Time to throw out some of the stuff in the boys' rooms. Already she'd made a little pile by the back door. Things they didn't need; things she didn't need.

It was incredible, and yet inevitable, that she would see a tiny figure on a bicycle appear at the turn in the road and advance slowly against the wind. Behind him great cat's tongues of surf licked at the sea defences. She watched his ludicrous zigzag along the track; if he once put a foot down then the whole unit, man and bicycle, threatened to topple over and be lost. The postman took five minutes to travel 200 yards.

As he drew level with her neighbour's house, she found herself leaving her seat and reaching for her coat where it hung by the back door. Ridiculous man: what was he doing? As she opened the door, she felt the force of the wind on her eyeballs. He was almost beneath the veranda before he could look up from under his cap, which was strapped tightly beneath the chin. His frown of concentration crossed paths with a triumphant grin.

Good morning, he mouthed noiselessly into the rushing air. She clung on to the veranda rail and waved a greeting with her free hand. He took it for an invitation, which it possibly was, and hauled the bicycle up the steps out of the wind. Catching his breath, he fished in his bag and brought out a single letter.

'Like the Windmill, we never close,' he declared, his usual salutation in adverse weather.

Quite, she said, offering him, for the first time in a decade and a half, a cup of coffee. To her consternation, he accepted.

Inside the doorway he laboriously removed his oilskin and unlaced his mud-spattered boots. As he leant down to pull the boots off, he saw the dusty pile of pictures, books and lampshades.

'I have always liked that picture,' he said, tilting his head sideways to get a better look. 'It's very impressive, the care he took with every detail of the animal. Its hair, and so on. Almost like a photograph, before the age of photography. You don't see it so much these days.'

You don't, agreed Daphne. And as soon as I get it to the charity shop, you won't see it around here either. Unless – and she grinned at her own pragmatism – I hardly like to suggest this, but perhaps you might like . . .?

'As a matter of fact, I would indeed,' he came back quickly. 'I would like that very much. Are you sure?' She nodded fiercely. 'I know exactly where I'd place it. Thank you. It's most kind.'

He drank his coffee and the wind fell a little, as if appeased by the break. Despite Daphne's protests that she would keep the picture for him, the postman insisted on forcing the print into the poacher's pocket of his coat. He rocked down the steps towards the bicycle, his chest square with the prize.

Daphne watched him crawl away along the path. She felt her duty was discharged.

Sometimes I wake in the night and I can sense my lists, my card indexes and files turning over. The names wash over me; like waves, they can't be stopped. The strange ones – the ones that sound oval or jagged, plump or sharp – come round again and again. Occasionally, there's one – a Tamburro or a Beschizza – that I can't shift.

There is so much to do, and when I can get to bed I have to sleep, I must sleep. Lying on my desk is the report I've not yet finished about the two dozen I saw yesterday. With most, it's fairly simple: they go on one side of the line or the other. Depending on the weight of evidence. I know I have to be clear; Gerald has shown me how to be clear. This is too important for anything else.

But now and then, I'm lost. When people don't answer the question, when they tell me things I don't want to know, about their jobs, their families, their workaday London routines, and these are the things I remember now.

Today was worst of all. I knew he would be difficult and precisely because he was strange and more exotic, a real outsider in fact, I was on my guard. But he was so young and so open. With him, there was none of the distance you would expect in this situation. It was a lack of respect, surely. He thought I was just a girl. But he spoke as if it mattered that I understood. I don't know people like this.

It was almost as if it was my future at stake, not his – as though I had done something that I had to account for. I should have put a stop to this at the outset. I should have been firmer, clearer. All that stuff about patriotism and nations – it was terrible nonsense, and yet I keep imagining that city. All those people with a mad idea that they could make something come true.

He belongs to a world that seems impossibly exciting, where people dare and bleed and weep. Joy and despair come easily. My world is bound about with instructions. Each day I pick my way carefully to avoid mistakes, always frightened of that moment when someone spots that I shouldn't be there and sends me back. It is so easy for me to fail; it is so early on. Sentiment is a luxury.

There can only be danger in gazing into someone else's

world. Anyway, the cheek of it, rambling on like that. I didn't need to know all that; I don't care for that familiar manner. It's not what I'm used to.

It's simple, really. You draw a line and you put the names on one side or the other. You have to rule out other possibilities. You have to be clear. There is no other way.

The characters in this book are entirely fictional, although the central incident – the internment of Italians in June 1940 – is fact. 717 Italians were deported at the end of June on a ship called the *Arandora Star*, which sank on the morning of 2 July, torpedoed by a German submarine. Only 271 of the Italians survived. There are several published firsthand accounts by internees. A moving testimony by Capt F. J. Robertson, one of the interpreters on board, was made available in the Public Record Office.

Lord Snell's contemporary enquiry into the *Arandora Star* disaster concluded that 'among those deported were a number of men whose sympathies were wholly with this country'. He had reservations about the compilation of the list of 'dangerous characters'. Steps had been taken to intern all male Italians between the ages of 16 and 70 who had not resided in Britain for more than twenty years. However, in selecting the 'more dangerous' for immediate deportation, 'the lists were largely based on membership of the Fascist Party, which was the only evidence against many of these persons. Apparently, the view was taken that those who had been only nominal members of the Fascist Party and those who were ardently Fascist were equally dangerous'. Whilst conceding the pressures of time and circumstance, Lord Snell could not regard this lack of discrimination as satisfactory. 'The security authorities must bear some of the responsibility for the results that followed from the acceptance of their list as a reliable list of dangerous characters.'

The primary source for the list is believed to have been the 1933 edition of the *Guida Generale*, a directory of Italian interests in London.